Caeia March was born in  industrial South Yorks[...] October 1980, and has [...] Cornwall. She is a countrywoman now and is a very keen gardener. She has published poetry, short stories and non-fiction articles and is widely known as a tutor of women's studies and creative writing. She is also the author of four other novels, all published by The Women's Press, *Three Ply Yarn* (1986), *The Hide and Seek Files* (1988), *Fire! Fire!* (1991) and *Reflections* (1995); and is the editor of *A Celebration of Courage: An Anthology of Writing by Women who have ME* (1998).

Also by Caeia March from The Women's Press:

Three Ply Yarn (1986)
The Hide and Seek Files (1988)
Fire! Fire! (1991)
Reflections (1995)
A Celebration of Courage: An Anthology of Writing by Women who have ME ed (1998)

CAEIA MARCH
BETWEEN THE WORLDS

First published by The Women's Press Ltd, 1996
A member of the Namara Group
34 Great Sutton Street, London EC1V 0DX

British Library Cataloguing-in-Publication Data
A catalogue record for this book is available from the British
Library

ISBN 0 7043 4471 8

Typeset in Times Roman by Contour Typesetters, Southall, London
Printed and bound in Great Britain by BPC Paperbacks Ltd

To Cheryl

ACKNOWLEDGEMENTS

So many people have given me help with the research and development of this book that it would be invidious to single out any one individual. I would therefore like to thank The Women's Press for enthusiastic support throughout the writing of this sequel to *The Hide and Seek Files*; the women of Orlanda Frauenverlag in Berlin for translating *The Hide and Seek Files* into German and publishing it there in 1992; friends who have offered comments on this sequel in the various stages of the manuscript; women in this country and abroad who have given me generous hospitality; women in Germany who were willing to share openly the issues explored in *Between the Worlds*; all those who sent and lent me articles and books and searched for obscure references; friends involved in ecology and conservation, who plant trees and rescue wild flowers; friends who tend herbs and learn their uses; and all women past and present who have been involved with women's land, in Cornwall and elsewhere.

This work of fiction arose partly from the experiences that Cheryl and I had as tenants living on the former women's land here. Some of the proceeds of this novel have gone into the setting up of the West Cornwall Women's Land Trust; and any readers who would like to hear more about women's land in Cornwall can contact me via the publishers.

Last, but by no means least, I would like to thank the many readers who told me that they loved Moss and Biff and asked me, 'What happened to Lerryn?'

Caeia March
Sennen Cove, Cornwall, 1996

BOOK ONE

Book One

Chapter One

The first of the Manx miniature daffodils which Taarnagh had brought from the island to Penzance were opening in the tub by the front door of number forty-three Lannoweth Road when she arrived home for lunch. She unlocked the communal door, shutting it quietly behind her, then checked her post which was mainly bills and circulars, except for one letter which had a Hong Kong postmark from Jocelyn.

Tarn let herself into her ground floor flat.

The afternoon sunshine was filling the back garden, from the south, and the rest of the jonquils would soon open on the rockery at the far end. Taarnagh made tea and buttered some saffron buns, her favourites, and sat in the bay window at the back from where she could see the flowers and read the letter from her younger daughter in Hong Kong.

She had developed a habit of reading Joss's letters sideways, not quite face on, as if to prepare herself for those arrows which might fly off the paper and embed themselves between her eyes. That way they zipped niftily past her left ear, landing in the cushions on the settee behind her.

She was half aware of this habit, and it wasn't without humour: an intuitive self-defence that most mothers and daughters practised these days. Even so the arrow-words were sharper than usual today. Jocelyn's letters were never easy, varying from mundane run-of-the-mill unease to the downright shocking. This one was off the end of the scale. Joss was returning from Hong Kong to live in London, hoping that her boyfriend was going to join her there within a month or two because she was now pregnant by him. She, herself, didn't particularly want the baby but it was what he had always wanted and she felt it would bond them together and improve things between them.

The phone rang just as Tarn was sighing with disappointment and frustration.

'Mum? Hi, it's me. How are you?'

3

'Hello, darling. I was fine, till I read this letter from your sister. Is that why you're phoning, love?'

'It certainly is. Though I wanted to talk anyway. Shouldn't really – not this time of day – but I'm on my break. Thought you might be too.'

'Yes I am. These split shifts drive me crazy. Anyway, how are things?'

'I'm fine. It's Joss I'm worried about. Why on earth is she doing this, Mum? I mean you'd have thought with all the independence you taught us girls after you and Dad separated . . . all that stuff . . . she'd see through this turd, wouldn't you? She never wanted a child. What the hell does she think a child will do? Make life easier? I know I'm a fine one to talk, with Yuki and everything. At least Jocelyn's older than I was when I had Yuki. But I've never been with a man who as much as laid a finger on me without my permission. And she's with this gorilla who has his brains in his balls and his anger in his fists. He can't string two sentences together! I can't get my head around this, Mum. She's driving us all nuts. That child is at risk before it's even out of the womb. It's horrendous!'

'I agree with you, darling. It's a living nightmare. But there's no point in you trying to change her mind, Helen. Joss has made her decision to get pregnant and have this child, and . . .'

'And I expect you'll say it's none of our business, Mum. But she makes it our business by writing to us all about it. She's with a violent man and has told him it is his baby so he'll never let go. This is worse than anything she has done so far . . . because he will never give up his ways. It's her and the child now, not just her.'

'I know. I'm just trying to take a deep breath and stay calm and not let it sabotage any more of my life. I don't know how to stay calm with this coming at me but this time I am going to. She loves him and he hates me because of my relationship with Sylvia. Even though that's long over now, he still holds it against me . . .'

'Mum, we'll never know why she stays with him or what she sees in him. I had to phone you. I always need to hear your voice when one of Joss's letter bombs explodes on us!'

'Me too, lovey. Me too. Is Yuki all right?'

'She's doing fine, Mum. Picking it up really well. She'll be tri-lingual before long and that's what she wants. It was a good move coming here to Cologne. There's a lot of racism, but she's a strong little girl, and she's used to being different. There's absolutely no one else who is half-Japanese, so she's lonely with that in a way, but used to it as well. We talk Japanese at home so she won't forget it . . . and she knows it's only for two years. She says she'll be all right. She'll be writing soon. I told her she could write in Japanese to you, Mum. Is that okay?'

'Of course. It'll keep me on my toes won't it? I'd better find my fountain pen so I can write back. Not a lot of call for it here in Penzance.'

'Listen this is costing me Mum – I must go. Love you lots.'

'Me too. I'm hoping to get over to Germany this summer, all right?'

'Oh please, Mum. We'd love that . . . Big Hugs from both of us.'

'You too. I mean you two, too.'

They both laughed. 'You sound like Brown Owl. Bye, Mum.'

Tarn sighed. She had been hoping that Jocelyn was at last going to leave her bloke. She was sure that he had a drink problem and that he was still beating Joss. Joss was such a strong loving girl – why on earth did she put up with it?

Again Tarn sighed. Then she stood up and stretched high and let out a huge yawn. It had been a heavy morning – French and German. She sat back down and leaned against the cushions. She was due back at the language department for the evening at six-thirty. She felt exhausted and, closing her eyes, she allowed herself a short rest.

When she woke it was late afternoon. Opening the french windows, she padded down the garden in her slippers until she stood atop the rockery at the far end. The other gardens sloped away from her to the station road at the bottom.

The sun had now disappeared round towards Land's End. Its late-afternoon golden light was now concentrated underneath a high curve of golden clouds, and reflected in the shimmering sea in Mount's Bay, as if pulled down from the underside of the sky. Had she not been at work this evening, she would have taken a slow walk on the flat sands of Long Rock, revelling in the blue-black waters there and the deep interplay of light and dark in the sea from the reflections of the quayside and town of Penzance.

From Tarn's town garden it was a long way down the hill and over the railway but it was good to have a framed fragment of the sea, a contained glimpse of a wider world. It was still the sea, and was calm today. Once it had been a vast forest stretching out towards the coast of Brittany and around to the southwest. It would have been the lost land of Lyonesse. But now it was just the sea, coming and going, changing mood and texture, reliable in its unreliability.

Back indoors with plenty of time while dinner was cooking, Tarn took her best fountain pen and began a letter in Japanese to Yuki.

Dear Yuki,
Your mum phoned me briefly today while she was at work and I sent lots of love to you down the phone wires across the miles.

I thought of you in your new school. I hope it's all going very well. Then I remembered what it had been like when I first came here to Penzance, though I was older than you are. I was about fifteen.

I was right in the middle of my O levels, as we used to call them. I didn't want to leave the Isle of Man and be dragged off here to an unknown place – so we're a bit different in that, you and I, because I know how much you were looking forward to going to Cologne with your mum. I'm sorry you haven't met any other girls who are part Japanese, but maybe you will because there is so much international trade and movement now and Cologne is a huge city.

This weekend you'll be meeting my old friends Liesl and Ingrid when you go to their house in the country. I hope you enjoy it. In the summer they'll put a hammock in the orchard for you.

Thinking of you made me remember my old school days back here in Penzance. I wasn't very nice to my parents about the move. I made up my mind to be as grumpy as possible and I was determined not to co-operate. I don't sound a very nice person, do I? Well, I wasn't.

6

My father had landed a very good job with a company that used to be here in Porthcurno called the Cable and Wireless company. Wireless is the old name for radio, as you know.

His work took him, as he said, from one Celtic land to another and when we arrived here I was astonished.

Everything was so like the Isle of Man – except for the horse trams which trundled up and down Douglas Promenade. I missed them. Do you remember the lovely long ride we had on them last summer?

Well, then something happened – actually a whole lot of things happened – and I fell in love with the land here. All the coves and headlands, little bays and wild moorlands, were so like my homeland that I forgave my father for uprooting me. I settled down quite quickly and got on with my O levels.

And I felt as if someone had put a warm Celtic shawl around my shoulders. It wasn't a real shawl but it seemed to be wrapped loosely round me to keep me warm and happy. It was a wonderful feeling. I hope this letter will be like that for you. A warm Celtic shawl around your shoulders, Yuki.

But there was more going on with that shawl, I think. It was as if the Isle of Man itself was a sort of mother or grandmother to me. As if the island had a personality and life of her own. She became very real in my imagination. A friend to me. We all need a special friend in a new place.

There's a name for the Isle of Man in the Gaelic – it means dear little island or something like that and the name is Ellan Vannin.

To me, uprooted and adrift in a new place, Ellan Vannin became my silent friend. I used to think of her as the island and an ancestor and a friend all at the same time. Whenever I sang in the choir I imagined myself singing for her and to her. I imagined her walking on the moors back in my birthplace or sitting spinning in her small turf house. I knew that she loved singing as well. I seemed to get my voice from her. As if she was singing as well whenever I was. I was very happy and I had the shawl around my shoulders whenever I thought of her. Does it sound silly? It was very real to me at that time and at night before I slept I'd say, 'Good night Ellan Vannin' as if she was a real person who could really hear me. She kept me very safe. I never told anyone about her till now. But it seems right to tell you because you have wonderful ancestors, Yuki, from Japan and from the Celtic places. A really amazing heritage.

I'd like to be your friend, Yuki. I know how hard it can be to be the new girl, even when you *want* to go to the new place.

I was a new girl in the school here in Penzance. In my year the girls all had their own friends already so that was hard. But I met some very kind girls when I joined the school choir. I made friends there, real friends. There was one girl I remember in particular. She was a couple of years younger than me and she used to disappear every summer up to Yorkshire to visit her aunt there. Her aunt was Cornish but she ran a sort of Arts Foundation in a Yorkshire village called Herton.

The girl's name was Lerryn. Isn't that pretty? It was from a Cornish village not far from Fowey where the writer Daphne du Maurier lived. Lerryn's other name was Trevonnian which is also Cornish. I never knew what happened to her, because I left the school after my A levels and went to university. That's where I met your grandad. Shortly after I got my degree, we went together to Japan and another whole chapter of my life started.

I am very happy to be back in Penzance now though, and it was lovely to show you my favourite places when you were here. Sylvia sends love to you. I miss her, but she is happy in Canada so I am pleased about that. I know I'm quite an unusual kind of granny – we are all very special people in our family, Yuki, and I like being unusual, and I very much like being your granny.

Oh, there's something else about Ellan Vannin. When I was in the school choir our soloist was taken ill and, at a moment's notice, they asked me to take her place. But I didn't know the song she would have sung and so they asked me if there was something else I could sing. I had a ballad which I had been writing for Ellan Vannin. One day I'll sing the entire ballad on to tape for you.

I stood there in front of a great blur of parents and teachers and pupils, with my friend Lerryn in the choir behind me, and I thought of Ellan Vannin walking on the moors in the island. She had green eyes and dark brown hair and I could see her singing there. She seemed so real to me. The warm shawl was around my shoulders and I opened my voice and I opened my heart and I just sang. I sang for her. I sang 'The Ballad of Ellan Vannin'.

So that's how I came to be happy in my new home. I was a new girl once like you. But we can get through. Think of a warm loving shawl around your shoulders and all those in the world who love you, and open your heart, and sing.

I love you, dearest granddaughter.

Love from Grandma XXX

CHAPTER TWO

All around me the world was grey. Low thin cloud, slowly dispersing, gave a ghostly quality to the thin air, and the heavy granite of the Cornish coast path seemed sombre, without any sparkle or warmth.

I trudged along the coast path from Raginnis in the direction of Lamorna, wearing thick winter clothing. My hands were stuffed in my anorak pockets. I carried a small rucksack but no map. I knew where I was going. I had been born in the nearby village of Catherine-in-Penwith in 1944, just before the war ended. This had been my childhood path, to the secret site where, above Catherine's Cove, I would sit on a stone seat, out of the wind, facing south, into the wilderness of ocean.

As a child I had so loved these cliffs which had seemed so full of delights and secrets, hopes and dreams, fantasies and legends. Down, far, far below my seat, according to local legends, smugglers' trunks and boxes had been been turned to stone and flung as huge granite blocks against the cliff by Old Catherine, the old woman of the sea, when the smugglers had disturbed her in her sleep.

But now, in the spring of 1994, the place felt as morose, cold, and empty of futures, as I did; and I followed my old, familiar route to my seat, with none of the earlier pleasure I had taken in this walk. There was no one about. I shrugged off my backpack and contemplated the long, long drop to oblivion.

From a side-pocket of my rucksack, I took several bags and a tough canvas belt. I pulled at the canvas belt and tested it for strength. Then I rolled it up and put it in my anorak pocket. I fingered the carrier bags which were the strongest plastic ones I had been able to find – the sort that people carry tins home in from the supermarket.

I folded them one by one and placed them under a loose rock so that they didn't blow away. Then I took a large bottle of brandy from my rucksack and had my first swig. It warmed me right down to the pit of my stomach. The glass mouth of the bottle felt cool to my mouth. Not like a woman's mouth, not like Lindsey Shepherd's mouth when I had first kissed her.

Six years ago, after sixteen years as lovers, Lindsey Shepherd walked out on me. I don't remember sleeping at all for months afterwards, though I must have or I'd have collapsed completely. I was fury and anger and fire inside. I worked like a demon. I danced like a dervish. I painted it out of me, covering canvas after canvas with the colours of fire, fear and despair; the textures of water, rain and pain; the shapes of earth, volcano and valley; the spaces of cloud, tornado and tempest.

I tried everything to move forward. I ran every workshop I could think of; I attended all the others that other women could think of. I didn't stop moving for years.

Fury and jealousy. Oh, those were undeniably action-packed days. Now I sat on my stone seat, my plans made, and peered down into the cool green waters. I was ready for the sea. From the sea and to the sea return me. I had made my plans, and I knew what to do. But first the brandy. I took a long swig at it, then another. I raised the brandy bottle to my lips again and watched the swirling seas below me.

As a young teenager, noticing the midsummer waters around these cliffs, I'd long for the end of school term and the chance it brought to spend time with my Aunt Harry in Herton. There, in the grocer's shop in that small mining town, I had met a girl named Lindsey. I'd loved Lindsey even then, when she lived with Moss and Biff who ran the shop – loved her without the means of knowing what it might mean for one girl to love another.

Later, I had searched for her . . . and had been lovers with her since I re-discovered her in London, in the summer of 1971, when I was almost twenty-seven.

The brandy bottle was huge. Pale green glass, one of the colours of the sea. I held the green glass curves to my face, cool green, smooth glass, and thought of Lindsey Shepherd.

We had been together so many years that I had forgotten to imagine life or a future without her. And then she fell in love with someone else. Almost before I'd had a chance to register it,

11

she had gone to live in Australia with her new woman lover, and all my crystal fantasies broke into shattered glass around my feet.

At night I dreamed glass, over and over again. Breaking glass. Silver and white and shiny. In my cheeks, behind my ears, inside the bones of my shoulders and knees.

Another swig of brandy. I was feeling warmer now. I leaned back against my stone seat. Images began to flow. I pulled a photograph from my pocket. Rosie – Lindsey's daughter, the child I had helped to raise – was a grown woman now, standing in the sun in Sydney, Australia. The brandy was doing its job. Clarifying the memories, but allowing them, sequencing but softening them.

After Lindsey had left I couldn't see much point in anything, but I had to earn my crust, as they say, and my paintings and etchings were selling steadily in outlets throughout Cornwall and the rest of Britain. Cards were a good money spinner, so I worked like crazy for the first couple of years building up a huge stock, like a squirrel hoarding acorns against forthcoming hard winters.

And they were hard, very hard. Life seemed to be a catalogue of losses, which tested me to the limit, until I became used to feeling numb. Then it was easy to stay shut down, closed off to all except my nearest and dearest friends, Tessa and Jules.

The others were all gone. In my everyday world I had only Tessa and Jules, Black women who needed their own lives, not my dependency.

From the outside I was a successful Cornish artist whose outlets clamoured for more, more. More of exactly the same. Paintings of Cornwall, in every season and every mood, in every hue.

It had been whispered during those awful years that there were those who envied me. Hints and innuendoes of jealousy would float in on the air currents now and then. Lerryn Trevonnian's got it made, you know. No mortgage, lovely studio in London, well-established career as a woman artist. Commissions left, right and centre.

If your name is public in whatever way, you may expect that

12

kind of thing. There's always someone ready to claim she knows you, did this or that favour for you, saw you here or there and with so and so. However tough you are or numb you feel inside, such little darts can pierce your skin, and you'd have to be a house brick to not notice. But by then I was well on the way to becoming a house brick.

If in doubt, work. But work hadn't filled all the hours of the day or night. The future was an empty canvas waiting for nothing.

It was all over. The fierce fast reality of the early years after Lindsey, hard but with their own momentum, had given way to an unendurable forevernothingness which had brought me at last to my old stone seat.

I'd been years arriving here on this cliff. Back to where I had started and with nothing left to do.

Behind me on the coast path the first flowers were trumpeting their sunshine sounds, calling me with a message that I couldn't decode. I had been long gone, from this land and my own self. I had no idea what to do except that some time between now and tomorrow I would simply and peacefully wade into the ocean, like my father before me.

My brothers had found his note and his body had been washed up exactly as he had meant it to be, after a long and happy life. He had come quite openly to the end of it, and he had claimed his right to quit on his own terms. We all thought it the bravest thing he had ever done.

My father had had a little one-up, one-down house which had been sold and my brothers had bought an old house in Penzance which they, being builders, were going to do up as an investment. When disaster hit the building trade, as the recession deepened, they found they couldn't afford the materials, and they couldn't sell it either.

My father hadn't left anything at all to me. I hadn't expected him to because the family had been so good about my having my studio from Aunt Harry. I had been a young woman when she had given it to me. It had given me security when I badly needed it, because I had to pay my own way through art college. My parents had not let me stay on at school. I had to leave and learn hairdressing. Aunt Harry, who was at that time married to a wealthy husband, had been appalled. She knew how I longed to be an artist.

I suppose that my parents had seen my determination by then. They had never given me any bad feeling about that gift of a studio to live in in London; nor had my brothers, to whom Aunt Harry had also been generous. However, they both felt guilty about my father's will. They offered me the chance to stay in the house, if I didn't mind the damp and the half-started projects there.

I didn't mind the damp because I didn't care much about my surroundings. I slept in the attic, without the blinds on the sloping window, so that the moon and stars were visible when the skies were clear. The moonlight would cast rectangles of cold light across the room, moving them around the floor until dawn.

Sometimes I slept, sometimes not. It didn't matter. I was back in Cornwall but not at home, neither in the land nor in my self. I couldn't make much sense of anything. Let alone care. I knew that I was loved – had friends – because I had Tessa and Jules. But I slept alone. There was no one at night just for me. No one special. Not since Lindsey left. I felt numb when it came to the future. And lost when it came to the past.

Sometimes I'd tell myself that there were people out there who needed help and that I was in a good position to offer it. Around me in Cornwall was a rural version of a weariness I'd witnessed in London. Folk were despairing. Years and years of Conservative government had ripped apart any of the support structures that the welfare state had offered. The fishing industry was gasping like fish do in nets when the nets are hauled out of water. Disputes abounded about how to survive the argicultural and fishing policies of the EC; and the bungling bureaucrats of both London and Brussels, who couldn't tell a kipper from a mackerel unless it was labelled on a menu, were making a thorough mess of things.

A third of my homeland was up for sale and a third was boarded up. But the pony-and-country-club brigades' blithe indifference belied all the homeless and hungry in Cornwall, and young riders trotted round the lanes, barely noticing the rest of the population there.

I used to care a lot. Demos and banners and campaigns. Used

to talk late into the night of my passions for world peace and lesbian nation.

But now my deepest longing in the heart of the night was to slip into ice cold water, a belt around my waist with shopping bags with boulders hooked around me, and sink, down, down as my lungs filled and I swam away to join the primal ocean as if into arms from whence we all came. I am after all a fisherman's daughter. From the sea and to the sea return me.

The first bottle of brandy was almost empty. I don't know how long I'd been there in my stone seat, and it didn't matter. Nothing mattered, though I seemed to want to let the film of my life run along before me, as they say.

In the years that had followed Lindsey leaving me, I had slowly, very slowly begun to rebuild my life. Not exactly a new life – some elements and people were constant: my Aunt Harry, Tessa and Jules, and my art studio in London.

In time I came to understand aloneness again and to try to replace loneliness with solitude. It sounds so simple, put like that. The process is anything but simple. For the artist solitude is essential, the one-to-one relationship between the self and the product. But solitude when it is chosen has a beautiful and magical quality to it. The inner peace, the outward calm. Whereas loneliness embodies an inner terror, in which you feel close to the descent to hell. A surging, nagging, rising panic.

I began the second large brandy bottle. I held up the other empty one to the last of the fading light, watching the shapes of curve and indentation form and re-form themselves as I played, tipping the empty bottle this way and that. Funny thing was I'd never been one for much drinking. Not even one for hanging around in women's bars. I was usually bored by all that. Much rather be on the dance floor alone in some far corner letting myself get lost in the other world of drumbeat and bass guitar.

The brandy warmed me. Melted parts of my brain. I'd have liked to find a bottle, like Alice did down the rabbit hole, which said, Drink me, and when I'd drunk it, I'd shrink to less than cork size and disappear inside the full bottle. Bottle-ottle-ottle.

15

Message in a bottle. Hear me. Hear me. From the sea and to the sea return me.

The nineteen-eighties became the nineties. Aunt Harry had died, leaving Hermit's Hut, her home in Cornwall, to a women's trust fund so that women artists, musicians and writers could stay for periods working in the inspiring rugged landscape there. Tessa and Jules worked closely with me setting up the trust fund to realise my aunt's dream. I spent a lot of time organising the schedules of women visitors, grateful for all the activity, the external pressure, the contacts and communication. It soaked up my time. Then reality hit me. There was nothing left to do.

I swigged again at the brandy, aware of the huge hard boulders all around me and underneath me. The sensation of hard granite, enormous, awe-inspiring, touched me somewhere, springing open the door to a memory of lying on similar boulders in another time and place.

Usually at Spring Bank Holiday the three of us, Tessa, Jules and myself, would travel together to Hermit's Hut to paint and draw, to walk the coast path, and to explore the mysterious land which rises in granite outcrops amidst heather and gorse inland from Hermit's Hut.

We had walked one day to the Witches Rock at Zennor and had lain there in the sun, relaxed and content.

'I don't know how I'd have survived these years without you.'

'We're family,' said Tessa. 'We brought up three children. We're bonded now. A Black and white family. That's who we all are. We're not just your friends, Lerrie. We're all of us nearer fifty than forty. We go back years. Do you realise how long it is we've known one another?'

We had had a wonderful time together. I had talked everything through with them. But there was nothing they could say that would give me back my sense of self.

In the early spring of 1994 I packed up my car with my art materials, gave Tessa and Jules my keys to my studio, which would temporarily provide them with facilities they badly needed in London, and drove west.

I was forty-nine years old and considering suicide because the rainbow wasn't enough.

I sipped from the second brandy bottle slowly. The brandy slipped down easily and brought me sustained moments of pure clarity. It flowed across my tongue smoothly, down the back of my throat warmly, and lined my stomach with gentle soothing fire. Slowly I filled the plastic sacks with huge stones, ready. Black, black and enticing was the beguiling ocean far below me.

I was warm, because of the brandy, I suppose. I watched the stars brighten as the twilight sky became the night sky. It was dry, a clear night. Not raining. That made a change. I thought of the past, the starry, starry nights I'd seen here from these cliffs in my early teens. The night sky over Herton when I was nineteen and had gone on my first search for Lindsey – only to be told she was in London, and married.

The London skies, starless and washed brown with the blurr of sodium streetlights, when I had found Lindsey again, a widow with a child.

The night skies on the cliffs over Hermit's Hut when she and I, lovers, had slipped away from London for a holiday, leaving Rosie with Tessa and Jules.

Now the skies held no hope. There was nothing. Nothing there. Only stars and the empty, empty places in between . . .

CHAPTER THREE

Tarn was completely exhausted when she arrived home from teaching her evening classes. She made a hot drink, flung the remains of the lasagne in the microwave and kicked off her shoes, but as the microwave pinged, the fax machine began to chug.

'I simply had to send you this. It's me, Liesl. I'm working late tonight so sending this from work. Yes I know that it's mega expensive to do it this way but look what was in the paper here today. Anyway here it is. I was sure you'd want to see it immediately – if not sooner! I've already cut it up and repasted it to A4 to fit so don't be surprised at the format.

Come and see us soon. Ingrid sends love. In haste.

Love Liesl.

PS Fax number + address are the library of the University of Cologne.

PPS Shall be delighted to meet your daughter Helen and little Yuki this weekend. L.

Tarn translated the article as she ate her supper. It referred to a stone box which had been found by builders working on foundations for a supermarket on the outskirts of Cologne.

Our local correspondent in Cologne dashed to the construction site of the new supermarket building in the west district today, when one of the men working on the deepest level spied a stone box about one and a half metres in length inscribed with carvings of animals and birds. All mechanical digging stopped while the university archaeologists were called in to examine the find. The box was carefully uncovered and subsequently removed in its entirety. It appeared to be of medieval design, one of a number of stone boxes with tight-fitting inset stone lids.

This afternoon the box was opened *in camera*. A film was

taken of the entire process as the famous archaeologist Professor Heinrich Schaffer took from the box a set of ceramic tiles engraved in Latin. They were wrapped in oiled leather and bound in wooden bindings encased in hand-worked leather. The tiles appear to have been written by a woman, Helga of Cologne, known to have lived in the Beguinage here in Cologne in 1318.

Professor Schaffer is quoted as saying, 'It is an extremely exciting find. We have only very rare fragments of Beguine writings. Moreover, the manner of burial of the tiles suggests that the author knew exactly what she was doing and longed for this to be found some time in the future. It is a miracle, an absolute miracle, for all of us involved in studying the history of the Middle Ages in Germany.'

Last night our reporters spoke to Ms Liesl Holz, one of the university librarians here. Ms Holz has published several articles on the Beguines and is currently working on a novel of the life and times of Helga of Cologne.

A television interview with Ms Holz is scheduled for Breakfast News tomorrow morning.

Tarn finished her meal and pulled on her anorak, suddenly and inexplicably invigorated. She opened the french doors to her tiny garden, clicked off the indoor light and went out into the dark.

Here at the back of the terrace of old houses there were no streetlights. Very few neighbours seemed to be home and only a sparse scattering of strips of light were visible behind closed curtains along the length of the row of buildings. It was a very dark night indeed, with an unusually clear sky.

Tarn climbed on top of her small rockery, aware that her slippers were a mistake for they were letting in the damp from the earth, and stood facing the distant view of Mount's Bay.

It was very quiet. Had Helga of Cólogne stood in her medieval gardens at the Beguinage hundreds of years ago on such a night? How had she really lived, there on women's land in Germany at the turn of the fourteenth century? Liesl's novel about her would ask that question and would be searching for answers.

Tarn wondered if Liesl was both overjoyed and slightly

overwhelmed at the discovery that the subject of her novel had left a record of her life and times. What would it reveal and how might that affect Liesl's creative process? What had life been like at the Beguinage? Had there been a true sense of solidarity there? Sisterhood, even? Or had the women fallen apart, bickered and fought when the pressure from male authorities outside their lands had been brought to bear? Tarn smiled to herself with recognition. Had they had hierarchies or collectives? Did it matter? Did they really have their children, mothers and aunts with them? Liesl had thought that they did.

The newspaper had said 1318. Tarn racked her brain for the details Liesl had passed on about her research. That must have been towards the end of the Beguinages. There certainly *would* have been male pressure at that time, she realised.

Thinking of Liesl and her research, Tarn's mind wandered to Ellan Vannin and Tarn's own search through Manx history for the realities behind the folklore. Tarn looked up at the powerfully enigmatic starry sky then rested her gaze again on the dark and distant bay. If she had not been so tired she might have walked down to that long beach which edged Mount's Bay. It would be low tide tonight and she could easily duck under the railway lines through the river tunnels and beyond Chyandour Cliff, not a possible route when high tide surged through. But she was simply too exhausted. Instead she imagained herself on the dark strand, at the edge of a night-black sea, the same colour as the dark ink with which she wrote, in Japanese, to Yuki. In the hush, she could almost hear once more the song which she had composed and had sung in school, calling her back to the island where her grandparents, now in their nineties, still lived. The island which was Ellan Vannin herself.

Oh, how strong was the call of the island on nights like this. Had Helga of Cologne responded to the call of the land in such a way? Tarn thought about the Beguinage, where up to two thousand women had lived side by side. They grew and cooked their food together, learned together, shared with each other. Helga would have been one voice in that community of voices.

But how different it must have been, at that same time, for the independent healing women who had lived on the Isle of Man. What had life really been like for them, on the island, in the twelve and thirteen hundreds? How had they lived there, those unnamed women, whose voices are not known, and whose lives, without written records, had been reduced to fragments passed down in the island's folklore? Who could they turn to for comfort and support when their lands were taken from them by the powerful local families? Who were they, those unnamed ones struggling to make a living as herbalists and healers? And how many of them were there, accused of witchcraft by the churches?

Women without names, without voices, without power, and without land?

Tarn found herself thinking of Eastfield Farm right here in Cornwall – a beautiful place with outbuildings and land. Land which had been set aside for women and was farmed and maintained by women.

Tarn smiled as she thought of her two friends, the current tenants of Eastfield Farm, who lived and worked together, maintaining the land, growing herbs and creating a healing sanctuary. As soon as she could she must go over and help with some more brambling and pruning. Hopefully tonight's clear weather signalled the onset of a good dry spell, so that plenty of land work could be done.

Tarn smiled again, returned indoors, fished Liesl's last epistle from the bureau and climbed into bed. Her old friend had sent chapter one of her strange, predictive novel. Tarn snuggled down, enjoying once again her bedtime reading: the story of Helga of Cologne.

I was thirteen, settled and contented when my father's words went like an arrow through my heart. From that moment my life changed.

I was now mature, my father said. Old enough to be betrothed to my friend Wolfgang. Wolfgang! whom I looked upon as my trusted companion, as if he were my own brother!

I was a fool not to have seen it coming. Had I not been bridesmaid to my elder sister Ulrike only within the year? She had been wed at fifteen, why not I?

I stood against the old tree for most of the morning, letting its deep strength hold me up, for if I had moved I'd have crumpled to the ground. Betrothal. Marriage. Children.

It wasn't so long since I'd been a child myself, but I wasn't unfamiliar with how children are formed or how they are birthed. I'd seen the bull being brought to the field at the right time, watched his great hulk towering up and over each of our milk cows, heavy and grunting, making all the noise he needed until he was done. Then he would be led away again, his great bollocks joggling against his raging buttocks.

I'd seen my father reaching his arm into the cow's passage to free the cord from around a half-strangled calf's neck. I'd heard the pain of birth and seen the miracle of it too. The one did not shadow over the other nor make it right. I didn't believe then and I don't to this day that animals or women are put on this earth to suffer, though I have seen my share of it, first hand.

Betrothal. Marriage. Children.

All the women in my family have a history of long and painful childbirth. By some quirk of fate we are made too small for the children we carry. We are birthed the wrong way round instead of head first and our family is famous for our triumph over this adversity.

My grandmother was born after two days of exhausted screaming by my great-grandmother. My mother was born feet first and had to be pulled out. My sister Ulrike was born bottom first with my mother almost dying of haemorrhage; and I took three days to arrive, by which time my mother's old scars had all ripped open.

In the fields and in the house I knew what my future held. Gruelling hard work and a child a year until I died.

I had to act and act quickly. As the shadows from the farmhouse lengthened, creeping across the yard until they finally reached the old tree, I tried to collect my thoughts and face the challenge ahead of me. Slowly I walked out from the farmyard and along the middle terrace to the sunken wall where the last rays of the sun lingered longest, warming the stones and colouring the vine leaves golden green. Small clusters of unripe grapes were hanging there, light green, jewelled, some in shadow already.

I sat looking down over the terraces, at the old worn stones, at the generations of human work revealed in the placing of each slab, as our mountain was carved and sculpted into fertile plots of warm soil How many hands had carried those stones, wielded the picks and mattocks, broken in this earth? How many feet had moved slowly, step by step along the rugged valley sides, defying the height and inhospitality, creating a vision here, making it into this dream, this everyday reality of sun and moon, rain and cloud, seedtime and harvest?

Countless numbers. I recall learning to count: *ein zwei drei . . . vielen*. My grandmother laughing and giving me honeycomb to reward my efforts.

Fool. I should have known this would happen to me. Hadn't I been aware of my destiny? This was my mountainside, my valley, my land, my grapevines, my homestead. Here I knew who I was and was meant to be. Helga daughter of Godfried, wife of Wolfgang. Mother of *ein zwei drei . . . vielen*.

I sighed, rested my elbows on my knees, my head in my hand.

As I did so, the sun dropped to just above the edge of the opposite side of the valley, sending up showers of red and golden, orange and apricot particles which caught the clouds and danced and shimmered there. I gazed at the spectacle, watching the disc fall steadily behind the mountain until, with a green flash, it left me.

I made my way slowly back to the farmhouse, knowing what I would never marry Wolfgang nor anyone else, and that I must now prepare myself to leave the Mosel for ever. I would go to live with the Beguines in the great Beguine lands on the outskirts of the city of Cologne.

CHAPTER FOUR

It was dark night as they set off, three of them from Eastfield Farm, with tripods and cameras. It was cold but the sky was full of stars in a coal-black eternity. The moonlight was bright, so they didn't need a torch on the rough lane which led up from the farm to the tarmac road at the top.

At the road they set off in the direction of the village of Sheffield. The name was no coincidence. It was said that some miners from the northern city had come here to find work in the quarry nearby, last century. Homesick, they had named their new place out of nostalgia.

Now the village was simply two parallel strings of granite houses along the road. The front gardens were always pretty and some of the buildings were strange shapes with corners missing, as if the miners – like the homebuilders in Ireland – had known that they must not build across fairy paths.

They were silent at first, the three women, content in each other's company, and each with a mind full of pictures – of the sky above and the falling stars which seemed to simply drop like rare fireworks in solitary manner from the bowl of the great Plough. The entire Milky Way was clearly visible.

It was an excellent night for photography.

They walked, companionably, for over a mile. The only sounds were of their boots on the metalled road and the heavy breathing of milk cows behind the Cornish hedges. They followed the road through Sheffield village and took the turning for Raginnis.

It was their intention to follow the coast path from Raginnis to the plantation at Kemyel. There, the old trees felled by the hurricane of '87 had been left where they fell so that nature might work on them. There, in the juxtaposition of old and new, lay many of the secrets of the night: secrets of shape and shard, texture and transformation, there where the land meets the sea.

It was a dramatic yet ordinary place. A nature reserve yet

unreserved in its regeneration. A complex metaphor of night and day, decay and delight, winter and wishes, death and hope.

They had been waiting for a cold starry night such as this, the three women friends from Eastfield Farm: waiting through weeks of wet and windy weather, mist and rain, and skies obscured by low cloud.

The two woman who lived at Eastfield Farm were not farmers, for it was no longer a farm as such. It was a collection of buildings which had been partly converted by its owner into accommodation and storage units, and it was surrounded on the east, north and west sides by three acres of fields which had been planted under the Cornish tree-planting scheme about twenty years ago. Now, deciduous woodland created screens and young growth, which gave enjoyment and privacy to many women year by year.

The owner was abroad now, and the two women who lived there were merely her tenants. They loved the place, run down as it was, an elemental place of strange boggy energies which could suck you in if you weren't careful so that you would never want to leave. A place which needed to be loved and to give love, which it did, in abundance. The two women, Cherry and Beech, who had come from up country to live and work on the land, were experienced land women used to gardening and coppicing. They had already recorded much of their progress on the land at Eastfield Farm in spell-binding photographs, the sale of which raised money for seeds and more trees.

Eastfield Farm was known throughout the circles of women who loved it as women's land.

The third woman, Molly, was much older. She was a widow, who now lived in her son's granite cottage not far from Land's End on the footpath to Nanjizal. For years she had run a small shop in Penzance known as The Gallery, which is how she had met Cherry and Beech, when they had been new tenants at Eastfield. But the farm itself was not new to her. Her own daughter had once lived there as a tenant, and Molly was part of the informal land group of women volunteers who came to tackle the brambles, hogweed, thistles and nettles – which waged a war on the quiet fields where the young trees had been planted.

*

25

There was no sound from the stones above Catherine's Cove as Molly, Cherry and Beech passed by en route to Kemyel. The huge boulders stacked down the cliffs were in shadow. Who is to say who had been there that day or what secrets were held there that night? A whole group of friends might have been cavorting there, and having made merry and settled down to sleep, might even now be dreaming there. No passers-by on the cliff path above them could have known. Only the deep beat of the sea reverberated there. Under the surface of the ocean Old Catherine slept undisturbed. This was no night of smugglers. Old Catherine slumbered on, neither roused in anger nor flinging boulders about in revenge. A calm night.

Cherry, Beech and Molly strode on with their tripods and camera bags slung around their shoulders. The path narrowed between bramble bushes then turned sharply right transforming itself into steep stone stairs which led up to a higher level for the final few yards to the plantation. The three women puffed upwards. There, in the starlight, the old and new trees breathed and sighed, black, brown and silver. Metallic reflection from moonlight on mirrored surfaces played chiaroscuro dramas among shadows. Shape-shifting forms arrived, paused momentarily then left the stage without telling tales. All was mime and mummery, cloaked in Celtic invisibility or sirened in silent song.

Experienced at working with each other, they set up and started in silence, soundlessly bound by the spell of the spinney.

Sometimes they, too, mimed. They might point, make arm movements, or simply take up the tripods and tiptoe to a trickier location.

They knew each other's signals for when the flash might happen, when they needed red lighting, when they must use zoom or wide-angled lenses.

In the background was the ocean dancer, she of the night, the friend of owl and of raven. In shimmering black watersilk she danced, moving powerfully to the rhythm of the tides. She who was the black horse of the salt sea, she who had a white mane which streamed behind her when she ran. She thundered her hooves on the ocean floor, her head thrown up above the surface. Enormous was she, dancing there, prancing there, in elemental night.

Beyond the trees the three women heard her but through the woods they could not see her. Part of the night, she hid her might, allowing only her echo which boomed when the waves met the granite shores, down down below the plantation, but she did not sleep. Boom, she danced. Boom, she pranced. She pounded at night to her heart beat, hoof beat drum. And the women worked on.

Until, at last, the star patterns dimmed and the night's performance drew to a close. There was a slow signal for the transition. It came upon the woodland naturally, steadily, a changing of the sounds of trees breathing. A quiet change. Almost imperceptible to anyone not watching closely. But they were women who worked with the dark and light. It was their job to notice, so that, eventually, they came to the end of their photography and sensed that dawn was imminent.

They were aware, before the first bird in a hidden treetop shouted it. They stood and beheld. They didn't move.

Call and response. Jazz notes and high tones. Wake up. Wake up now. Don't dilly-dally about it. Wake up. Wake up.

Across the plantation the sounds of the birds opened into the air between the trees and multiplied until, tree by tree, bush by bush, from the path to the edge of the cliff where the trunks hung over at crazy angles, the shoreline seemed to shake with song.

'Time for food,' said Molly, yawning and stretching. They packed up their equipment.

'I'd like to be out in the open,' replied Cherry. 'How about if we make for the boulders back there?'

'Good idea. We can brew up and make toast,' said Beech. To Molly she added, 'We haven't shown you our new stove yet, have we? Thrilled with it. It packs down to six inches but s'got full power. We can make hot coffee or hot chocolate, easy.'

'Sounds great. I'm colder than I thought. Come on. Look at the light now. It's going to be one of our rose-pink clichés. Come on.'

'We're right behind you. Lead on.'

*

27

They were about ten minutes trekking with the gear out of the canopy into the open. The sky was now washed by brown and beige deepening to pink to their left. They humped the tripods carefully down the stone stairs back on to the gently undulating coast path which rose again to the junction by the secret path leading out above Catherine's Cove.

The friends settled down on top of a great outcrop where they had a good vantage point of the ocean below and could watch the effect of the dawn across the waves. They made breakfast, laughing and joking as they talked on about the night's work and their plans to return sometime in a different season to discover the changes.

Presently, while Molly downed hot chocolate, Beech declared that with all that real coffee she needed a pee, so she grabbed tissues from her backpack and set off across the rocks to find a secluded crevice.

Back at base camp the others heard her shout, 'Hey, you two. Hey! Hey, come here. Quick. Oh, my God! You two, hurry up, come quick. Come here. Come quick.'

'What on earth?' They scrambled to where Beech stood, alarmed. 'Down there. I think she's dead. Oh my God, a body.'

Rapidly they climbed down to the stone seat where a woman lay face down, with huge empty brandy bottles near her outflung arm.

'Here, let me,' said Cherry who had done first aid. She hurriedly undid the woman's zipper and collar and felt her neck. 'She's alive, there's a pulse. Oh hell, she's so cold though.' She rolled the woman over and, as she did so, the woman made muttering sounds.

Molly arrived and peered closely, her face recording astonishment as Beech said, 'There's a whole bundle of folded carrier bags under this stone and others with huge stones in.'

'I know who she is,' said Molly in a strange, shocked voice. 'You've got her cards on the wall of your living room. This woman is Lerryn Trevonnian and she's only just alive. We have to move very fast, very fast indeed.'

'Lerryn Trevonnian?'

'The very same. She's the niece of Harriet Mulliere who founded my shop The Gallery and left us the Hermit's Hut Arts Trust.'

28

'The niece. But . . .'

'Whoever she is, we can't call the air ambulance from here. It'd be quicker to get her back to Eastfield.'

'She's muttering and grunting. That's a good sign,' said Cherry, thinking rapidly. 'More drunk than anything else, it seems. We have to get her off these cliffs. She's damn lucky. If she'd slipped into unconsciousness it'd have been a police job. No way could we've brought her round. She's conscious – well – just – but how the fuck do we get her out of here?'

'Should I rub her a bit? Get her circulation going? What about a hot drink?' asked Molly.

'No. No drink. It would do more harm than good. You could try talking to her. She's murmuring. I'd like her a bit more aware.'

'Okay. I'll try.'

'She's well-clothed,' Beech said, 'but she had all that alcohol. Do you think she's going to make it?'

'Luckily it wasn't a wet night or she'd have been soaked through.' Cherry was rubbing the woman's hands. 'She's got top quality waterproofs on. Whatever she was intending to do here, it wasn't to get hypothermia.'

'It was something to do with those bags. Check her pockets, see if there's anything.'

'Well, let's see. There's nothing with writing on, if that's what you mean. But there's this heavy canvas belt, all rolled up. Seems purposeful. She's no obvious need of a belt, unless . . .'

'Shades of Virginia Woolf it seems. Stones in the pockets . . .'

'It was in the papers,' said Molly. 'Maybe you missed it. Her father did it like that.'

'Oh, I remember. But I never realised it was her dad. He had carrier bags on a belt and huge stones in them, didn't he?'

'Whatever can have brought her to that?' said Molly, and she began to talk to the stupefied woman.

'Come on, lovie. Talk to me, Lerryn. It's me, Molly. You remember Molly. Lives by the footpath to Nanjizal. Come on, Lerryn, talk to me. Come on now, me 'andsome. Talk to me, Lerryn lovie. Come on now, me 'andsome. Time to go home. Come on, Lerryn. It's me, Molly.'

For many minutes Molly talked to the murmuring form. She kept up a constant run of words, on and on, talking and talking.

'It's not good,' said Beech. 'She doesn't seem to respond. Come on, Lerryn. Wake up and talk to us. Come on.'

'We'll give it another five minutes, then one of us must go for help to the houses at Raginnis,' said Cherry.

'What about Kemyel Crease?'

'I don't know the people there but there's the Harper family at Raginnis and they're quite friendly.'

'Yes, but are they discreet? This woman is a well-known artist,' said Molly. 'It'd be all over the *Cornishman* before you could say rescue team. We don't want that. Lerryn must be in deep despair or she wouldn't be thinking of following her father into the never-never, would she?'

'Her eyelid flickered. Keep talking,' said Cherry.

'Come on, Lerryn, wake up. Come on, me 'andsome, we have to get you home.'

'She's changing tone. Lerryn?'

The woman groaned and opened her eyes.

'Thank God for that,' said Molly.

'Mmm. Oh. Oh dear,' sighed Lerryn, opening her eyes.

'That's better. Hello, Lerryn, it's me, Molly from The Gallery. I knew your Aunt Harriet. Talk to me, Lerryn.'

There was another different groan: 'What's . . . what's . . .'

Molly kept on talking. 'It's me, Molly. You're all right. Come on. Keep your eyes open. You're doing just fine now. That's it, Lerryn. Open your eyes. That's a good soul. Come on, me 'andsome. Lerryn? Try and say something. Come on, lovie.'

'Oh, oh dear . . . Where . . . what'ssss?'

'We found you. We're friends. You'll be all right, Lerryn. Come on, lovie. Come on, me 'andsome. That's it. There now. You've had a long long sleep. You'll be all right.'

'I . . . I was . . . I was . . .'

'Yes, we know what you were going to do. You didn't do it. You're here with us, Lerryn. You're going to be all right. Everything is going to be all right. You didn't do it, me 'andsome. You didn't go through with it. And we're glad. We're so glad. What a waste it would have been. Look, here's my friends, Beech and Cherry. We'll help you now. There, now. You'll be all right now. We're friends here. You're going to be all right.'

'Beech, I've got an idea,' said Cherry. 'You're the fastest

runner. Could you make your way back to Eastfield as fast as you can and bring Molly's car to the junction at Raginnis? And our folding wheelbarrow? I know it's bizarre, but she's going to be heavy in this state and it's a long way! Then could you come back and find us. Meanwhile we'll put that canvas belt around her and try to hold her and steady her back over these rocks so we can start back with her along the coast path.'

'She'll be a dead weight. Look at the state of her.'

'Yes, I know. But she is conscious and that should help. It's not that far up the very rough bit, then we can use the wheelbarrow.'

'It's so steep . . . But you're right. I can't think of any other way – not without involving the police.'

'No,' said Molly rapidly. 'We do this ourselves.'

'I know. Okay. What about all the cameras and stuff?'

'We could hide all the cameras and tripods under the brambles here. No one will find them. Then this afternoon we could come back and collect them.'

'Okay. We could wrap them in all these carrier bags to keep them dry and they're all in their cases anyway. I agree the priority's to get her home – a warm bed with hot-water bottles. Okay. She must get warmed up, yes?'

'Exactly. I'm sure the stuff will be all right for that short time and the forecast is for very dry weather or we couldn't . . .'

Beech interrupted, 'But I think I should just take out the films, surely? I could do that in a mere five minutes before setting off.'

'Make it so, Number One,' said Molly, who was a Star Trek fan.

They laughed, and soon Beech was disappearing back up the cliff leaving the others to attend to the drunken Lerryn and make sure she stayed awake and aware.

Beech worked very quickly. She hid and protected the photographic equipment under the brambles and bracken by the coast path.

Molly and Cherry struggled to get Lerryn moving, pulling her to her feet and manoeuvring her up the narrow track.

Lerryn was drunk and heavy and unsteady, but she seemed to know that they were doing their best. They steadied her, moved her feet one in front of the other, steadied her again, shoved her a little bit, then hauled her forward with the belt round her waist.

On the steepest aspect of the path, with one of them in front of her and the other holding her from behind to stop her falling backwards, they lifted her knees one by one on to the next stone.

Eventually, after what seemed like hours, they placed her on part of the coast path where Beech could arrive with the barrow.

Then the three of them together lifted her, half-seated, into the barrow, which was used on the land for heavy stones and could easily take the strange bundle's weight.

In that manner, they barrow-loaded her all the way along the bumpy path to the car, talking to her all the while to prevent her from slipping into unconsciousness.

By early morning the whole mission was accomplished and no one except the four now resting in front of the log fire at Eastfield Farm knew anything at all about the events of that very strange night.

CHAPTER FIVE

For several days I slept and recuperated at Eastfield Farm, watched over by Cherry, Beech and sometimes Molly when she came to see how I was.

My room was on the ground floor bordering the lane. It had windows on the northeast, southeast and southwest sides so that, as I lay there, I could watch the movement of daylight around white walls, from early morning through to the evening, and the shadows of an ash tree whose leafless branches tossed and swayed in the wind. The room had low walls and its focus at the southeast end was a round-bellied black-painted wood-stove. It had a curving black stove pipe leading up to the point of the roof slope. The stove door could be opened so that from my single bed I could look into the small fire through a six-inch square aperture. This was the heart of the room, which in other ways reminded me of Mondrian's art studio in Hampstead, where he had fled from the Nazis before the Second World War. He had painted it entirely white just like his room in Paris had been, and he had joined the community of modernists described so vividly in Marion Whybrow's book of St Ives. Later, when war broke out, some of the modernists, including Barbara Hepworth, had come to St Ives. Now in St Ives there was the new 'Tate of the West'. Times change.

I loved that white-painted room at Eastfield Farm. From time to time Cherry or Beech would slip in silently and place another piece of wood into the stove. Just as silently, they would leave again, knowing that I was mid-thought, mid-shadow, mid-journey back to life. I had made my choice there on the cliffs. They had found me, resuscitated me, rescued me. But I had made the choice. I had not followed in my father's footsteps. I had chosen to stay alive.

During my night on the cliffs above Catherine's Cove I had, somehow, chosen to drink myself into a stupor rather than end my life by drowning myself in the ocean. I had, even if it seemed by default, taken action which had not ended my life.

33

Sometimes in the white room, I'd be shuddered from a reverie by an unfamiliar shaking sound but, after the first shock, I came to recognise the hooves of approaching horses in the rough lane and the accompanying voices of the riders moving towards me and fading away again. There were no cars except that of a woman who took care of Hazel Banyer's old farmhouse which formed the fourth side of the erstwhile farmyard.

On my second day I was loaned an old pair of wellies and taken on a tour of the buildings and the adjoining acres which Cherry and Beech loved as if they too were trees growing there rooted in the fertile soil.

After that, each day, I would go out from the white room just to stand on the land and feel it under my feet behind me ahead of me and all around me. I too began to take root there.

It was so very very quiet. Although inside that quietness were a million fragments of earthsound. I was reminded of a beautiful passage in one of my favourite novels, *A Thousand Acres*, of how the deep soil on the American farm was created over millions of years by layers and layers of dead leaves, fish scales and birds' wings.

This soil on which I now stood, alive and coming to terms with being given this new chance with new friends, was not deep nor had it ever – to the best of my knowledge – been under water, but it was beautiful. It sloped gently to the southwest, facing a ring of hills – Sancreed Beacon, Chapel Carn Brea, Bartinney and more. A few miles over those hills lay the end of the land and the wide Atlantic sea.

Around me were the young trees which the owner of Eastfield Farm had planted and, although some were too close together and others slightly misplaced, the combination of natural landscape and mixed woodland with one or two stunning specimens of larch and lodge pole pine, was breathtaking.

In the mornings the fields steamed under the spring sunshine as the dew evaporated, sending up shimmering layers of mist. In the lower field, bordering the lane but hidden from walkers and horseriders by the high Cornish hedge, Cherry and Beech had worked like human dynamos, hour after hour, to reclaim the land. They had freed up the blackcurrant bushes, raspberry canes and thick clumps of comfrey which had been hidden, like the secret gardens at Heligan, under an invasion of brambles and hogweed.

Beans grew there again, and parsnips, turnips, peas and potatoes had all been planted, though field mice in profusion thought the beans were for their benefit. It was a human-against-inhabitants battle of wills, especially as Cherry and Beech were organic gardeners who would not put down poisonous chemicals. The mice chomped merrily and went forth and multiplied, Cherry and Beech shrugged and went on planting.

I listened. Birds' wings overhead. Rustling in the branches. Patterings in dried leaves under the young trees. And every-where a sense of eyes and insects moving, humming, flitting, searching.

On my fourth and last morning at Eastfield Farm, the day I was due to return to my brothers' old rundown house, which I was ready to do, happy to do, I made my way very early in the borrowed wellies up through the middle field towards a secret new woodland which now covered the whole of the third field. It became a day of magic for me, one of those days when you know you're turning a corner.

That morning Eastfield Farm was enveloped in thick mists, but at first they didn't reach down as far as the grass so I walked up through the middle field inside a layer of luminous light which seemed to bounce between me and a low swirling overhang of damp air.

I stood a while under heavy, leafless trees in the hidden heartland of my homeland. All around me the mist moved, clinging to the hawthorns, wrapping around the pale green lichens, entering every crevice and cranny of the granite hedges, soaking the curving fields, cobwebbing the low bushes where, among red winter bramble leaves, the minutest green buds were visible.

I was caressed by the mist, delighted by its ethereal quality as I heaved the farm gate on its hinges and, replacing it, stood leaning against it, listening to the silence.

A dripping enclosing silence. No farm machinery could be heard that day. No cars, no wind, no birdsong. Only the creak of the farm gate against its stone post as I leaned on it; and then, only the slow sound of spongy waterfilled grass receiving each bootfall as I entered the secret woodland created for women on Eastfield Farm.

The sounds changed: a ripple of water in a spring from the woodland, a slow drip from young overhanging wild cherry in an earthy environment lit by a single clump of early Lamorna daffodils, someone's planted gift.

I breathed quietly, waiting unhurriedly by the tiny spring, taking it all in. Wetness. It was a watery day. No rain. Water and earth, the elements. No fire, except the daffodils, no air, only water. I did not have a belt around my waist with shopping bags with boulders hooked on. I was standing on firm earth. Breathing water as if through gills, as if I were the first creature to emerge from the sea, crawling on the earth, adapting to the changes. Alone but connected. Solitary but loved.

The gate to the secret woodland is attractive. Old, practical, carefully made in cast iron. A working gate with horizontal bars and easy swing. No fuss or curls of iron. An old gate. Simple and useful. A storyteller's gate. Come in, be safe, I have something to tell you.

The woodland was enclosed, young, deep, and peaceful. The story was short and to the point. I crouched by the spring, listening, balancing on my haunches to avoid soaking the knees of my jeans, glad of a waterproof jacket that protected me from overhead drips.

Remember your connection with this homeland, said the water that flowed from the earth. Wild garlic and primroses clinging to the cliffs. Summer heather and the wind in the grass. Blue skies of autumn and the dazzling winter light. Your stone seat at Catherine's Cove and the pounding ocean scattering itself on the rocks. Sea birds calling and the adder that suns itself on the coast path. Mist and rain, and fast-flowing streams from the moorlands down to the shores.

I am the spring that never runs dry from the earth beneath the wind. I was the voice of all your rainbows, here before you and there beyond you. I came from every well spring and can be seen after many a storm, here on your western shores. Forty thousand years ago I was there in other lands for other peoples. They named me. Julunggul. Yulunngur. Aido Hwedo. The rainbow serpent. I am famous worldwide. I am untameable. Know me. I lie along the cloud ridge waiting for the rain to cease. Know me. I dive under the earth and emerge in other valleys. Know me. I am everywhere. I am older than you can comprehend. I am available. I am a restless artist. I am a shedder of old ways. Know me.

I was here before you and will be here when you are long gone and I am here for you now, part of you, your rock strength along the length of your spine. I am echoed in every curve of your body, envisioned in a double helix in every cell, and drawn in circles by your ancestors with stones upon your land.

I am wisdom and origin. Know me. I am the idea itself. The original concept. I am the process of transformation.

I am calling you, here in your land to create a full circle. My tail is held in my mouth. I join you to yourself. I am your colours that flow when you paint. I am creativity. There is no place I cannot be. I emerge from every water hole and return to every sea. Trust me.

I don't know how long I stayed by the tiny spring in the secret woodland on Eastfield Farm. It must've been a good while, because when I returned through the storyteller's gate back into the middle field I could see the distant ring of hills, which before had been enveloped in mists.

Indoors again in the low-beamed living-room with Cherry and Beech, who were about to start the morning's gardening, I had a late breakfast and then took my time tidying the white-walled room, and helping with the washing-up. Then Molly arrived to give me a lift into Penzance so that I could take up my life again in residence in my brothers' old rundown house.

Molly oohed and aahed happily over the dilapidated old place and I knew, by then, that I would come to love and cherish it as my home. We hugged warmly as she left and I whispered thank yous in her ear. The thank-you-for-everything kind of thank yous that are the only ones you can say to someone such as Molly for the part she and my two new friends had played in helping me save my own life.

Chapter Six

It was a perfect spring morning and it was Monday, her day off. Tarn pulled back the curtains by the french windows to let in the sunshine. She ate breakfast lazily and then took a long slow bath. Then, ironically, already up to her neck in warm bubbles, she realised that what she most wanted to do was a spot of gardening. It would have been sensible to have the bath afterwards, but that wasn't the way she felt like doing things. Ever since she'd lived alone she'd relished the luxury of being able to decide to do simple things in the wrong order, if she so pleased. It was wonderful.

So, after her bath, she dressed in her gardening gear, made fresh coffee and took the mug out the back, where she stood on top of the small rockery watching the glittering sea down the hill in the distance. She was perfectly happy with the day and with herself.

Despite the sunshine it was chilly. She decided to go in for her gardening jacket, which was good timing because it meant she heard the postman ringing the bell.

'Parcel for you, Tarn. *Guten Morgen.*'

She laughed. 'Thanks, David.'

'Day off?'

'Yes, *es ist wunderbar.*'

'*Auf Wiedersehen*, Tarn.'

'*Auf Wiedersehen. Danke schön.*'

'*Bitte schön.*'

Much laughter. He was still chuckling as he went down the path. It was an easy ritual, performed ever since he'd been to one of her evening classes and had gained his German GCSE. He'd been thrilled to bits.

Indoors Tarn opened the parcel which was a book she'd ordered from her book club; and sat by the french windows with the latest letter from Liesl.

Dear Tarn,

Thanks for your last letter. It's all so exciting, isn't it? The tiles are now translated and I have an advance copy because Professor Schaffer is at the university here. It's amazing for me because I was very near the truth about the life and times of Helga of Cologne in my new novel – people who know me are talking of 'magical reality'. I've heard of it for other novelists, of course, but for it to happen to *me*? It's just wonderful! So I'm posting this to you immediately with the translations and I'm asking you to embargo it until the public have got access to it, dear Tarn, or I'll be in some bother. I know you'll understand but it will be published very soon so it's not a lot for us to 'hold' – otherwise we'd be bursting with it, wouldn't we?

I wonder if the weather is still sunny in Penzance. If so, I imagine you going into your garden and reading these outside because this is a story about women and land – land which the Beguine women loved and needed here so desperately in the late thirteenth century – land which, as you rightly say, women still need today.

It's a shame that your back was playing up and you were unable to go over to your local women's land recently but I am sure the women understand – they are good women at Eastfield Farm – and if you do manage to get over there now that it's better (very glad the pain has gone now, hope it stays that way) to do some brambling again, please give them my best regards. There's a group of women in Berlin who have begun to save up and to look for land and maybe next time you're here we could go to women's land at the holiday house, Moin Moin, near the border with Holland. Flat country very calm and incredibly peaceful. The women who run it are lovely and there's so much going on there, massage and healing weekends and so on. The older lesbian group also stays there from time to time – I think I might make contact and go along. Maybe I'm ready for groups again but, well, it's always a bit of a risk. Me and groups – I'm not sure if we mix really.

I went with Ingrid to see the tiles at the university, before they go on display in the museum here. I was astonished, Tarn. They are larger than I had imagined – about twenty-five centimetres square – and they are SO blue. The blueness generated deep, deep responses in me. All the colours of blue, gentian blue, swirled in my mind. Hills at twilight, distant, calling, which made me think of the hills of the Mosel in my novel and Helga as a young woman watching the blue distance, planning to leave her home for the long, uncertain route to the Beguinage. Blue, blue hills. Then, the inside of a magpie's wing against the sun. Blue feathers, shimmering. Then, peacock feathers and blue glass bottles in antique shop windows. My old blue sandals – many a long journey wearing them. Blue also for the colour of meditation, and many herbs in flower, blue for healing and blue for joyfulness. So, lastly, the intense blue of a candle which Ingrid gave to me at midwinter, with the light shining through the melted wax.

I know that I sound emotional – because of the tiles. So blue, so compelling. The colour reached into me in a most unexpected way. I seem to thrill with it; to resonate with it. The tiles seemed to say to me, Liesl, write your novel. Tell my story, for I am Helga and I haven't much time. Hurry. Hurry. Soon they will come for us.

Then I thought of you, Tarn, and your folklore research on the Isle of Man. You *must* continue with it, my dear friend. Do your research on the witch accusations. Let us not forget these women.

On the tiles, the writing is in Latin, of course. Helga of Cologne was educated at the Beguinage by some of the most wealthy, independent women of Germany. Some were widows, who had sold their lands to set up again at the Beguinage, sometimes donating their money and sometimes the lands themselves if they were nearby. There was already the tradition, on the Continent, that wealthy women could learn from their brothers and fathers even if they did not themselves have their own tutors. The role model is, of course, Hildegard of Bingen about a century earlier. I heard some of her music on the radio this week, incidentally.

When I looked at the square tiles I felt as if they were video screens, behind which I could imagine Helga in the film of her life. She was planting and working, illustrating the Beguine manuscripts in her exquisitely fine calligraphy, and sitting under a bower beside the walled herb garden with Ilse and

Ilse's daughter, Hilde. They were wearing the long, grey, simple clothes of the Beguines. There was a bank of blue rosemary, purple sage and deep blue hyssop behind them.

But I digress! The tiles are well over two centimetres thick. One of them was cracked across the corner and had been left like that on display to show the cross-section, which was very interesting. The base was the traditional grey German clay, which is very strong and can be dried flat without buckling. It was about one-and-a-half centimetres thick. On top of this was a thin layer of white fine china clay which may have been imported, or transported from somewhere else in Germany itself. The women had money, after all, and so the cost wouldn't have been prohibitive. Those two layers appear to have been fired to what is called a biscuit. Then the tile may have been tilted slightly and what today we call a slip may have been poured over it.

Opinions here vary as to exactly how it was done in those days but today the slip would be made of wet clay with pigment added. We would leave it until it was 'leather-hard' or 'leather-dry', then the writing would be cut through the blue layer into the white clay below. It would leave a little ridge around each letter and this would fill up with glaze in the final stage, thus making a flat shimmering surface. Wow!

Now here's the fascinating point. The pigment was copper-based and Ilse, who appears to have been the potter, must have known that if she applied a lead glaze to that it would go a greenish colour and that if she wanted the vibrant deep blue, even though it has a magnificent sea-greenish tinge at the edges, she had to have an alkaline glaze. Because alkali plus copper pigment makes blue. So the two women were taking the German ceramic development into a new stage by making these tiles.

For the final glaze, these days, a potter might combine soda ash, or some other alkali, by heating it with silica, into a molten form of glass, which would be poured into cold water. The glass would shatter into tiny globules which could then be ground up finely to make what is known as a frit. This ground glass would then be applied over the blue pigment layers and the tile would be fired again. When the glaze and pigment layer fuse together the final colour is created. The second firing would be at a lower temperature than the biscuit but would be high enough to melt the frit and fast enough to avoid evaporating the copper pigment and thus accidentally reducing any of its intense colour. It fascinates me, all this. The purpose of the second firing is simply to put a thin layer of glass across the written tiles: glazing! I never even connected the word glazing with glass-covered tiles before. But I am learning fast: it's interesting to me that techniques which are one-offs like this can take place but may be lost across time, until they reappear later, somewhere else. In this case Professor Schaffer says the knowledge had to have come from the Middle East – that was the centre of excellence for blue tiles in this period of history.

Oh, I love these Beguine women! To me it seems obvious that they really wanted the colour of their herbs on those tiles. To me, it's part of the message across time and space.

I have been rattling along at a pace in this letter but it is my dream to write that novel, and I must make it come true, especially now, mustn't I?

Anyway here's the bumf – let me know how you feel about it!! (I was going to say enjoy, enjoy, but it's not quite the right sentiment!!) Love from Ingrid and myself.

Liesl.

Tarn pulled on her gardening jacket. She trusted Liesl's intuition. She would read the translations sitting outside, connected to her own special plot of land. She stuffed the rest of the letter in a deep pocket and found the key to the garden shed.

The hinges were well-oiled and the padlock likewise. Even so, she would have to buy a new padlock again this springtime because nothing much withstood the salty air – things left outside rusted so fast here.

She stood on the threshold of the wooden shed and looked in, smiling, letting her eyes move slowly to and fro, deliciously slowly, the sort of slowly that comes naturally to seasoned gardeners, tracking across the shelves, and up and down the lined wooden walls. Her gaze rested momentarily on a small trowel. She remembered her old Aunt Ginny back on the island: a place for everything, dear, and everything in its place. Aunt Ginny, who was actually her great-aunt on her mother's side, used to make amazing summer puddings from the raspberries, redcurrants, blackcurrants, loganberries and blackberries in her garden. Aunt Ginny had given Tarn her first gardening trowel, with a warm wooden handle. It was hanging there now in the shed, clinging upside down poised on two thin nails, like a small metal bat resting by day on thin twigs. Inspired by Aunt Ginny, Tarn would come by collectors' items of old tools. She lovingly sanded their handles and primed their metal shafts. Her favourite was not used much in this garden, which was what they call a pocket handkerchief, though Tarn perceived it rather more like a huge plant pot. Her favourite was a very old real pitch fork. The rusted tines in an old shaft had been a gift from a friend who'd gone to an agricultural auction. Tarn paid a blacksmith to mend it and fix a new handle. It was a perfect tool, its balance and proportions created by those who knew exactly what was needed from its use. *Wunderbar*.

Tarn stood at the entrance to the shed. A workplace. Had the Beguine women kept their garden tools neatly like this? Had they also loved the ordered symmetry of their other workshops, such as their pottery? Wooden boxes of clay, different colours, different compositions? Wooden benches, one with a stone sink, great vats of water that had been collected from the well. Rows of plates and mugs, huge bowls for kitchen use, storage jars with enormous lids, rows of them, and, on shelves right up to the roof, lines of earthenware plant pots, all sizes, rows and rows of them, on planks of wood, waiting for their turn to be fired?

Had the sunlight striped in across the pots, illuminating flat beds of wooden frames for making tiles? Work benches with potters' tools laid out ready for use? How had it appeared, the Beguine pottery at the beginning of the fourteenth century? Had it been a pretty place where a woman had taken a series of glazed pots and filled them with fragrant herbs? Would you see a stool with a cushion on it where the potter's friend had sat, catching up on a morning's gossip?

What had the panic been like, creating those tiles? Could they hear the sound of hammer on stone, nearby, in the sculpture workshop where someone else was carving birds and animals on to a huge stone box with an inset stone lid? Or was the box already sitting there, waiting?

Tarn loved the calm, unhurried intensity of the interior of her garden shed. It smelled of cedar, well-treated. Her tools shone, in neat rows, their blades oiled and evenly cleaned. Washed plant pots were stacked in graded towers like grown-ups' toys, which is what they were really. Count them, sort them, size them, place them, wash them, get them all muddy, start the whole playful game again. And if you planted the sort of seeds that children love, easy grow and instant success seeds, such as marigolds and nasturtiums, you could watch every part of the miracle *and* eat them at the end. Nasturtiums tasted like sweet hot chillies. And so dramatic-looking around the edge of a green salad. From this shed you could grow order out of chaos and chaos out of order, mixing and matching, ducking and diving, any time you liked, any way you liked. The whole shed was just one big toybox, really. Better than any old doll's house. You couldn't do anything with a doll's house. Nothing grew in a doll's house.

In the pitch of the shed roof horizontal slats held the bean poles and long handles of the hoes and rakes. A string bag, suspended from a high hook, revealed two or three thick pieces of waterproof foam.

Thoughtfully, willing to enter into the world of Helga of Cologne, Tarn took out a thick foam kneeler from the string bag, and left the familiar shapes and patterns of the shed, closing the door respectfully behind her. She placed the foam on a low part of the garden which was, despite its small size, expertly designed on different levels.

Now she sat surrounded by herbs and spring flowers in a patch of sunlight trying to imagine the Beguine women with *their* favourite trowels, hoes and rakes among their flowers, herbs, fruit bushes, vegetables and orchards. Beside her the first butterflies and bees of the season were now busy on an early rosemary bush. Tarn reached to its nearest branch, stroking its needles firmly between finger and thumb, then drew the rubbed fragrance to her face. They do say that where a rosemary bush grows there's a strong woman living.

She didn't know much about the Beguines. But she had talked to Liesl about them and often wondered how they had lived so many centuries ago. The first women's movement in

Europe and a very powerful one at that. No wonder the men had been so threatened.

She pulled the papers from her deep pocket, ready to read the translations, after which, she promised herself, she would spend the rest of the morning pottering about out here.

The Ceramic Tiles of Helga of Cologne

Tiles One to Four

We make our protest. We are old women now. Writing to you the people of the future. Read our tiles and know our power. I am Helga, a manuscript illustrator at the Beguinage. She, Ilse, is the widow of a potter, from Frankfurt. We combine our skills at this time in this place.

Tiles Five to Nine

We use new techniques to create these objects. Ilse learned this from an itinerant Persian potter, who, escaping conflict, came east and north by sea and land, and found shelter in her husband's house.

Tiles Ten to Thirteen

The usual tiles hereabouts are caustic tiles from grey clay. Inlaid with coloured clays, fired until stoneware. Ours are unimaginably new here. Unknown, except at the Beguinage.

Tiles Fourteen to Seventeen

We have the blue, intense and luminous, coloured by copper fired under a soda ash glaze. Two firings to make something rare. Exceptionally new. Beautiful. We create new forms here. In every way.

Tiles Eighteen to Twenty

We are Beguines. We are women with land, time, money, and imagination. Old skills. New knowledge. Old wisdom. New ways of being. So the Church of Rome hates us, one and all.

Tiles Twenty-one to Twenty-three

They will destroy us. All of us. It is a simple fact. Ilse walked here with her daughter on her back. Sold her house. Gave her money to the Beguinage. Now we shall lose our home and our lives.

Tiles Twenty-four to Twenty-six

The men have taken Ilse's daughter, Hilde. She is young

enough to conceive a child. She is in the house of the head of the Weaver's Guild. His son has the pox and is disfigured. He has none of his teeth left. No one will have him. Three men dragged Hilde away.

Tiles Twenty-seven and Twenty-eight

Hilde begged us to leave her and take a boat along the Rhine to a safe village. However we have had all our belongings confiscated. No means of supporting ourselves.

Tiles Twenty-nine and Thirty

All of our land is forfeited and handed to the church and leaders of this town. The men scorn and vilify the old women like us, but we are free from marriage. We give thanks.

Tiles Thirty-one and Thirty-two

We have shared a gentle and frugal life. The calligrapher and the potter. Here we worked the land and gathered harvest. We watched the moon rise and the sun veil herself behind clouds. We have no wish to leave. We will take strong herbal poison together.

Tiles Thirty-three to Thirty-nine

Protest. We protest. These superb tiles are our new creation. There are none others throughout the length and breath of this land. Ilse takes the secret of this technique to the grave. On Ilse's tiles I inscribe from my experience with my hand-crafted words. We glaze the tiles with soda ash. We fire the tiles with passion. Fast. To keep the colour's intensity. The only set of such tiles made here. I write with a bamboo wedge nib down through deep blue pigment: inscribe our life through the leather-hard slip. White marks I make. Protest. Now, you read our story. Absorb the blue which dazzles your eyes. We live again. Beyond the blue distance. Strong. Luminous. Do not forget us. We made new lives, we make new deaths. We shall live between the worlds and shall return when it is safe.

CHAPTER SEVEN

The large old terraced house is on busy Lescudjack Road, part of the hilly aspect of the town, and from the mezzanine back bedroom window I could look down the length of the quiet back gardens of Baron's Hill with a narrow but uninterrupted view of the sea in Mount's Bay. The east light of early morning was glorious in that tiny room, which had a protruding old casement window, now rotted and wobbly. I set up a dining-table in there and it was from there one morning over breakfast that I saw her.

I couldn't call out to her because the window wouldn't open but I was so delighted to see her after all these years that I was almost tempted to break the glass and lean out.

That seemed a bit excessive. She was obviously not a visitor because she was bending, wearing gardening gloves and sorting out old pots from a cedar potting shed about three gardens along and down the hill from me. She wasn't behaving as if she was working for someone else, and I quickly came to the conclusion that she must be living in one of the flats, one with garden access, or at least it must be a holiday home that she often visited. Behind the closed, jammed-shut window I couldn't even leap up and down to attract her attention. If I'd banged on the glass she wouldn't have heard at that distance.

Nothing else for it. I sensed an energy running through me that I hadn't felt for years. I ran. Down the stairs, along the passage to the back kitchen where my old duffle coat hung by the Rayburn, kicked off my slippers and pulled on my boots, grabbed my key and left the house.

I ran. Up Lescudjack Road to the corner, and turned right, pulled up short by the dazzling light on the water in Mount's Bay at the foot of the hill in the distance.

Then I counted. One garden. Two. Three. This had to be it. I unlatched the gate and ran up the tiled front path.

These were old huge Victorian houses, genteel, now mostly flats and holiday apartments. A list of names by the bells.

Hers was the bottom one. Either she hadn't married or she had returned to using her maiden name. Callister. I rang.

Damn. If she was in the garden she mightn't be able to hear the bell. I waited. I rang again. I waited. The door opened. It was her, all right. I had been twelve and she fifteen when she arrived at the grammar school. She came from the Isle of Man. She had green eyes. One of the few schoolgirls with eyes the same colour as mine. Celtic green.

We'd always liked each other. We met in the school choir and she had a wonderful Manx voice, for they are a musical culture like the Welsh and we were always friends across the age gap. She'd had dark brown hair, but her hair wasn't brown any longer. We forget, don't we, that if we are women of the same age – or roughly the same – we are probably both looking time-worn. I was grey-haired too, by now.

We knew each other at once. Her face registered surprise and delight. In my mind, as she smiled hugely, opened her arms to hug me and invited me in for coffee, I saw her standing there on the stage in front of the school choir singing 'Ballad of Ellan Vannin'. The first lines came to me:

> Listen to the ocean, the ocean, the ocean
> Early morning tide slow surging washing clean
> Sunlight on the low waves; listen to us speak.
> Calm tide and sea birds. Calling, calling, calling
> You. Listen to our voices. Your heart longs for peace.

She hugged me again as we entered her flat. She was an inch taller than me and I'm tall. She was the heavier one, with a lovely wholesome body, a solid feel to her, a grey-haired white woman with green eyes and lightweight glasses that suited her, giving her a highly intelligent, slightly literary appearance, offset by her practical down-to-earth shabbiness. She had no grandeur, no aura of wealth or class, although I soon learned that she was a seasoned traveller and had lived abroad for many years.

I also learned that her main love was folklore and she had studied the form of the ballad and folksongs worldwide for her Masters in English. She had made her living by teaching English as a foreign language and was fluent in French, German and Japanese.

Currently she was making a comparison of the Gaelic languages, including her native Manx, which she had never learned as a child.

It was wonderful to meet her again. For the first time for ages, I cared about something new, and about someone new. I felt, I was absolutely clear to myself, very drawn to her. Perhaps if I'd known what was in store for us I'd have run a mile. But, '*Je ne regrette rien*'.

I went home from that first meeting humming to myself, then I took out my paints and began a painting on the theme of Ntozake Shange's poem: For coloured girls who have considered suicide when the rainbow is enuf.

I painted intensely for the rest of the day.

That night I lay thinking for a long time about women's friendships. Tarn was an old friend, met now in a new life. I had other new friends, Cherry, Beech and Molly. And always I was nurtured and sustained by my long, long friendship with Tessa and Jules.

I lay in the candlelight, in my attic, with my Moon Circles tape playing softly, and moon squares from the attic window sliding slowly across the floor. I was glad to be back in Cornwall, and curious about Tarn's ancestral connection with her homeland, symbolised now in the woman whom Tarn called Ellan Vannin.

I slept soundly and next day when Tarn arrived as planned for morning coffee I asked her what she felt nowadays about the island and how often she went back there.

'Only once a year, if I'm lucky,' she said. Her eyes were warm and smiling, her hands quiet and still as she leaned towards me slightly, her elbows on the table and her chin cupped in one of her hands. Sometimes she would look at me directly, with an intriguing sideways look, but at other times we watched the movement of the waves in the bay in the distance as we spoke. 'Something is pulling me back there,' she said. 'The call to return to the island comes like the tide. Ebbs and flows. It flows urgently, it flows peacefully, but always it flows. It begins with my thinking about the ballad. I think my first glimpse of my ancestors came all these years ago, when I sang 'The Ballad of Ellan Vannin' for the school choir.'

There wasn't much time before she had to leave for work but we managed to talk about a great deal. It turned out that Tarn knew Cherry and Beech, and had worked on women's land at Eastfield Farm. I promised to introduce her to Molly as well. She told me about Liesl, her friend in Germany, and her research into women's land in the thirteen hundreds, and the women who lived there. I had heard of the Beguines and had seen a Beguinage which still exists in Brugge. I promised to ask Tessa and Jules to send my photos of the buildings, so I could show them to her.

We arranged to go for a drink together that evening, and hugged warmly before she left.

After that, we met every day, learning about each other's lives. Tarn hadn't known that my parents, being traditional Cornish fishing and mining folk, hadn't understood my need to study art. Their idea of taking care of me and my future had been, quite rightly in their kind of lives, that I should learn a useful trade. I had been sent to work in hairdressing and not allowed to go on to higher education until I could pay for myself. I told Tarn about my aunt, who had been a wild girl in her youth and had met and married a wealthy businessman, and become a patron of the arts. Through her I had the confidence to hold on to my dream of becoming an artist. She had helped me make my dream come true.

On the other hand, I hadn't known that Tarn had spent years in Japan having married an engineer, nor that she had two daughters, Helen, who now lived in Germany, and Jocelyn, who was now in London expecting a child later in the year.

Of my recent night on the cliffs above Catherine's Cove I said little at that time. Later, I was to tell her all the details along with the decision I made there, but for the time being, I was only too pleased to be alive, friends with Tarn, and revisiting Eastfield Farm with her. I needed to move forward and not keep feeding the negative images that had led to that night. I knew intuitively that Cherry and Beech would allow me that freedom: to talk about my past, present and future by myself and for myself. Some things you just know – I knew that they would let me reveal my story to Tarn in my own way in my own time.

Of her women friends, Tarn spoke with loyalty and affection. She did not talk about loving women from girlhood onwards in the way that I did, though she was open to hearing about my years of South Yorkshire summers with Lindsey, and our subsequent love story.

Tarn listened with careful attention to the life and death of Lindsey's grandparents, Moss and Biff. I fetched the pictures I'd drawn of them both all those years ago.

'But this is wonderful,' she said. 'A search for Biff's true identity – a search through history for women's lives that have been hidden. It's just what I need to do for the Isle of Man. It's so exciting. And the research process really interests me, too. How *did* you find out that Lindsey was brought up not by her grandma, Moss, and grandad, Biff, as everyone thought, but by two "grandmothers"? I mean, how did you do your research?'

'It took me a long time to put together the pieces of the puzzle, although I had suspected for some time that Biff was a woman. After Biff died, Moss began to drop hints. She never told me directly, of course, but I felt sure that she wanted me to track down the truth. She said: Manchester. I was sure she meant that Biff had been born and raised there. That was the nearest that Moss ever came to revealing it.'

'Manchester always means "suffragettes" to me. Is that how you started?' asked Tarn.

'Yes. Manchester was too much of a hint to be ignored. And, many years before, Biff had told me in a letter that her family had been suffragettes. By now I was certain that Biff had been a woman. Someone in disguise. I had all the pictures that I had drawn, and I had seen a very old photo of Jessie Kenney, a suffragette, dressed as a post office telegraph boy. That's what confirmed the idea that Biff might have been a young suffragette. So there must be archives of her. But I didn't know her real name. If she had had to take a disguise, then Bernard Ian Ferguson must be her assumed name. So I started at Somerset House as then was, when it was still the registrar's office of births, marriages and deaths. Eventually – it took ages – I found an entry for Barbara Imogen Farley born in Manchester in 1896.'

Tarn's eyes shone. 'Go on, this is great . . .'

'Then I took myself to the Fawcett Library and I worked my way systematically through their suffragette archives. I found a record of a Mrs Farley who had been in Holloway and died later on. But no one else, though I knew that Biff had sisters because she'd also said that in her letter.

'After that I went to Manchester to the Pankhurst Centre. That's when I found Lucy and Sarah Farley in the archives. They had been mill workers – working-class suffragettes – who I think were Biff's older sisters.

'By now Moss had also died and Lindsey had gone to Australia, but I had something very precious to me. Not just a warm and loving memory of Moss and Biff, who had always been kind to me, not even just these drawings that I've shown you – I had far more than that. I could trust that the warmth of Moss and Biff came from their relationship as two women who loved each other. Biff was a woman and a lesbian! Biff was real.'

'That's amazing! It makes me feel all ziggy,' Tarn laughed, wide-eyed and shaking her head.

'And now I'm free to think about Moss and Biff again because Lindsey is fading now. I always liked Biff – even when I was a young woman without a clue as to what was really going on.'

'Which is that they were lovers and they were two women,' said Tarn. 'It is a wonderful thing, isn't it!!'

Her tone inspired me to ask, 'Have you ever had a relationship with a woman, Tarn?'

'With Sylvia,' she said, softly.

'When was that?'

'Two years ago, in London.' She smiled and paused. Then she said, 'She was already with a woman, back in Canada. They'd made a commitment to one another. It was a beautiful time, even so. It was my coming out – to myself and to the world. When Sylvia returned to Canada I came here to settle. I wanted the sea, some work came up in the language department here, and the land here – is like my island. Something familiar. Despite the call of Ellan Vannin, the Isle of Man's too far and far too expensive. As they say in German, *Es ist zu teuer*. Price too high. And frankly, for anyone like me who lives and works with attitudes that are international it's simply too small. I couldn't live there.' She shrugged, dismissively.

'Yet the call of Ellan Vannin is still very strong?'

'Yes. And the call draws ever nearer. I will want to go there soon, despite Jocelyn's pregnancy, despite my love of Cornwall. Although my home is here, now.' She sighed, rather sadly.

'Many years ago,' I said, picking around my words as if they were boulders on the moors, 'I saw a stone that I thought was a person. It's a bit like your island also *being* Ellan Vannin. I thought it was Biff there, though I knew she was at home in Herton. It gave me such a start when I turned the corner and saw it the first time. The slope of the shoulders, everything. After that I called it the Biff stone. Now, I can go and see Biff there whenever I like, just as you can visit the Isle of Man.'

'Maybe we could go to the Biff stone one day together,' said Tarn gently, with a question in her voice.

'Oh, yes. It's a long trek – very remote – we'd need plenty of time.' I looked at her intently.

'Then there's not enough time today,' she replied, smiling. 'But I did wonder if you might like a breath of fresh air. I certainly would before I start work. It's a long shift today. So I wondered if you'd like to take some lunch up on to the north coast road and show me the view with Hermit's Hut, your Aunt Harry's old place? I realise we can't call in or anything – if women are staying there and working – but I'd love it if you'd simply point it out to me. What d'you think?'

'Great idea. I'd love to show you Hermit's Hut.'

So, very shortly after that, we were driving over the moors. It was a bright day in early February and the first primroses were just peeping here and there in the hedgerows. Around the horizon, in every direction, was a bank of opaque mist like an upturned pudding bowl with the top sliced off. Above us was a light blue lid of curved sky over barren moorland, shining blue with high wisps of icy cloud like a pattern painted on the lid, bright in thin sunshine. A day for feeling glad to be alive.

In the rugged beauty of the north coast road we parked in a lay-by and, shouldering our mini-packs with our lunch, we climbed swiftly a short way up the rough area above the old road, until we could sit on a rocky outcrop looking down over the old field systems that were still marked out in granite boundaries between us and the sunlit, ice-cold sea. Under the strange bank of mist it glittered and shimmered as it often did on these end-of-winter days in West Penwith.

I pointed to the different farms and buildings, naming them one by one until, finally, there in a hollow with its wide windows on the ocean side of the house hidden from our view, was the cluster of granite buildings that had once been Aunt Harry's retreat and, in her later years, her home.

'There it is,' I said. 'The Hermit's Hut Trust Fund for Women Artists.'

'What a lovely setting. Oh, it is beautiful, Lerryn, but I'd never have found it by myself. This really is remote, isn't it!'

'And bleak. The wind is like a knife sometimes. You couldn't possibly have women's land down there. It's no place for fruit trees or a market garden. There were some tourists one year who tried to buy a farm at Pendeen. They were going to grow peaches. Honestly! Some hope.' I laughed. 'Can you see that curved extension at the back?' Tarn nodded. 'That was built when my aunt retired and the enclosed yard was filled with tubs by Denny, her housekeeper. There were flowers everywhere. My aunt and Denny fell in love, but then my aunt suddenly died. Denny flew out to New Zealand and stayed there. We still write.'

'Your aunt didn't leave Hermit's Hut to Denny?'

'No. No, it wasn't like that. Denny didn't want it, though she could have stayed for the rest of her life as warden if she had wanted to. But Cornwall wasn't the right country for her after the shock of loving and losing so quickly. So she made a new life for herself.'

'I can understand that,' said Tarn, gently. 'You miss your aunt very much don't you, Lerryn?'

'Very much. She was always there for me.' Then, in the silence and beauty of the moors and, in a rare moment of trust, I heard myself say, 'When I went in search of Lindsey, my childhood sweetheart, I was nineteen and I was sure of my feelings. But I was too late. Lindsey had gone to London with a boyfriend. I felt bereft. Abandoned. Then I met a lovely friend of my aunt's. Her name was Anna von Schiller and she was very much older than me. We fell in love. I suppose I was on the rebound, but it was a profound love. I feel a great warmth towards Anna, even now. It's not simple, these things never are. My warmth towards her has also some unresolved anger in it. It's partly class – Anna was very wealthy, a patroness of the arts, and she wanted me to travel with her and live with her all over Europe. But my dream was to study in London and live my own life to the full. I didn't go with her. My life was here. My work, my aunt, everything. So Anna and I parted and my aunt was wonderfully kind to me. But . . .' I paused and sighed. Tarn waited, keeping her gaze on Hermit's Hut down below us. 'What I didn't know was that Anna had been Aunt Harry's lover. She left my aunt for me. I couldn't possibly have known because I had simply never thought of my aunt as sexual, somehow. It had never ever occurred to me that Anna and my aunt had been lovers.'

'It must've been an incredibly strong bond between you and your aunt to withstand that!'

'It was.' I smiled at her warmly. 'This is a lovely thing to do today, Tarn. Thank you.'

'I'm glad,' she said, simply.

'We'd better eat up, hadn't we? I don't want to make you late for work.'

'There's enough time. Don't worry.'

We ate in companionable silence. I thought of all the things we were beginning to share and her simple words: I'm glad.

CHAPTER EIGHT

The first lambs were bleating in the fields when I decided one day, while Tarn was working, that I must not neglect my own personal journeys. So, with my well-worn copy of *A Week At The Land's End* in my rucksack, I parked the car on a grassy verge by a road above the Bosistow Valley and, following a newish sign that said Footpath to Nanjizal, I opened the gate to someone's back yard and made my way respectfully towards a cottage on the left a few feet from a granite stile. As I approached, an upstairs window opened and Molly waved to me, calling out, 'I was just cleaning this window and there you were! Let yourself in. It's open. You've time for a quick coffee? You're looking so much better.'

I opened the front door as she arrived a bit breathless from rushing downstairs. 'Come in, come here and let me hug you! You on your way to Nanjizal?'

'Molly! Lovely to see you. It's such a good day I thought you might be over at Eastfield Farm, brambling.'

'I was, yesterday. But I must sort out my bedrooms today. I haven't run the hoover round for ages.'

'I was going to knock to say hello, anyway,' I said following her into the low-beamed room. It was beautifully done in blues and greens. The colours seemed to be a reflection of the peninsula itself, which was surrounded by the sea on six out of seven sides. Molly had been given some stunning art work over the years by friends she'd made through The Gallery. And the nooks and crannies in the walls were adorned with wood carvings.

'How are you, Molly?'

'I'm fine dear. Actually the reason for all this housework is a delightful one. My son owns this house, as you know, and he and his girlfriend are coming next week. Such a treat.'

'Ah! That's why I can smell fruit cake. One of your specials – I wondered as I came in.'

'You name it I bake it, me 'andsome. Now what have I got in

this tin today?' It was a shining tin, oval, with a red-and-gold pattern. 'Flapjacks. Nice with fresh coffee. Have you got time?'

'You spoil me.' I nodded, smiling.

She shrugged merrily. 'Won't do you any harm, to be a bit spoiled, eh?'

'No, it won't. But I might get used to it. Then I'd be here every day.'

'I don't think so, Lerryn. A little birdie told me you're busy these days . . . you and Tarn?'

'Yes. It's wonderful to be getting to know her again after all these years.'

'Well, I look forward to meeting her, my love. Soon, I hope.' Molly smiled. 'You are looking wonderful, Lerryn. I'm so pleased to see you. By the look of that rucksack it seems you're off on a day's outing?'

'Yes, I'm feeling the need to touch the land. To visit all my old places.'

'Well, the land here will heal you, Lerryn. You have your ancestral spirits here.'

I laughed aloud. 'Not you as well, Molly! Everyone I meet seems to be talking about spirits these days. Aunt Harry used to say that Cornwall's like a Christmas stocking, all the nuts drop to the toe. Not you as well?' I grimaced and rolled my eyes.

She laughed lightly. 'Don't worry, Lerryn. I'm not trying to convert you to spiritualism.'

'You'd have a job.'

'I realise that. But I've always been that way minded. I'd say I'm quite religious. Not church; nor chapel. But I do love the earth and when I'm over at Eastfield Farm, clearing brambles, I feel I'm in tune with the spirits of women everywhere, past, present and future, who love the earth as I do. And of course there's my spirit healing circle.'

'I love the earth too. And I suppose that women's land at Eastfield Farm was a healing sanctuary for me, in a way, but I don't want a spiritual way of life. It wouldn't be real to me. I'd be pretending, you know? I'd feel out of touch with the harsh realities of most women's lives. I've always felt like this. I used to talk to Aunt Harry about it. After she died I missed those conversations.'

'Well, it takes all sorts, me 'andsome. It takes all sorts. No rules . . . each to her own I always say,' replied Molly, offering the red-and-gold tin again. She smiled lovingly at me, confident of how she wanted to live in the world and not the slightest bit concerned that I felt differently. An easy silence opened up in the room. I relaxed in the armchair, thinking how delighted I was to be becoming part of women's land at Eastfield Farm; and grateful that I wasn't going to be put under pressure to pretend to be something I wasn't – into spirituality like my new friends seemed to be.

'Maybe Tarn and I will meet at the weekend,' said Molly, sipping her coffee. 'When I was over at Eastfield yesterday, Cherry mentioned that it's her birthday on Saturday and she's got open house from midday. All invited. She was going to ring you both last night, I think. Did she talk to you yet?'

'No, the phone was busy all evening, what with one thing and another. I expect there'll be a message when Tarn gets in.'

We finished our elevenses and Molly wrapped two flapjacks in a paper bag for me 'for the journey'. I thanked her and we hugged closely. She whispered that so long as I was all right now, that's what mattered.

I left the house and climbed the stile and was soon striding out in the thin, clear sunlight across stiles and open fields. Passing through another farm yard, the last scattered buildings now all behind me, I found myself beside a dark brown ploughed field, in the Bosistow Valley. With only the songs of birds and calls of distant lambs for company, I stood and listened. I was in a wide and undulating valley, its lines and shapes sensuously female, with well-placed soft, hairy areas, luxuriously erotic, tantalisingly available, resting there in the sunlight.

Behind me, to my left, was Sennen Church. I let my gaze sweep across the skyline to the north until it came to rest on the tower of Buryan Church, a quarter of a circle round the horizon. Between the two churches were low hills and ridges and furrows and stone walls marking out quiet farmland in the first stages of spring. Smudged trees, their branches not yet leafy but blurry with bursting buds, nestled in the creases of the folds, but I was too far from them to hear the water that I knew gathered there, flowing south towards the sea. Above me were blue, blue spring skies, bright and clear with the translucent light that Cornish skyscapes at the coast always bring to welcome me at this time of year. Home. Great surges of delight rose through me like a song.

Ahead of me, the ploughed field had a wide, earthy stripe across its furrows where the farmer had marked out the right of way. I stepped forward on to the muddy surface, my boots squelching slightly, without sinking in, as I crossed over to a smart new wooden gate with blond-coloured posts.

Now the track narrowed and I turned right between shoulder-high blackthorn bushes, their spines and buds just beginning to trust the weather, not taking any chances. They were no-nonsense, don't-mess-with-me bushes. They reminded me of some of the stroppy women I'd known in London, and Lindsey when she was premenstrual all those years ago. I stopped walking.

I stood again, grounding myself, willing her image away from me. Most of my memories were vague now, separated from the emotion that used to encase them. I reminded myself of all the significant journeys I had made since then – to Yorkshire, to Herton, to the gravestones of Moss and Biff. The missing pieces of all the puzzles had been found, sorted, placed in position, their pictures reconstructed, the stories told and retold. Now I had reached the time for a new relationship; I could give and receive real love, here, now, in the present. I wouldn't let any of that old bitterness creep back to sabotage me.

Suddenly I realised I could hear the streams, swollen by spring rains and surging down the valley, and I ran forward along the narrow path until there, the sea opened before me in Nanjizal Bay. The waterfalls that drop so beautifully into the sandy cove were jumping and jostling for space and light.

It was that time of the afternoon when Land's End turns itself to meet the sun and none of Nanjizal Bay is in shadow. Sunlight played over the boisterous waters of the bay, and sunbeams pushed hard through the stone arch that was filled with light and foam and spray.

From Carn les Boel in the east to Carn Boel in the west not an inch of blue sea could be seen. All was white foaming billowing surging and falling floating water, light upon light, air upon air, layer upon layer. Breaking, retreating, returning, the waves came again and again at the cliffs; and over the whole surface a dazzling silver-white yellow sunlight bounced and shook itself in frills and curls and turns and swirls of white silk and satin, lace and flounces. There was no wind and the skies were calm blue and friendly. It was an outpouring of light and a rejoicing of water upon air upon water greeting the land with showers of bubbles interchanging and combining, shifting and dancing.

Stony cliffs observed the water pouring over them and recorded each sound, each moment, each movement in fragmentary shifts of rock. No single molecule of stone was unchanged by the sea's communication. Nothing was left to chance in this dance. It was orchestrated and choreographed there in front of me. Every particle of felspar, mica and quartz responded. Smoothed or cracked, chipped or grazed, worn out or worn down, the imprint of the sea was left there in its memory. But it was still granite composed of its parts, yet more than the sum of them, and I was still Lerryn Trevonnian, with memory and meaning, structure and purpose, even though waves and waves of events and incidents had been impinging on me since the day I had been born.

I had lines on my body and imprints and memories. I had knowledge of hands that had flowed over me and wetness that had delighted me. I had been changed by this and was still in the process of transformation.

There on Nanjizal beach I was part of everything and everything was part of me. I was home. Where I belonged and longed to be. On the land. Not in the sea. Of the earth and from the earth and flesh and blood, not stone. I, too, could record every single event that happened to me. An artist, I had the power to transform some of my realities, and, at the least, to understand those I couldn't make much impression on. From out of every experience I could create some artistic response, with paint, pencils, prints, whatever medium seemed most suited.

I was small, smaller than any of these rocks that made these soaring cliffs, but no less important nor able to withstand. I was as capable of giving and receiving love as they were. They were loving me that day and I loved them back fiercely, gladly, openly, rejoicing with them that I had returned.

Tarn was waiting for me when I arrived back at the house in

Lescudjack Road. She'd let herself in with the key I'd given her and a meal was prepared, with candles alight on the table, some fresh flowers in a little pot, and a bottle of Chianti. We hugged closely and then ate listening to tapes, talking about my day's walk, and enjoying the wonderful food. She liked to cook, which was something we could share since it was one of my favourite pastimes, too.

However, there was a shadow about her and after dinner I asked carefully if she would like to tell me what was troubling her.

'Jocelyn's asked me to go and see her in London,' she replied. 'I feel I should go because she rarely asks, but the timing's not of the best.' She gave a wry smile. 'Not that that's anything new where Joss's concerned.'

'You mentioned to me that you would want to see her, though, didn't you? I seem to remember you saying that you chose not to live in the Isle of Man partly because it would have been difficult to get to see your daughters. It would have been more difficult for you there than here, I think you said. Am I right?'

'Yes, it's true. The island would have made it all much harder. But even so, I'm finding it difficult enough. It's the contradictions, I suppose, that tear me apart,' she said.

Tarn was quiet for a while, watching a candle flame that was multiplied around the small room wherever there was a shiny surface. The window which looked down over her garden had no blinds or curtains. Now, after dark, the candle flame flickered in each of its panes at different angles. It was pretty and alluring simultaneously.

Tarn began again, 'It seems as a mother that it's never ever about my timing. Whatever happens in my life can be interrupted or intersected at any time by something that happens to Helen or Joss. I feel settled here at the moment, and . . . Lerryn, I'm enjoying our new friendship very much. It's just about timing, really.'

'I still keep in touch with Lindsey's daughter, Rosie,' I began, 'We love each other dearly. If Rosie was in trouble I'd have to respond.'

'Yes, but Rosie seems to be accepting of you and very loving. But unfortunately, Jocelyn and I have had such a strained, difficult relationship recently. I was just getting my head around the timing of her pregnancy. I don't really feel ready to dash up to London. She'll only want to see me for a day; anything else would be, well, she'd feel it was too intense. And we'd get to disagreeing – even having a row, which I really don't want. I can't stand the idea of her having a baby by a violent man. It's a nightmare . . . it spins round and round in my mind and I'm not sure I'm calm enough to give her what she wants.'

'Why not see Joss in a week or two, maybe at half-term, and then have a break? You could go to spend a few days with Liesl in Cologne perhaps? I *know* you want to see the wonderful tiles that have been found, and talk to Liesl about her research and her novel. A break might do you good, help you relax again after a day with Joss.'

Tarn's troubled face lit up. 'What a good idea! It would be wonderful to see Liesl. I know I'm over-reacting to Joss's request and I know I need to calm down. I've been going round and round. Like Dougal on *The Magic Roundabout*.' She laughed and did spinning actions with her hands. 'You're right, Lerrie, it's a great idea. And . . . our friendship will keep . . . won't it?'

'Of course it will. Yes, it will. Besides, it's not cheap to go to London. If you're going all the way there, from here, and you're near Heathrow, you're half-way to somewhere else. That's how I'd feel if I had to go back to London right now. Though I'm glad I don't. I'll miss you very much, but it's only a week or so. Go for it . . . take time out for yourself.'

Remarkably, she reached for my hand, held it whilst replying. 'You mean a lot to me, Lerryn. This,' she hesitated, 're-connection means a lot to me. It's been good to talk. Thanks.'

'It's fine. Really.' I squeezed her hand and, self-consciously, we both let go.

'I can't possibly ask for time off work,' Tarn said. 'But I don't work Mondays and there *is* half-term week coming up. It would make financial sense for me to fly to Cologne from Heathrow. It's quick and easy, and I'll be able to see Helen and Yuki too. They'll be delighted.'

'Good. That's great, isn't it?'

'Yes, wonderful. And I've been bugged about something to

do with those tiles. I'm dying to talk to Liesl. Somehow I think that talking about her research is going to help me with mine on Ellan Vannin.'

She was quiet for a little while, and I could almost hear her thinking about Ellan Vannin. I had read her 'Ballad of Ellan Vannin' many times since meeting Tarn again. She had given me a copy of it, and it now lay permanently beside my bed. In my mind I could hear the sing-song words of the chorus as if Tarn was walking in the countryside in the Isle of Man, singing aloud on the moorlands, and the hill farms, the cliff walks and the glens running down to the sea.

Into the silence, Tarn said quietly, 'She was a healing woman, my Ellan Vannin. Like Liesl's Helga of Cologne. You're right, Lerrie, I should go. I'll go and see those tiles in the museum. I'll go talk to Liesl. After that, perhaps, you and I could put our heads together about my Ellan Vannin?'

'Sounds good to me,' I said. 'Meanwhile we have an invitation to a party on women's land – shall we do some cooking together for it? We're more than ready for a women's party, don't you think? It'll be perfectly wonderful, I just know it. Let's cook something really special.'

'Another brilliant idea, Lerryn. Now, where are my recipe books?'

CHAPTER NINE

As soon as we arrived at Eastfield Farm for the party we heard the sound of drumming. Following it, we made our way around the house up to the camping field where a huge bonfire had been lit.

There, despite the end-of-winter weather, which wasn't exactly warm, a group of women were making music and singing. A large tent had been put up at the side of the field and Cherry ran forward to greet us. We laughed and hugged and wished her happy birthday.

'Isn't it great?' she said. 'They're down from Bristol and they always were a hardy bunch. They're lined up like sardines, sleeping in your old room, Lerryn.'

We had all brought food and drink to share and we put ours on the trestle table in the tent.

'I hadn't realised the party was going to be outside!' I said, smiling and stamping my feet to increase the circulation.

'Well, it wasn't exactly planned but this lot are a load of good fire-raising witches, you know, and they all piled into the house last night laughing and joking and declaring we would have a fire today for old times' sake. So here it is! All we need now is the skies to stay clear for us, yes?'

'Yes. Oh yes. It's so long since I went to a bonfire!'

'We collected the wood all morning – and we had a barn full of dried gorse. It just blazed up at once. And the old Greenham plastic sheeting to sit on was still in the roof of the barn, and there were old mats to lay on top of it. We got filthy fetching it down. But there's nothing like drumming with your feet on the earth. Come on, I'll introduce you both to my old friends.'

The bonfire was wonderful. We kept it going as the afternoon light faded and the skies darkened to clear dark evening. Beyond the circle of the fire and the silhouetted dancing figures, the skies were full of stars and we stood with Molly for a while picking out the constellations.

Tarn said, 'I've been coming here to do brambling but I've never sat down and asked anyone what the history of this women's land is. How it got started.'

'Oh, I'd love to tell you the story, my lover,' said Molly, with enthusiasm, lasping into the Cornish idiom. 'Let's find ourselves a nice warm space on a soft rug near the fire.'

So we tromped back down the field in our heavy boots, called in at the food tent for a plateful and a large mug of warm mulled wine, and settled ourselves down in the warmth of the enormous bonfire. I was amazed that it was possible to be so warm at that time of the year. In fact, we had to keep quite far back from the fire, because it gave off so much heat. We chose the opposite side to the drummers, where we could hear Molly easily.

'It all began,' said Molly, 'in the early seventies, while you were in London, Lerryn. There was a young woman here, the daughter of an old friend of mine who is herself an artist. The young woman's name was Madeleine Gerrard. She was a local weaver of some renown, a woman without a studio or workshop of her own. She used to sell her work in my friend's shop in St Ives. It was a perfect tourist outlet and she made good money doing so. But she was under a lot of stress: a workshop rented in one place, a flat rented with some women friends in another place, and the long trek to St Ives to sell her wares.

'Anyway, into the shop in St Ives one day strode a tall, lovely, older feminist woman academic from London. Then the magic began.'

'Did they become lovers?'

'No. That was never part of it. The woman, Hazel Banyer, was recently divorced and was looking for a place down here that would be her base. She travelled abroad a great deal for her work, and she was to retain an office in London, but she wanted a more tranquil home the rest of the time. The two struck up an immediate bond which was to last many years. They began to search for an old decrepit farmhouse with outbuildings to be converted into separate places for each of them, with land for each of them attached.'

'Did Hazel have money, then?'

'Yes, she did. Hazel would buy the whole precinct with money from her recently ended marriage. She would give some outbuildings to Madeleie and Madeleine would pay her back over the years. Each would have first refusal if and when the other wanted to sell either the buildings or the land.

'One day, when she was on the way to her weaving workshop, Madeleine took a different route. She found herself walking past an old farmhouse. A very romantic setting. She thought – ooh just the sort of place that Hazel and I would love to buy.

'It was this very place – the old house over there with that cluster of buildings there around the yard. Then the magic happened again. Into the shop that week, in St Ives, came two people talking about that very farmhouse, saying, between themselves, that the farmer's old mother had died and that he, left alone now and also old, was going to sell up and retire.'

'Molly! All these coincidences. They sound unreal, as if it really was magic. It's very Cornish, but is it true?' I smiled at her.

'As true as we all sit here now, my love. The next day Madeleine put on her oldest clothes and pulled her shabby country hat down over her ears. She went to talk to the farmer, saying she was so sorry to hear that his mother had died. She didn't mention the farm at all. Instead, as is the way in the country, he asked her if she'd like to walk through the fields to see his pride and joy – his pretty handmade goldfish pond. This she did. She talked only of his goldfish, the building of the pond and the care it took to look after them. Then, as they walked back, he said if she liked he would sell the farmhouse and land to her for cash. He said he'd trust her not to resell and turn it into a holiday home or caravan park. He could see that she was local and loved the land as he did and would do her best for the land.

'That afternoon, Madeleine's solicitor advised her to go back to the farmer and ask him to write on the back of an old envelope that he did intend to sell to her. This she did and he complied.

'So the sale went through for Helen and Madeleine amidst some kerfuffle . . .'

'I should think there was a hoo-hah,' I said. 'There'd be some noses out of joint round here.'

'Absolutely. It was a remote and beautiful site and some local people were jealous. But Madeleine and Hazel carried on.

Madeleine was to have the derelict cow byres, which is where Cherry and Beech live now. There was no proper roof, no drainage, no electricity, no doors, no windows, no floors, but it was a solid granite building. Madeleine and her friends camped out and did the place up together, with a little help from Madeleine's brother, who was a carpenter. Madeleine agreed to pay Hazel fifteen grand over time.

'Meanwhile, Madeleine got involved with some women from Greenham. She got into feminism and singing all the old witch songs that the women sang around the Greenham fires. She fell in love, came out, came home and turned her fields here, all three acres, into women's land.'

'How come I never heard about this women's land?' I asked.

'It was a Greenham thing. You weren't at Greenham, were you?'

'Only at the big demos.'

'But you'd have thought word would've got round, even so,' said Tarn, 'I was abroad, of course. But Lerryn was active in politics in London.'

'Madeleine didn't want too much publicity for this place,' Molly replied. 'It was word of mouth only and you had to be in Greenham circles really to be on the inside. It's still like that really. It's a kind of protection, which Madeleine and many of the other women felt was essential.'

'Well, it's a marvellous place,' I said. 'I love it here.'

'So do I,' said Tarn. 'Where else hereabouts could we have the wonderful freedom to meet and have a bonfire party like this. I mean the beach is wonderful at night in the summer, but it's not women only like this. That's the thing I love about it.'

'So what happened next?' I asked.

'Well, Madeleine lived here for many years. But finally her spirit grew restless. She had always been a restless soul. Even when she was a small child, she used to skip school and wander in the woods learning the wild herbs and flowers. She knew where the wild leeks grew; she collected spinach off the beaches; she gathered garlic and she stole cabbages. To her the abundance of the earth was there for everyone; field boundaries never contained her. As a young woman, she had travelled in the States, camping out in the wilds. She had always hated the thought of restriction. After a while, inevitably, I suppose, she began to feel contained, even within the three acres of Eastfield Farm.

'In the end, she packed hurriedly and left West Penwith with her woman lover for the United States. That's where I came in. My daughter's friend Maizie, two other local women, and I, became an informal land group, left in charge of women's land. We want, eventually, to create a women's trust for the land. To make sure it is held in perpetuity for women. Just before she left, Madeleine said to me, "This land is for wild women and wild animals for all time."'

'And how is the Land Trust going now?' asked Tarn.

'Well, it seems fine. We wrote to Madeleine a while ago about a couple of things we need to sort out, but we haven't heard back. You know how it is,' Molly sighed, 'She's so busy with all the work on women's land in the States.'

'Is there anything I can do to help with the Trust? I'm interested, really I am. I love coming here to do the brambles, but what I'd really like is some kind of proper involvement with the Land Trust.'

'That would be great,' Molly replied, smiling. 'As soon we've heard back from Madeleine and sorted out the smaller matters, we can start to progress again. I'll let you know just as soon as we hear something.'

'Thanks. I'd like that. It's just wonderful here. So special.'

'You know, it's interesting,' Tarn said to Molly. 'I'm going to some friends of mine in Germany for half-term. One of them, Liesl, has been doing research into women-only communities in Germany, called the Beguines. She's just come across a major find. All very exciting. The Beguines did exactly what Madeleine did – created a separate space for women, women's land, which they then maintained and farmed.'

'Get away!' Molly exclaimed. 'What did you say they were called – Beguines? I never heard of them. Now it's your turn to tell me a story – and I want all the details.'

So Tarn told Molly about Liesl's research, Helga of Cologne and the finding of the carved stone box and the amazing blue tiles.

I listened lazily, warm by the great fire. A new tune started up, one I hadn't heard before. I listened carefully to the words, words which the Greenham women had composed and which these friends of Cherry's, many of whom had been at Greenham with her years ago, were now singing lustily. It was a song about the witches.

I glanced over at Tarn, remembering what she had told me about her research in the Isle of Man. All the unnamed women accused of witchcraft in the early period. And the later trials, which were recorded.

I found the reality of the witch hunts very frightening. I found the hatred frightening. The two hundred thousand interrogations, frightening. The one hundred thousand murders, frightening. I found the knowledge awesome. Meanwhile, as I sat by the huge bonfire at Eastfield Farm that evening, the pieces of the puzzle fell into place for me and I knew why it was so important for Liesl to write her novel about Helga of Cologne who had lived on women's land; why Tarn must some time this summer visit the Isle of Man and do more of her research on what had happened to the witches there; why we needed to know that awesome history of women across Europe; and why I loved being here, now, alive and with Tarn at a women's party on women's land, in the heart of my homeland.

The tune stayed with me and will always do so. I could sing it in my sleep, and if ever, ever I was lonely again, alone and bewildered, I could call upon its power to sustain me.

Oh, who are the witches, where do they come from, maybe your great-great-grandmother was one – witches are wild, wise women they say, and there's a lot of witch in every woman today.

After the others had left the bonfire for the wood stove indoors, and yet more more wine, women and song, and with the shifting coral and amber light from the embers behind us, Tarn and I walked into the enclosing darkness of the quiet woodland, and paused by the storyteller's gate.

This land, said the gate as the hinges swung gently, is for wild women and wild animals for all time.

Then she took me in her arms and kissed me.

We stood kissing sweetly, aware of the crackle and hiss of the mature log fire far off down the field; and, nearby, of the crack-snap of dried twigs and the swish of an unseen animal on a nightly prowl. In the distance came the hoot of a barn owl.

Nearby was the occasional flurry of wings. Above these sounds and behind them, forming a musical backing for the surface patterns, we heard the stream, flowing from the woodland, full and steady in its end-of-winter mode.

Alone but together in the night, on women's land, we reached for each other, recognising what had been forming between us.

She kissed me again. A simple kiss, followed by an easy joke: your place or mine? Hers, we decided, but I don't remember the short journey back and I think I floated all the way across the field, past the heavy-embered fire, down the lane to the car and all the way to her flat. Hers, for its touch of luxury: warmth, thick carpets, the homely atmosphere, ease of being. It was strange to think that she would soon be going away for a few days. But we knew this wasn't a brief fling. Time seemed to be irrelevant, because we came from different worlds to this new time when the arching rainbow seemed to touch the town of Penzance, especially for me, Lerryn Trevonnian, falling in love again.

CHAPTER TEN

Dearest Lerryn,

How are you, dearest, and how are they all at Eastfield Farm? The fire, the women, the colours, the loving – are all still with me. Your loving arms, your voice, your face and hands, the touch and smell of you. I love you, Lerryn.

I felt about seven years old going into a shop to buy bubbles for Cherry's birthday – but I like blowing bubbles – and, oh, how glad I am for that day of play!! And that night – the first of many nights of loving as our relationship unfolds. I knew then, as I know now, that our bonding process is deep and fast. I feel that I have found something and someone rare and precious, to be recognised and cherished.

I'm glad this isn't a long separation – it's quite long enough for me! I'm having a lovely time but it will be good to be home again. Keep the bed warm for me. I'll be back soon.

It's wonderful to be here and to be staying with Liesl and Ingrid once again. It was a good idea to do this. I was feeling so anxious about Joss, but now that I've seen her I feel relieved. At least we've been able to start talking to each other, though it won't be at all easy when her man's living with her again. He makes a fuss if she spends time talking to 'that dyke' on the phone.

As to Joss herself, she has a haunted look in her eyes. She is hoping and longing for this baby to bring peace to her household. Jeff (I find it hard just writing his name) arrives from Hong Kong in about ten days' time. I have no illusions of it working out. I don't have any trust in him at all. He has written lovey-dovey letters about their baby and how he will respect Joss as the mother of his child. Can you hear my cynical laughter? It's all been said a million times before in households like this, and I know from all those friends who have worked with Women's Aid over the years how hollow such promises usually are. At least I was able to see her without him – she was right to ask me to come to her before he arrives. And she was all in one piece. No bruises. The worst thing I think in my life *ever* was to see her with bruises. It was heart-breaking. It made me so unbearably angry. I wanted to kill. Real mother tiger and her cubs stuff. I hope I never have to see it again, but I don't hold out much hope.

Anyway, I've done all I can for her just now. I'm relieved to have got through it without too much trauma, and to be safe in Germany learning about Helga of Cologne!

Liesl and Ingrid met me at the airport. Helen and Yuki had arrived earlier and were waiting with them. So apart from the fact that you're not here – a huge absence which feels strange to me all the time – apart from that I'm surrounded by most of my nearest and dearest, which is only a little way short of bliss.

Ingrid drove us straight from the airport to the museum where the stone box and the tiles of Helga of Cologne are now on display. Ingrid doesn't talk at all while she's driving but Liesl, beside her in the front, did a half turn so she could talk to Yuki who was seated between me and Helen in the back. Yuki was chattering all the way. She was asking Liesl non-stop about the Beguines and Liesl was answering her so carefully and patiently, I was really touched by it all.

'The Beguines were the first nurses here in Cologne. They had the first women's movement here in Europe in the twelve hundreds.'

'A women's movement?' said Yuki. 'Like my Grandma's one in England?'

I suppressed a chuckle at the thought of owning the women's movement in England – and a sigh that it was falling apart now . . . followed by a touch of nostalgia for the good old days. Ho hum.

Liesl was saying, 'Yes, a real one. Full scale. Very big. They did a lot of nursing and not just of the relatives of wealthy folks like in the nunneries, instead they nursed the poor and the elderly women – those who had no one to care for them. The whole movement was called the Beguines.'

Helen cut in with, 'I thought they were in Flanders. I never associated them with Germany.'

Liesl said, 'Düsseldorf, Frankfurt, Magdeburg, and many other cities had Beguines. I think ours was the largest though.'

'Why were they called Beguines?' asked Yuki.

'It came from the French *Le Begue* from the Old French *Li Beges*. It means one dressed in grey. It was a sort of put down, really. It also means heretic. Do you know what a heretic is, Yuki?'

'It's somebody you don't like at all. You don't like what they are saying. About churches and God and things like that.'

'That's right. Well, the men didn't like what the women were saying because some of these women didn't want to get married and they wanted to live close by each other.'

'Like you and Ingrid?'

'Sort of. But some of them were just good friends – and some of them were lesbians like me and Ingrid, but we don't know how many.'

'Men in churches don't like lesbians do they?'

We all laughed. 'Not a lot. Not usually. Sometimes they do.'

'But they didn't like the Beguines, did they?'

'No, they didn't, especially as time went on.'

'Why?'

'Because they thought they were too big for their boots, I suppose. They wouldn't do as they were told. And they were very, very good at weaving and spinning and embroidery so some of the men were very jealous.'

'Did they want to do the sewing themselves?'

'No, they wanted their wives to do it and get the money instead of the Beguine women.'

'But they were better at it.'

'Yes, they were.'

'So that's not fair.'

'No, Yuki. It isn't fair. It's not fair at all.'

'Are we nearly there at the museum?'

'Yes, we just have to go in this multi-storey car park.'

'Oh, good. I want to see the box.' She turned to me, adding, 'It's got bears on it, hasn't it, Grandma?'

'Yes, it has,' I replied, and whispered conspiratorily, 'D'you think Big Ted would mind staying and looking after the car for us?'

'No, I already asked him. He doesn't mind.'

'That's good then. Here we are.'

When we arrived in the brightly lit room the glass cases were reflecting the light at different angles. But the tiles were tilted so that we could easily see them, and beside each one was the translation.

The box stood there with its exquisite patterns. We could pick out bears and boars, deer and domestic animals – cats and dogs and cows. There were chickens too, and ducks on a small pond. Around them were twined some leaves, sheaves of corn, branches of fruit and vines with full bunches of grapes. On the narrow end there was a wonderful traditional beehive with tiny bees alighting on their platform. It was absolutely magical.

Despite Liesl's letters, I was unprepared for the luminous beauty of the thirty-nine tiles. Blue, so blue, deep blue, with white writing cut into them. I was transfixed. All the deep blue things I had ever seen paraded before me, just as they had for Liesl.

For me, the first thing that came into my head was, of course, the ocean's horizon on a deep blue day. And the sea by the caves at Nanjizal, cobalt waves when you look right into them with luminous green edges inside. Oh, the blue of them! Gentians in the old granite wall by the gate to St Loy Woods. The spines of some of my favourite books. The blue velvet curtains by my french windows. Colour on colour, fold on fold. The woven blue tweeds of Ellan Vannin's long winter skirt. I looked at Ilse's tiles and saw my Ellan Vannin and wet was running down my cheeks and history was shining there in glass cases in front of me.

The white markings reminded me of the white marks on a seagull's wing. The scratch of a thin white line on the deep blue sky of my favourite painting of yours, my love.

The tiles were so perfectly square, framing the words. The words were so contained. They had to be so carefully chosen, to fit the limited space.

I found myself thinking of Virginia Woolf, centuries later, writing *A Room of One's Own*; pointing out that the novelists of preceding centuries often had to beg money from men for their paper and plead for their pens. Standing there, I thought how things had deteriorated for women in the centuries since the Beguines. As if the tiles and the story of the end of the Beguines, told in such a condensed way, symbolised the loss of women's freedom. For the Beguines themselves life had not been restricted. Women there had been free to learn, and to teach others, too. Free to be real, to be themselves. These women could read and write and speak and think. These women could garden and sew and make honey and make music. These women could eat and sleep and dance and make love.

Then the soldiers came. And the priests. Soldiers of God. To destroy and to rape.

I had prepared myself for the fact that everything would be in glass cases. I can cope with the glass cases. I've read Barbara Hepworth's handwriting through glass cases in her studio in St Ives. I've read Virginia Woolf's handwriting on display in the University of Sussex, years ago.

The power of the tiles shone through the glass, undiminished.

Empowering me through the life of Helga of Cologne.

After the museum we drove through the countryside beyond the city up into the hills to Liesl and Ingrid's old house that they're busy doing up.

I'm in the attic room, close to the wild old trees behind the house. The hill slopes up at the back of the yard and my window looks on to the hill, almost into the heart of the canopy of branches. They rustle at night as if they are broomsticks with twigs on. Quite spooky it was, the first time I heard it, but now it puts me in mind of Ellan Vannin and Helga of Cologne and makes me feel peaceful and calm.

Well, dearest Lerryn, it's late now and I need to sleep. I'll write down everything that happens, and send it to you in batches. Then you'll know what's going on with me.

I miss you, darling – and this is doing me so much good here – so I feel so close to you and will be home soon.

All my love, Tarn XXX

Dearest Lerryn,

It's a wooden walled room with windows on to the hillside. The curtains remain open – we're not overlooked here – and the tall trees outside move in the wind.

Tonight after we were wined and dined, we sat around the wood stove by candle-light in comfy armchairs, eating grapes and chocolate mints. Yuki was on the sofa, her knees curled underneath her, arms wrapped round Big Ted. (He is HUGE. She asked me if we'll be charged extra if we take him on the tram!)

As Liesl talked, centuries came and went, images flowed, not comfortable, but compelling.

'When the women founded the Beguines it was a response to their need. For somewhere safe to go,' she said. 'Some stayed married, in those early days, living with their men folk but visiting the Beguine buildings on a daily basis, whilst others were marriage-resisters from the start. Widows might sell up their houses and move in together and buy up land near one another, perhaps clustered, at the start, around the hospital or a favourite church. One of their strengths was that they didn't have hard and fast boundaries about exactly how each woman should choose to live.

'The buildings called Beguinages were a development from the clusters of women in the early groups. At first, the church thought they were convents and the church authorities were fairly relaxed about it. But then, as time went on, the Beguines started to claim independence from male authority, and independent women, of course, are a threat.

'Slowly things began to change. Firstly, on the one hand the groups became very large and looked more like villages; but on the other hand they weren't enclosed or very rule bound. Some of the Beguines lived communally, others didn't.

'When the women who were not living communally were still with their husbands, the church authorities didn't turn a hair. But as time passed, the non-communal ones were often widows or single women living alone. Maybe in their own dwelling near to the Beguinage. Maybe in their own place *within* the Beguinage and its grounds. This was much more problematic, it seems. Individuals were viewed as wild and unruly both by the church and by the other Beguines who didn't want to be tainted with the image of the beggar women or the individual mystic who might write heresy.

'Then the guilds began to see them as competitors. As well

they should! They wove and spun, producing a good amount, but perhaps more dangerously, as far as the guilds were concerned, their work was of a very fine quality. Their embroidery was beautiful. Even the churches used Beguine needlewomen to make the altar cloths and vestments.'

'It's amazing,' said Helen. 'A whole movement of women. Self-sufficient, creative.'

'Yes, it is, isn't it? Very exciting. The Beguines grew their own food and many were brewers and made mead. They did all the jobs that women had done for years. There's a wonderful list. It's in a book I read.' Liesl stood and went to the deep recess where her books were, and ran her finger along until she found the well-known spine of the book.

Then she sat again and flicked through and read to us:

'They were brewers, fortune tellers, healers, midwives, pharmacists, milliners, seamstresses, spinners, tavern keepers, thatchers, road workers, lace makers, caterers, wet nurses, weavers and sellers of their surplus on the market – oh, and receivers of stolen goods!'

We all laughed.

'It's a mighty good list, isn't it! And that was just the extras. They also,' she took a deep breath dramatically and began again 'kept gardens and cared for domestic animals, preserved food, chopped and carried wood, transported water, cared for and educated the children, nursed sick family members, and prepared the dead for burial.' She let out her breath and said, laughing, 'That's all!'

By then it was past Yuki's bed time, so I took her up to bed and tucked her in with Big Ted. She was sleepy but not too sleepy to ask, 'Grandma, would you like to be a Beguine?'

I said, 'Ooh, I'll have to think about that. Tell you tomorrow. Night, night. Sleep tight.'

'Night, Grandma.'

I kissed her and I think she was asleep by the time I pulled her door to, leaving a crack so that the light on the stairs would shine in.

When I went back down to join the others, I found Liesl taking time out from storytelling to scoff some grapes. Helen was putting some logs into the stove and Ingrid was busy bringing some beer from the fridge. I topped up my glass and passed the wine bottle round, followed by a box of mint chocolates, then we settled down again for more of the stories.

'So,' Liesl continued, 'they were competent, self-sufficient and a threat to the male authorities. The Beguines started being persecuted from 1311 and 1312 when the pope put forward a Bull telling them to stop.

'In Europe, at that time, the church wouldn't accept that any person, man or woman, might not be religious. So the Beguines were only acceptable at the beginning because they were semi-religious and wore a grey habit. But they weren't an enclosed order, so the church couldn't fit them into the three models that men had of religious women – virgin, martyr and mystic. Beguine women didn't make perfect virgins, martyrs *or* mystics. Though there are examples of all of those among the Beguine women in different places at different times. The men's praise for them was superficial. A veneer of praise for their apparent piety.

'I think that under the men's false praise there was a deep undercurrent which was what men really thought and felt. That attitude was fear. The truth lay in a hidden model of women – a fourth model – that semi-religious women or any independent women were perceived as witches.'

I leapt in, excitedly, 'The same thing comes up in the folklore of the Isle of Man! Exactly the same! Going way back in time. If you can't control a woman then you fear that really she is a witch. It's the subliminal, unspoken fear. Wicked witches were invented by frightened men!'

'You sent me a badge with that on,' said Ingrid. 'I wore it till it wore out. The pin fell off. Do you think it's a sign?'

We all laughed.

'Was the word witch applied to Beguines directly?' Helen asked.

'No, I don't think so,' said Liesl. 'They'd be more likely to use the word heretic at that time. But it amounts to the same thing, the same phenomenon. Men felt threatened. That's why they wanted the Beguines removed as time went on.'

Ingrid said, 'Because they were organised and strong.'

'Yes. And that made them visible. Vulnerable to backlash.'

I jumped in again, 'So there was definitely a link – even in the thirteen hundreds – in the minds of men between uncontrollable women and the fear of witchcraft?'

'Yes,' replied Liesl. 'It would be foolish to imagine that the witch hunts of the sixteen hundreds simply happened out of the blue.

'There must have been precedents in one way or another and we need to know the historical context of the preceding centuries. Nothing happens without a history. And whether we like the history or not we need to know it, if we are to understand how cycles become established and maintained.'

We all nodded and I asked, 'So when the Beguines were broken, and the Beguinages were sacked and closed, do you think that it set the scene for subsequent generations of women becoming vulnerable to being accused?'

'Yes. I think so,' she said simply. 'For a start, after the Beguinages closed, women had nowhere to go to resist marriage. Secondly, they were now known to be a threat to the men's guilds – the rules were tightened about women's work from then on. But the oppression of women had a long history here before the Beguines, during the Beguines and afterwards. Individual women had been accused of being heretics for a long time. That wasn't new here on the Continent.'

'Were they isolated cases?'

'Yes. To burn a heretic in Germany wasn't new. What was new after the Beguinages were closed was that, over time, the word heretic was changed to the word witch. It took about a century to become really established and for "witch" to become a crime mainly attributed to women. From then onwards the accusation of being a witch increased until it peaked in the mass witch hunts.'

Liesl paused. All eyes were fixed on her. I was leaning sideways, elbow on the chair arms, my chin in my hand, listening intently. Helen was leaning back in her chair, with one knee bent up and legs askew, running her hand through her hair in a gesture that's very familiar to me. Ingrid held a beer glass tight, her rings and the rim of the glass catching the light of a candle from the alcove.

Part of me wanted to back away. To be on holiday. Not to

have to think. But the other part of me was already intent on understanding the chronology from the Beguines onwards.

Then I felt so close to you, Lerryn, it was as if you were here. Everything you had told me about your search for the identity of Biff was here, too. As Liesl talked I had, in my mind's eye, all the time, a parallel moving film of the story you'd told me of Biff's sisters as young suffragettes, their hair being pulled, their bodies shoved, their faces and breasts beaten, their bodies thrown from a car and found by New Year revellers at the wayside. And of Biff's mother, who had died from forced feeding. And how you had been compelled, like I am, to search back for the history and the truth.

All those women. We must have land, I found myself thinking. We must have land. Safe land for women for ever.

We could have heard a feather float down in that room. We were all there, wrapped up in what Liesl had been telling us and, simultaneously, away elsewhere on other journeys. We were visiting all those places and times when women have had land denied to them, education and creativity blocked from them, votes and housing and security forbidden them. We all had different journeys in our minds and the room was spinning with silent stories there because of Helga and her way of life.

Liesl resumed quietly, 'When the Beguinages were forcibly closed, many of the women were, against their will, married to local men. Women who had been with other women all their lives, suddenly shoved into heterosexuality. Women who were virgins hurriedly forced into some man's bed. Women who were celibate, likewise. Women who were widowed, content with their work and status, cast out into a rough and cruel world.

'Before the Bull there was a famous case in Paris – the Beguine and mystic, Margaret Porete, was burned. Her visions and writings were considered to be heresy. She was an example of an early case.'

'There was persecution of all those considered to be heretics throughout the Middle Ages,' said Helen. 'I know that much. The question is what counted as heresy, I suppose.'

'Yes. Jews were among those considered to be heretics. Here in Germany public execution by fire was usual. It was the standard way of purging heresy of any kind. Trials of heretics were carried out from the eleven hundreds onwards. And mass executions. The witch hunts came at the end of a four- or five-hundred-year period of executions. What was different in the witch crazes of the sixteen hundreds was that, for the first time, women as a group, across the whole of Europe, were criminalised. They died because they were women, poor women, beggar women who would formerly have been village healers.'

As if speaking in my mind, Ingrid said, 'The Beguines were destroyed because they were strong women; witches were destroyed simply because they were women; how many other attacks spring to mind – historically and right now – without our even having to think about it? What can we do to make ourselves safe?'

It's late now my dearest Lerryn, so I must sleep. I'm thinking of you and our wonderful women's land at Eastfield Farm. Such peace and safety there. Give my love to Cherry, Beech and Molly.

All my love, Tarn XXX

Dearest Lerryn,
Here the land is alive with the crops that Liesl and Ingrid have planted, the house is alive with the sounds of Yuki and Helen laughing, and I'm alive and in love . . .

Liesl has been in touch with someone – a friend of a friend of a colleague – who may be able to help with my research about the Isle of Man. She is a woman who works at the University of Oslo in the library there and although there are no coherent archives for the thirteenth century there are fragments of manuscripts which refer to the control which Norway had at that time over the Isle of Man.

We are going to try that avenue of search for traces of the lives of women brought before the ecclesiastical courts in the island in the reign of the last king of Man, under Viking rule.

It transpires that the whole of Europe was under the rule of the pope – and the Bishop of Norway ruled over the Isle of Man in the form of the North and South Suderies. That included all of the western isles as well – split into a north and south grouping with the most southerly island being the Isle of Man itself.

Today I searched along Liesl's bookshelves for references to the history of German women and I read for the first time a terrible story about a poor woman who became accused of being a witch, just as the unnamed women in the island's folklore had been, so many miles away.

It will stay with me, always, because it is an extreme example of what can happen when women are forced into poverty, without resources, without education, without work, without housing, without freedom, without land, without justice, and without each other.

I was told this story differently when I was small. They called it Cinderella; told me a fairy tale about a little kitchen maid who found a kind and handsome prince who rescued her from poverty and married her and they lived happily ever after. I passed on the fairy tale to Helen, and on down the line to Yuki.

Now I read the truth behind it. I read about the real Cinderella whose real name was Anna, and it is not a pretty tale and the prince was not kind. I shan't tell Yuki. Not for a very long time. If I had three wishes I would wish first of all that the reality was only in the past: that there were no modern versions. However, since I know there are, I study here in Liesl's home, preparing myself for my research on my own homeland – and I call to my ancestral mother, Ellan Vannin, to pass on to me her strength because her story is, I am sure, not dissimilar to this one concerning 'The Real Cinderella'.

I won't fax it – I'll write it and bring it home with me, because it's not the kind of story I would like to send you in a letter.

Home very soon. Oh, it will be wonderful to be with you again.

Thinking of you dearest,
All my love, Tarn XXX

Once upon a time there was in the duchy of Bavaria a young and handsome duke called Maximilian. He was already married and his marriage had been idyllically happy for five years except for one small thing. He wanted a son and heir but however hard he and his wife tried, his wife did not get pregnant.

So, with just one year left of the sixteenth century he realised he must find someone to blame for this terrible misfortune and that someone, somewhere, must have put a curse on himself, his wife, their castle and the lands all around.

So he talked to his advisers and sent them out into the highways and byways to search for any evidence of witch-craft so that he could punish the witches and get the curse lifted.

They searched and searched, but no evidence could be found.

They returned to the palace and told Maximilian.

The young and handsome duke had set his heart on finding who was to blame. He was extremely put out by the lack of information. His wife was still not pregnant and the new century was coming nearer and nearer like the hands of a clock approaching midnight. He issued further orders that the witches must be found. The advisers rode forth once again. This time they talked amongst themselves and told one another that if they didn't find a witch their heads would roll, such was the power of Maximilian.

They came to one of the small towns in the duchy where there was an old prison. They had not searched every house or tavern, shop or prison on their first visit. They hadn't thought it was necessary. They had been looking for women freely and actively going about their practices. Poor women, healing women, begging from door to door and known by local people.

This time, however, they talked to the prison warder. He said he knew of one prisoner who might be able to help them: a convicted murderer who was being held in the cells. He was their last chance. Perhaps there was some witch that he knew of. The prisoner told them, and gladly, that there was a woman whose name was Anna and she was a vagrant with a licence to beg.

The advisers to the young duke were told that they could look for Anna in the poorhouse. She was indeed a witch, the convicted murderer insisted. Of that he was quite certain. He had many tales he could tell of the things she was supposed to have done. The advisers talked amongst themselves. She did not sound at all ideal and they were sure the prisoner was lying to please them and save his own skin. But time was pressing hard upon them and they had searched everywhere else without avail, so they agreed together that she would have to do. They had expected her to be a widow or single woman but Anna did not quite fit their expectations.

She was still married and not a widow. She was fifty-nine and had been married for thirty-seven years to a travelling privy cleaner called Paulus Pappenheimer. Her father had been a grave digger, which made her an outcast in the villages around.

In the early hours of dawn they came upon her in the poorhouse where she had settled for the winter with her husband and three sons. (In the summer they all wandered from town to town to clean the latrines.)

She was a quiet, thoughtful woman, who had held her family together for many years, despite abject poverty. At other times she might even have been thought of as respectable, but the work the family did was disgusting to the duke's young and well-to-do advisers, who could not bear even to be in the same room as people who lived with the pollution from that kind of work.

Anna was arrested and bound and thrown, with her husband and sons, into a cart and the whole entourage set off in triumph for Munich. The hands on the calendar clock struck midnight as Anna was flung into prison in a separate cell from her family. The year sixteen hundred had turned. The new century had begun. In Bavaria, as in all the German lands at that time, there were many, many people with hardly any work. There was general unrest.

The young duke, Maximilian, was well pleased with the discovery of Anna Pappenheimer and her family. Now he had someone to blame for his terrible misfortune. He and his wife still hadn't conceived a child.

Maximilian thought that the devil had cursed both his wife and his marriage bed. He prayed hard in his Catholic chapel that now that Anna had been caught, and was going to be punished, her sins would be atoned and his son and heir would be born. So the witch hunters had an urgent need to come up with a confession from Anna, her husband Paulus and their three sons. The youngest was a little boy of eleven called Hansel.

There was one terrible piece of evidence that was held against Anna. She and her family were devout Lutherans in a Catholic land. The young duke had had a Jesuit education and was determined to stamp out any kind of heresy in his part of Germany. He firmly held that all Lutherans were heretics and capable of withcraft.

In prison Anna's conditions were appalling. Her cell was filthy, and she was chained to the wall without enough to eat or drink. At first when Anna was questioned she would not admit to witchcraft or using folk medicine or folk magic of any kind. So the torture began. She was tortured repeatedly. In between she was kept chained to the wall.

For days and nights the ordeals continued. Finally, she confessed to flying on a piece of wood to meet the devil, having sex with a demon lover, murdering children and using their bodies to make ointment, and making demonic powder from dead children's hands.

The young duke, Maximilian, was pleased with the confessions.

He gave orders for a public trial. It was long and many people attended. At the end of it the entire family was convicted of witchcraft.

All over the beautiful lands around Munich the minstrels and storytellers announced the story of Anna Pappenheimer and what she had confessed to doing with the devil. News spread fast throughout the villages and towns.

The date for the execution of the family was set and, as it approached, people could be seen with carts and bundles making their way into the city of Munich for the spectacle, as if they were going to a fair. Rich people got dressed up and went in carriages as if they were going to a ball at the invitation of the young and handsome duke.

So they attended, rich and poor alike, at the place of death.

The poor brought their whole families with them. Thousands gathered there ready to watch the death of the woman who had caused Maximilian to miss the chance of a son and heir.

Among the crowds there were many women. Women whose stock-in-trade – folk magic and folk medicine – were now an executable offence. Women with breasts and labia – the parts of a woman's body that had previously been precious and loved – now named as models for the devil's 'teat' on which he liked to suck. Poor widow women who were no longer allowed to carry on their husbands' trades; poor single women who were refused apprenticeships or other entrance to the guilds; and women without land who could not grow their own food and had before them a clear example of what might happen to a woman who is forced to beg. Women who had had abortions and others who had performed abortions, were now very frightened of having this secret revealed. For these were now serious crimes in the eyes of men like Maximilian, who controlled the courts and the legal system. The trial was turning the handsome young duke, Maximilian, into a man with Godlike power. All the women must on some level have known that any woman could be accused; that anyone might confess under torture, naming someone else; and that anyone showing signs of rebellion, anyone challenging the authorities, anyone who spoke out, was especially at risk.

The execution, under the young duke's orders, was to be slow. First the Pappenheimers were stripped and their flesh torn off with hot pincers.

Then Anna's breasts were cut off and the bloody breasts were forced first into her mouth and then into the mouths of her sons to humiliate her. Maximilian had introduced this new custom into witch trials himself.

Following this was a long procession to the place of execution led by a municipal official carrying a wooden cross. Church bells were ringing to demonstrate the power of Christianity over the devil. The crowd sang hymns; and pamplets were for sale describing the sins of the Pappenheimer family.

They were refused the privilege of being strangled before being burned.

A heavy iron wheel was dropped on Paulus till his bones broke, and he was impaled through his anus with a stick.

Anna's small eleven-year-old son was made to watch his mother, father and brothers being burned. He cried out, 'My mother is squirming.' For this he was executed three months later.

After this trial there was less unrest in the duchy. But until 1631 there were still many accused witches in Maximilian's prisons.

Once upon a time there was a handsome young prince who found a poor woman called Cinderella and searched for her and married her. That is a fairy tale. But there was no fairy godmother who could save the real Cinderella. Her name was Anna Pappenheimer and hers is the true story. There were one hundred thousand women who died like Anna. There were two hundred thousand accused, tortured and tried. Between the world of legend and the world of reality there lies the world of those whose names have been lost.

CHAPTER ELEVEN

Wet and windy weather ravaged the Land's End peninsula; up country was sleet, hail and snow.

February and early March could be strangely contradictory in West Penwith. We might have glorious blue days with mild temperatures and hours of sunshine – but it could suddenly turn, even though it was supposed to be approaching spring-time, and snarl at us with unexpected teeth of intense cold, and growling gales or hostile rainy squalls.

Tarn was home again and back at work, so, one special morning, during a brief respite from the savage weather, we took ourselves to the area of Nanquidno. As we drove along, she said, 'Look, Lerrie. No daffs this year. The bulbs have only put up leaves – they've got no buds or flowers over this side. How strange.'

The clusters of greenish-blue leaves were very pretty and I thought: the life force seems to be reneging on its promises here, but I feel so alive with a life force that's promising a whole year of springtime. I'm opening up; learning to love someone new. I love Tarn and I can learn to trust again.

Turning off the St Just to Land's End road, on to a narrow lane which ran alongside the airport, we were facing the sea, and entering a shallow valley of gently curving fields. The lane, which I knew so well from childhood walks with Aunt Harry before she bought Herton Hall in Yorkshire, wound its way past isolated farms whose lands sloped towards the coast path and ended in dramatic cliffs, which had crumbled into endless boulders. We parked inland on a grassy lay-by and, shouldering mini backpacks which held our coffee and biscuits, we stood for a while, taking in the rural scenery.

A tarmac path ran past us towards Nanjulian Farm, which had by now been bought and was being done up slowly, though it still had a look of dereliction and neglect about it. Next to the tarmac a wide, fast-flowing stream was rushing onwards, swollen by recent rains; on the fields to the west there were dottings of silent sheep and a couple of goats. Further inland towards the airport we could hear a tractor in the cauliflower picking fields – on the way down the valley we'd seen stacks of telltale white boxes waiting for the crops and the packers.

We stood there, arm around one another, kissing and absorbing the countryside with its contrasts of soft fields and hard rocky outcrops, slow silent clouds and teeming tumbling streams.

There was water everywhere as we began to follow a rough track beyond Nanjulian Farm leading us over a footbridge with the water flowing on our right. Again the blue-green daffodil leaves but no buds or blossoms. Never mind. There were new honeysuckle leaves in the hedgerows and new buds on the blackthorn bushes. I marvelled again at the ancient Monterey pine tree spreading several huge curved branches like extra trunks, many feet in all directions across the stream. There the track ended by an old granite mill, that was converted into someone's holiday home.

'In all my visits to this valley,' I said, 'I've never seen that house open to the sunshine with breezes blowing through its windows.'

She squeezed my hand and smiled at me. 'It's like a book that's never been read, shut tight with a gold clasp and an exquisite lock with no key. You can't read its story, however hard you try.'

'Puts me in mind of that conversation I had with Molly.'

She had phoned to arrange to go brambling at Eastfield Farm with me. Whilst we were chatting on the phone she'd mentioned that her daughter Sally had applied recently for one of the National Trust houses in Penberth Cove, because it had become available for rent. But Sally was a single parent with four children, not someone the Trust favoured for a des. res. They'd rented it to people from up country.

Similarly the old/new mill house in Nanjulian seemed not to be lived in these days by the Cornish. Owned perhaps by rich up-country folks who rented it out or used it twice a year. Then I thought of Tessa and Jules who could certainly have afforded to move to this area if they could have found work, but once when they'd been to see a couple of places locally with a view to moving out of London, they're more or less had the No Blacks treatment. Not in so many words of course. Even the Cornish have realised that they have to be discreet about their prejudices these days.

I sighed, watching the old silent pine tree. Its cones were tight shut, revealing no secrets, no gossip, as if its motto were, Hear no evil/Speak no evil. Its central branches were crusted with grey lichens, the huge furry spectacular sort.

I loved it then as I always had and thought of an old photo of me and Aunt Harry taken by Anna von Schiller on one of their visits to Cornwall when I was a teenager, with us sitting laughing on the lowest branches, my legs dangling, my feet in sandals and my hand shading my eyes from summer sunshine.

The weather around us as we walked on was misty and very atmospheric. Against the distant roar of the sea we could marvel at the nearby sounds of moving water as the stream began to fling itself fowards and downwards. Granite outcrops formed the spectacular frame of the water colour being created ahead of us where the valley prepared itself to meet the sea.

On each of the valley sides great grey boulders lifted upwards from old bracken and sleeping brambles. Bright dark ivy clung in places and lime-green clumps caught the light in the misty air where the bladder campions would colour the countryside white, in April.

The sound of water. All around us. There was no wind.

The stream had split into three parts, each full and coursing downwards, creating islands of mossy ground from which sprang branches of knife-like, foot-high montbretia leaves, with a strong luminous yellowy green resembling no other colour hereabouts. Their bases were dark russet, composed of last year's montbretia leaves which covered and protected all the bulbs underneath. Stringy and fibrous in texture, the base coverings were as bright as doormats in Brixton market, back in London where Tessa and Jules would be shopping, amidst dozens and dozens of people, all colours, buying yams and plantains, melons and mangoes.

Tarn's hand was in mine – she was here, with me, and we were in love. We chatted easily and I loved her voice in that between-the-worlds place, where the waters of the valley met the waters of the sea.

By the waters of Nanjulian I spoke my love of Taarnagh. By

the waters of Nanjulian I heard her singing there. By the waters of Nanjulian I felt my love of Taarnagh. By the waters of Nanjulian I loved her being there.

We sat for a while on the boulder beach, enjoying the sounds of falling water, and the waves crashing on to the rocks. Such a variety of shapes and colours of rocks, some smooth and rounded, others jagged, lying at crazy angles where they had broken away from the cliff.

Black, orange and pale green lichen bands were clearly visible, adding to the dramatic scene. We absorbed the fluid beauty of the shore and were steady, contented and happy. I felt strong, empowered by the sense of continuity which I felt was integral to the moving melting blending of the stone and water landscape.

It had always had that kind of effect on me. It was a place of continuity, change and danger. It was a place of edges and ledges. A place to go when I needed to walk along the edges of my mind, without losing my balance. It had always been like that for me. At Nanjulian, where the sky meets the sea, where the streams meet the ocean, where the cliffs break and splinter, where the lichens grow in ferocious conditions, where the montbretia flames red in summer and the wild roses fringe the path.

A place of contrast, where history belongs.

It could be dazzlingly blue and silver and bright. It could be wet, wild and whiplike. A place of such dramatic meetings that, within them, the land, sea and sky changes could maintain a long-term continuity. It comprised the contradiction of security within danger. Was it Gertrude Stein who had said, 'Considering how dangerous everything is, nothing is really very frightening'?

We were aware that the mist was quiet and the sea was loud. That the brief interlude in the run of bad weather was something to be glad about, for it had given us the morning that we wanted. Deep inside me was the love of Tarn Callister. All around me was the ambience of being loved again, the knowledge that she was home and we would have time together.

We walked back up the valley towards the converted mill house. The mist was patchy on the hillsides but the valley and the path were clear. It was still damp everywhere and there were many minute spiders' webs along the hedgerows with misty droplets on them, picking out the geometric forms and the perfectly woven strands.

Then something happened which later seemed to have significance. In the distance, on the bank the other side of the stream which tumbles past the mill house, we saw a vixen, sitting in a quiet mist-free patch under the old Monterey pine. She was wary and watchful, looking straight at us. We stood stock still, meeting her gaze and not moving a finger or toe. Eye to eye across the stream we regarded one another.

I was just wondering how long she might keep this up when a sound from the land behind her caused her to jump to her feet. She looked directly at us again then swiftly turned about and made off through the bracken. She disappeared over the brow, making for the wild moorland beyond.

I had seen many foxes in West Penwith over the years but this vixen so near at hand and so consciously staring at us unnerved me for some reason. I was learning to trust my intuition, despite setbacks, and something told me that the vixen came with a message, but I didn't know then what it was.

We followed the path past Nanjulian Farm, then drove to Penzance to drop Tarn off to work. I went on to Eastfield Farm to spend the day with Cherry, Beech and Molly.

You have to park down the lane and walk from there. I had barely pulled up by a low granite barrier, where the milk churns used to stand, when a dozen Jersey milk cows came curiously to greet me, all pressed up against the other side of the barrier, leaning their necks across, wanting to have their noses stroked. They were so pretty, with liquid brown eyes and false eyelashes like film stars, so I took my time, though I didn't know their names.

Then, as I walked up the lane I recalled that Cherry and Beech's stone house used to be cow byres, and I imagined the cows indoors, some giving birth. Cherry saw me through the kitchen window, so we waved and I rounded the corner and entered the old farmyard, now full of daffodils and crocuses.

'Sorry I'm a bit late. I was saying hello to Mr Mace's cows!' I said as she opened the door.

We hugged warmly. I took off my muddy boots and padded indoors in my thick socks, into the wonderful granite rooms, where a lunch of hot soup and new bread was waiting for me. But, almost immediately, I realised that something was terribly wrong. Into my mind, quite abruptly, came the image of the room as cow byres, and there was blood in the straw on the stone-cold floor. I shivered, involuntarily. The others came to greet me, 'Are you cold, come on, sit here by the fire.'

'No, it's okay. I'll be fine.' I paused. 'There's something wrong, isn't there?'

Cherry spoke immediately, 'This arrived this morning,' she said.

'It gets the Gold, we think,' added Beech. 'For letters that arrive on International Women's Day.' She looked across at Molly, who rolled her eyes.

'What is it? What's going on?' I asked. Then, looking at the handwriting and the postmark, I added, 'Is it about the Land Trust? You've been waiting to hear, haven't you?'

'Read it, Lerrie . . . See what you think.'

It was on thin airmail paper. Quite a short letter. I read it twice, hardly able to comprehend it.

It was a letter of eviction, asking Cherry and Beech to vacate the house and lands at Eastfield Farm within the two-month term, as specified in their contract. It was signed Madeleine Gerrard.

I sat down, shaking, and the weird sensation that the rooms were cow byres intensified, and images chased one another through my mind, so that I was overwhelmed and I couldn't speak. It happens now and then, but it was horrible. The room seemed to be very cold, like a stone tomb, and some of the animals were struggling, and their calves were having to be pulled out, and there was blood everywhere, as if the calves were being evicted from their safe, womb-like existence.

I handed the letter to Beech who placed it on the table against a vase of daffodils, where it stood isolated on the expanse of old wood. All eyes seemed to be focused on it, then I was aware that the women were setting out soup bowls and bread on a huge tray on the rug so that we could sit around the open fire.

I recovered my composure quickly and the animals faded until the place became Cherry and Beech's living-room again.

'We've been uneasy for a while now,' said Molly. 'No letters arriving, the long delay in news from the States. This letter is the worst scenario . . . for all of us. For me,' she shrugged unhappily, 'well, Madeleine's mother has been a friend of mine for years.' She paused and we all exchanged looks. I was thinking, How do Cherry and Beech feel with that damn letter there on the table?

'Here, have some soup, and bread,' said Cherry. 'Help yourself, won't you?' So, we sat by the fire, drinking wonderful soup, and feeling totally churned up inside. I smiled gently at Cherry and Beech, who were on the old two-seater settee. They were trying to smile for me too, but they looked a grey-white colour, and appeared sickly, as if someone had kicked each of them hard in the solar plexus.

Despite everything, I was very hungry. We ate quietly for a short while, each with her own thoughts which was eerie as there was so much to say. Probably, the silence lasted only seconds, but it was real and strange. I recalled the vixen, that morning, but I couldn't say anything.

I sipped my soup and refilled my soup bowl and as I did so, we sat for a brief moment in a collective silence, as if we were Beguines waiting for a violent raid of some kind, at the end of the Beguinage in Cologne. I was trembling now, recognising that that's what this place – Eastfield Farm – had been for women. It had been a safe, nurturing place. It was being changed into a stone-cold tomb.

I shook myself as I heard Molly's voice breaking the silence. 'I don't understand it,' she said, 'Clearly she needs to sell Eastfield Farm. It must be something pretty dramatic in the States – it's a matter of survival for her, I expect.'

Molly's eyes were unusually restless, and her body was tight with a tension that I'd never seen before. Her gaze darted from the fire to new tears on Cherry's face, then passed around the well-loved room, with its low roof and heavy beams, the old and new pine wood, coming to rest, finally, on the table.

The reality of the thin-papered air letter was enormous now. It was huge. Unbelievably real.

Molly continued, 'I can understand Madeleine's need to

survive, but, why, oh why, didn't she tell us about it? Why her long silences? And how on earth did she get her head around this terrible Letter of Eviction?'

'She must've decided that she has to sell this place,' said Cherry, 'and she couldn't, or wouldn't, face us. It's a cop-out for her – and a disaster for us! We wouldn't wish something like this on our worst enemies.'

'No, we wouldn't,' said Beech. 'We're both incredibly hurt; and many more will feel betrayed by the selling off of this land after all the promises, hopes and dreams. It's privatisation. That's what it is. And it seems, that's what it always was. In the last resort it belongs to Madeleine. I have no quibble with her selling her own property. But I feel that I and others have been deceived about her intentions.'

Cherry's tone was urgent as she interrupted, 'What's upsetting me most is that her promise all those years ago was a false promise. Many of us worked extraordinarily hard for that. And all we've achieved is doing up her land for her, maintaining her property. I feel so very bitter about it.'

'All that brambling!' said Molly. 'All those hopes for the Land Trust. It was delayed right down the line and then never came about. She must be in a terrible state to let this happen.'

'Well,' said Beech, 'state or no state, I can't help feeling that she never wanted to relinquish the land to women – in the end it was always hers. Hence the letter.'

'Why, if she needs to sell,' I mused, almost to myself, 'why doesn't she offer us all the chance to buy the woodland and the field beyond it? Then she could sell the middle field and lower field with the house and still get a good whack.'

'The top field will go to the local farmer,' said Molly. 'He's been after it for ages. He has the money. If she needs a quick sale, and it looks like she does, that's the best way to do it. We couldn't possibly raise four grand instantly.'

'At least we could be given the chance to bid for those two fields – the top one and the woodland – to keep as women's land,' I exclaimed.

'Presumably,' said Molly, 'Madeleine needs the highest price possible. Mr Mace would offer that in order to get it. And who knows how we could possibly buy those fields? We're all on the dole, or semi-retired, aren't we? We're poor and she knows that.'

'Okay, but what about Hazel Banyer. Why can't she buy it? Then at least it'd be going to a woman who is sympathetic – she might even want these two as tenants.'

'I'm sorry to be such a wet blanket, Lerryn,' said Molly, 'but I rang a friend of Hazel's who comes into The Gallery. Madeleine did try Hazel, some time in the winter, it seems, though it was all very hush-hush at that time – but Hazel simply can't raise all the money. Madeleine needs to get substantially more than Hazel can find.'

'She won't drop it, for Hazel?'

'No, she won't. I'm sorry. I know it's awful. It's not how things were meant to happen, not at all.'

'Let me get this right,' I said, because the shock of it was beginning to cloud my mind. 'Correct me if I'm wrong, but what we're saying is that these two women here will be homeless in eight weeks' time and any old patriarch can buy Eastfield Farm and take away the land we have loved.'

Three silent heads nodded solemnly.

Another sharp intake of breath and a knee-jerk response.

I looked at Molly, a question in my face. I looked at Cherry and Beech.

'You can come and live with me at Lescudjack,' I heard myself say.

BOOK TWO

Book Two

CHAPTER TWELVE

I was waiting at Tarn's flat for her mid-evening. She was late home from the sixth-form college where she'd been asked to do some urgent end-of-term supply work due to the sudden illness of someone in the English Department.

Eventually I heard the front gate and then her key in the lock. She staggered in through the door appearing drained and exhausted, with stress lines around her eyes and mouth.

She held me close. 'Oh, it's good to be home. Good to see you, what a day.'

I hugged and kissed her. 'You look awful, love, whatever's the matter?'

'A row. Major row. In the staffroom.' She kicked off her shoes. 'I need a drink.'

'Sit down. There's still some Sangria in the fridge. Will that do?'

'Thanks, love. You're a treasure.'

'Here you are. Swig that down. I'll run you a bath.'

Soon she was soaking in deep warm water. I perched on a stool nearby and she told me what had happened.

'I like the A level group. The first years. They're a nice lot. Friendly. We've just finished the unit they were doing and it's slowing down a bit, you know, for Easter, so one of them had brought in a copy of Robert Hunt . . .'

'*Romances of West Cornwall*?'

'Yes, the legends . . . and said could we have a look at some of them because she was fascinated. We'd been talking about storytelling as an art form – it was fine. It all fits very well. Anyway, she asked me about the White Witch of Zennor. As you know it's a long legend, lots of elements. All that smuggling and tinning up on the downs. You know the one?'

'Yes. It's a very complex one with lots of layers. The witch had hares for pets, as I recall?'

'Yes, and there's all that about her friendship with one of the

99

smugglers and the role of a witch in a close-knit community. It's a thoroughly good legend!'

'So what went wrong?'

'We were having a good in-depth talk about racism in legends and in the language of the legends. It was all going well, though there was one guy who said he didn't see any problem with calling some witches white or black witches – and that we needn't be doing any stuff on racism because it didn't concern us here in Cornwall. There were no Black people here anyway, that sort of thing.

'Some of the others got quite animated about that and they wanted to know how the idea of white and black witches got started. So I referred back to Peter Fryer's book, *Staying Power*, and the times of Queen Elizabeth the First. I said that she was thought of as an exceptionally pale-skinned woman, i.e. queen, and pure, the virgin queen – so whiteness came to be seen as standing for her purity, youth, beauty and intelligence during her reign. All that basic stuff. Very basic. But it seemed to be new to some of them.

'I told them that the chapter in *Staying Power* was called after one of Elizabeth's favourite phrases – because she called the Black people "those kinde of people" and she tried twice unsuccessfully to have them deported, but she liked to have them as entertainers at court. I said some of the nobles like Raleigh had Black children as pets in the family – and one lad then said that he thought Elizabeth had got it right, and no wonder the witches were divided into white and black witches . . . He was just going on about witches when in walks Bob Greenaway, who's a born-again Christian.'

'Shit. Perfect timing.'

'Yes. Perfect.' Tarn swallowed some more Sangria. 'Then later I went into the staff room and all hell let loose. Bob said I wasn't on supply to discuss witchcraft, that the parents would be horrified, and the Cornish legends were not on the curriculum, end of term or not. Then he said that I had no business linking it with racism. Who did I think I was coming from up country and doing a number on these students, that's exactly why he'd come back home to Cornwall to get away from all that kind of thing in the cities.'

'He meant "those kinde of people", did he?'

'Yes, he did. But he also meant that you don't have to bother talking about racism in the education system here. You can just leave it to the teachers in the cities. Appalling! You remember that article in the *Western Morning News*? About hidden racism here; people coming from up country to get away from Black people. It was horrible. It was like that. He was coming up with all that.'

'Oh, Tarn. Oh, love. I am sorry. You don't deserve all that.'

'It was awful. I lost my cool. I'd done fine in the tutorial. I really had. It was a good discussion and one they had been wanting to have, they said so. But in the staff room Born-again-Bob was the last straw. It was really front line stuff. I remember when I first came here from London to live and someone in the street who had come from Scilly (because her husband was too ill to make the journey from Scilly regularly for hospital treatment), told me that if she'd been living in London she'd have done the same as me. Too many Black people, said in that awful half-whisper. You know? When whites know it's racist but they don't want to show it openly?'

'What did you say to Bob?'

'I gave him it straight out. Told him he was a racist git and that as far as I was concerned the more Black people that came here to live the better and I wasn't going to have Black friends insulted; and that all our language is based on racism and as a linguist it's my professional commitment to challenge it. That was my job and I was going to continue to do it as well as I possibly could. I tried not to mention the witches, concentrated on the legends, because it's inflammatory enough what I was saying. If I'd added in about witches that'd have been another red rag to a bull, and by then I'd had more than enough. I wanted to get home.'

'Sounds as if you did really well. I'm proud of you.'

'Yes, but it really takes it out of you. I feel completely wiped now.'

'I'm not surprised. So, did Bob's interruption wreck the tutorial? Or did you carry on?'

'Oh, I carried on! He just looked thunderous – he didn't actually say much until I was in the staff room. When he'd gone I told the students that I was happy to discuss the origin of the language and the concepts, but that I wasn't going to have any of them expressing racist ideas. I won't provide a platform for racism. If they didn't like that they could leave and have a free period, but they couldn't stay and mouth off in my tutorials. The guy decided to stay and his girlfriend too, who was saying the same sort of thing and obviously agreeing with him. So I started to talk about my research on the origin of the witch hunts and the case of Petronilla de Meath – she stood as scapegoat in place of her mistress Dame Alice, who was wealthy enough to leave Ireland; and that there were already Black people living in Ireland too, because in one of the follow-up trials there it's on record that one of the witches was actually a Black person; I told them about what had happened to witches in the folklore of the Isle of Man.

'Then we all talked about the folklore of Cornwall. They all knew about Maggy Figgy, she's the most famous, but not all of them knew of the White Witch of Zennor; and they didn't know that nearby – in Plymouth – John Hawkins started the slave trade in Elizabethan times. Nor that the coat of arms of Plymouth was three Black young people, the same age as them, in chains.

'Then I went on to say how the ideas of blackness or whiteness in Elizabethan times reinforced the beginning of the slave trade, since it was used to justify the idea that Black people weren't human and that the whole economy became based on greed – backed up by racist ideology. Then that it was the same ideology that was transferred on to women and witchcraft – backed up by Bible fundamentalism.

'Then I said that Black people who came here later, as free people, brought their own knowledge and remedies with them, and those cures would be used in everyday life.'

'That would have been underground stuff though, wouldn't it? Hidden realities.'

'Oh, yes.' Tarn paused. 'It was a terrible era and it's crucial to examine the interplay of language and culture. Racist language supported the exploitation of Black people for economic gain. That's part of what the tutorial was about. I did not need Born-again-Bob muscling in on it.'

'I wish someone'd taught me all that in school,' I said.

Tarn replied. 'Tell you what I wish. I wish the modern books on witches would deal with this issue. All you ever see is a couple of inverted commas "white witch", "black witch", as if that's enough. It's a racist concept that we need to deal with, not behave as if a couple of inverted commas will solve it.'

'Well I think it sounds as if you did splendidly, love.'

'Thanks. I hope so.' Tarn was beginning to relax. She managed a smile. 'The irony is that to Christians like Greenaway it wouldn't matter whether the witches were labelled white, black or sky-blue-pink. They're all anathema to them. Past, present and future.'

'Well, I'm proud of you. I bet you gave him a real run for his money.' We smiled at each other. 'I do love you so much, you know.'

'I do know. It's been an incredible few weeks, Lerrie.' She yawned loudly, ran some more hot in. 'I love you too. It's wonderful. The equality, companionship, understanding . . .'

'Fun, lust, sex . . .'

'Not right this minute.' She yawned again, splashed me with water, and we played then, laughing and splashing for a while.

The next evening, Tessa and Jules rang me from the studio in London. They'd taken a call for me. A call with a message from Anna von Schiller – the first woman I'd been lovers with, before I'd re-discovered Lindsey. Anna, whom I hadn't seen for years, was now in her seventies, living in Hamburg, in a flat, overlooking the central lake.

'It was Margret who rang, Anna's housekeeper,' Jules said. 'She speaks almost perfect English. She says that Anna is ill and is going blind; that Anna begs that you'll come and visit her; and that she wants to make peace with you before she dies.'

'Is she dying?'

'She's not critically ill. She's not fading fast or anything like that. But she is ageing, and she would like to see you. Oh, and if you've a lover, do please bring her. All expenses paid.'

'That's my Anna.'

'Be fair, Lerrie. Sounds more than generous to me.'

'It is. That was mean of me. I'm sorry. Old hurts and all that. When we parted there was some unresolved anger between us. It's never been that easy to maintain a friendship, though we have tried to keep in touch. We still care a lot, but it was not a simple break-up because she wanted me to live with her in Europe. It was a class thing – she's very wealthy.'

'Begs was her word, by the way, not mine.'

'Okay, thanks.' I took a deep breath. 'How much time have I got to think about it?'

'No immediate crisis. I said I'd phone you and you'd get back to her, to Margret I mean. Anna doesn't use the phone much these days. She has some bother with tinnitus.'

'Did you give her this number, here at Lescudjack?'

'No. I wouldn't. I don't know these people. But I promised I'd phone you. Margret said that what Anna would really like was you to fly out there to see her for Easter. She knows how busy you are, and she didn't know if you were doing any teaching right now, but she worked out that if you were, then maybe you could come in the Easter break. Anyway it seems all rather predetermined to me, but I didn't say so. I said I'd pass it on. Was that okay?'

'Wonderful. Thanks. How are you both, anyway?'

'Good, yes. Jean's been staying with us with little Mark – that was lovely. He's nearly two and he's going to be a performer when he grows up . . .' Jules laughed. 'We gave him a pair of maracas – he knows just what to do. His feet are going and he's standing there, his whole body keeping time, and shaking . . . and speaking . . . Talk about a rap poet.'

'He's only two, for godsake!' I laughed at Jules's enthusiasm. She'd obviously got it bad for Jean's little boy.

'Yep. A child prodigy. Did I tell you that Tessa's going to be a granny again?'

'No, you didn't! I bet she's thrilled. When's it due?'

'In the autumn. Hey, are you still okay for us to come to Hermit's Hut for Spring Bank?'

'Yes, we are. Tarn will be very busy but I can take the whole time and want to go to the caves. There are some low tides around that week.'

'Great. We're looking forward to it. Very much. Jean's due on the fifth of September, by the way. A baby on your birthday, Lerrie.'

'That'd be an honour!' We both laughed. 'How's the band?'

'Good. But we're up to our necks in rehearsals. There are

eight of us, plus a new singer. She's ace. She has a fine, fine ear, and she's used to a cappella.'

'Is she? I'll have to come up to hear you, won't I?'

'Yeah, shame we're not on in the next month or so – you'll stop over if you do decide to go and see Anna, won't you? But we won't be ready by Easter. Ah well, it's all very exciting. I'm loving it. It takes my mind off work – don't know how much longer I can go on in residential care – the pressure is never ending. But money's money, isn't it?'

'Yes, I must start some workshops soon. But the cards are doing so well, it's all right at present. Couldn't you do a job share, like Tessa. That might take the pressure off?'

'Not really, Lerrie. She got hers when she was already high up in the Housing Department – she got a bloody good deal – but things have tightened up so much. It's just not on. I can't see a way out at present, so I just carry on and try not to fret about it, and I concentrate on the band. It's wonderful! Do you want a word with Tessa?'

'Please, if she's not busy.'

'Here she is. Bye then, Lerrie. Lots of love.'

'And you Jules. Big hugs. And thanks.'

Jules passed the handset to Tessa whose voice glowed down the line: 'Hello, you. We're missing you.'

'Me, too. How are you, Granny?'

Tessa laughed. 'Old. But wiser, of course. Actually I'm feeling ace. I've finished that painting and I'm really pleased with it. I've started something new already and it's looking good. What about *you*? How do you feel about the voice from your past?'

'Well, I'm not sure. Going to see Anna's no simple thing. I've got to think about it.'

'I hope you do go, then we get to see you soon.'

'I know. I'm missing you both like crazy.'

'Us, too, Lerrie. It's just not the same without you.'

'I know. It's awful. I keep trying to kid myself I can pick up the phone, like in London. But I daren't get into that. I'd run up an astronomical bill. You know what we're like – we talk and talk.'

'We do that. How's Tarn? You two still . . .?'

'Yes, we are. She's lovely!'

'I was thinking about you, Lerrie. It was such a new thing for you both. We were delighted for you. But then to be suddenly parted like that at half-term must've been hard. We hoped to meet her in London, but of course the timing of her flights was so tight. Is she all right?'

'She's fine. Tired. She's doing shift work and there's been a bit of bother with a racist born-again git at the college. We'll tell you about it all when we see you. But she's hanging on in there. Her younger daughter, Jocelyn, is very difficult, as we said. She won't leave this man. We can't get our heads round it. The violence, you know. So there's a fair bit of tension here.'

'I can imagine. It's a really hard one to unravel. Tarn must be worried about the baby. I would be. It's any grandmother's nightmare. Can we do anything?'

'I don't know what can be done really. But it helps to have you to talk to, it really does. Joss and the baby are both very vulnerable. But what can we do? Joss's boyfriend's in London now, with Joss, and gawd knows what's going on. Tarn loves Jocelyn, and we both feel that Joss must be in a bad way to be with this turd who beats her up. He hates Tarn because she's close to Joss and also he hates lesbians.'

'That's horrible. Tarn's such a strong woman, you'd think a bit'd rub off on her daughter, wouldn't you? It doesn't make a lot of sense, does it?'

'No. It doesn't. That's part of what Tarn finds so hard.'

'It's very sad. We've been so lucky, haven't we? You with Rosie, us with Sharon and Jean.'

'Exceptionally lucky. Jean's obviously fine – is Sharon okay?'

'Oh yes. She loves her work, very professional and dedicated. This is where the theatres are – there seems to be more funding here – and she loves London, so we're all together, which is nice. Things are great.'

'Good. I'm glad. Give her my love, won't you?'

'Yes, sure. Can I make a suggestion, Lerrie?'

'Yes, of course, what is it?'

'Why don't you *both* go to Germany – you and Tarn – have some time there together. You'd get to meet Helen and Yuki ... and to see Tarn's friend, what was her name, Liesl, out in the country . . . and besides, Tarn speaks German fluently, I think you said. That'd be a help.'

'Yes.' Pause. 'I think you're right. I was going to suggest to Tarn to take a break over Easter – it has all been rather intense for her lately. This Joss thing really pulls her down. I'll talk to her and see how she feels. She has two weeks at Easter, so we could do the trip to see Anna in a leisurely way. Yes, I'll talk to her.'

'Let us know then. You can either stay over with us, or at the studio. Everything's kept aired.'

'Bless you. Love you lots. Give Jules a hug from me.'

'Okay, talk to you soon then, Lerrie. Love you. Bye now.'

By the next evening, our tickets were booked. A short while later, we were on our way to Germany.

CHAPTER THIRTEEN

We approached Hamburg airport in the dark, dropping height over a city of ships and tankers, water and docks, rivers and lakes. Tarn was reading a German newspaper in the seat beside me. I was an artist by a window, absorbing urban night and liquid light like a dry sponge, filling up and expanding joyfully.

Margret, Anna's housekeeper, was there to meet us with her lover Renate. It was a lovely, warm welcome. We liked one another from the start. Margret and Renate became our new German friends, the first friends we'd made together.

It was about half an hour's drive from the airport through the busy city streets. The first time I'd come to Hamburg I'd been very puzzled. All the streets seemed to have the same name – *Einbahnstrasse*. I shared the joke with Tarn. *Einbahnstrasse* is German for one-way street.

Presently we arrived and juggled our way into a tight parking place. There were cars everywhere, but also very, very old trees, in bud but not yet in leaf. Daffodils – *Osterglocken* – rang the bells of their flowers across wide grassy banks under the trees, which lined the roads around the old buildings. It was now midnight and Anna was asleep. We four ate a meal together, drank some good white wine, and slept soundly till morning.

My first full conversation with Anna von Schiller took place in her beautiful, light and airy two-storey apartment surrounded by old trees in a densely packed, attractive area near to Hamburg's central lake.

Anna was frail, white-haired and thin, sitting up in bed with a shade of green plastic around her forehead. It reminded me of the shades tennis players sometimes wear and put me in mind of Martina and it gave Anna's eyebrows a rather eerie glow.

Her eyes were faded now, but she could see me and she reached for me. I sat on the bed and held her closely and gently, the years and memories melting between us in a flow of compassion.

Her face had been a perfectly proportioned lesbian face as a younger woman. Perhaps that seems a strange description. It depends on your point of view. No one could have mistaken her for anything else but lesbian. I don't mean that she looked butch or femme. 'Look at the faces of those who have chosen it,' Adrienne Rich has said, and that somehow describes Anna exactly. There was a distinctive sense of the erotic. A movement in the turn of her head. A wisdom in the corner of her smile.

Now as an old woman there was a suggestion of crone. A shining intelligence which could not be hidden; a lifetime of womanfocus which gave depth and meaning to her expression; a breadth of understanding that was international and home-centred simultaneously.

But there was also a different word that came to me directly upon entering the room and seeing her, face to face, after all those years. It was not a shocking word because I didn't think of it as negative. Her face had changed. She had been ill – though she was not dying from a terminal illness, merely from natural causes – and this gave her mouth and nose an unmistakable shape. The word was witch.

I took a deep breath. I had seen many representations, over the years, in children's drawings, of witches. They are taught to perceive the word witch and the idea of witch as something horrible. Anna herself, smiling at me with life and joy and peace in her whole countenance, was splendidly positive. A woman of life and living. A woman of depth and loving. Someone who, by touching me, could pass something worthwhile on to me. That's what I mean when I say that on looking at Anna the word witch came to my mind.

The room was high ceilinged, with a carved border around the top of the walls and wooden, old, external roller shutters on the elegant windows. Long, off-white curtains were draped there and there were no nets so that the room was full of light. Two enormous fig plants in pots reached almost to the ceiling and the furniture was exquisitely carved, in the old German style. The bed was a rich deep wood with a wooden frame that hid the mattress and had carved head- and footboards with oval, burnished knobs at each corner. It was a single bed and had been so highly polished that it gleamed. It was very beautiful to look at, set off by an embroidered duvet and pillowcases in cream on white. On the walls there were one or two hand weavings and an original Chagall. The room was not over-furnished, a cross between a bedroom and a gallery. It was very peaceful. I felt at home there, which surprised me.

We sat with our arms around each other for a few minutes.

In that brief space of time I recalled the last time I had held someone so old.

My mind flew back to South Yorkshire and I could see the village of Herton with its pit tip and the small buckets endlessly cabling up and down. I had been there with Lindsey, just after Biff had died. I had sat like this on Moss's bed, and we had held one another for a while. My conversation with Moss returned to me, there in Anna's room, with astonishing clarity, across the years.

'I can feel Biff's presence here,' I had said to Moss, and I had continued, 'The whole house has both of you in it. Not in a sad way. It's positive. I was looking at the garden, from the upstairs window, while I was dressing, you know this afternoon. It was already getting dusk. I was thinking about all the troubles here in Herton. How it's all building up. How Biff would have been on the spot with the analysis, as always.'

Moss had replied, 'Yes, I miss that. Biff would have been able to mesh all the details of the history together.' She had sighed, then added, 'It was a particular gift Biff had, to make people understand the history. Like Lindsey. She says sometimes she's never forgotten the lessons on the packhorse bridge, but she didn't know they were lessons, just stories. Biff was such a one for stories.'

'Wasn't Biff's mother a suffragette? And two of Biff's sisters? I remember that from one of Biff's letters. I expect that made a difference in Biff's life really. Being part of it as a child.'

At that time, during that conversation, the effort of using Biff's name all the time had exhausted me. I had become conscious minute by minute of the energy it must have taken Moss and Biff always to be so careful, without selling them-selves short. Had they really decided all those years ago for Biff to pose as a man but only to take on *some* of the disguise and not other parts of it? How much maleness *had* Biff taken inside herself? How had she struggled with that?

Moss had taken her time replying. 'Yes. Biff was born and raised in Manchester. Alongside the working-class suffragettes there. Biff lived in two different centuries, was only four when the twentieth century began. Oh, I'm tired. It's been a lovely day. I'm going to sleep now. Sleep well, Lerryn. Pleasant dreams.'

'I will, Moss. And I hope you do as well. Dream whatever you'd most like to.'

That had been ten years ago. Now I was in Germany, in the home of my ex-lover, my first lover, before Lindsey. I had changed so much in the intervening time.

Presently Anna let go of me and I pulled up a comfy armchair beside her bed so that I could be very near while we talked. Talking was something of an effort for her. Anna was not yet eighty, though she seemed much older than that.

I sensed that Taarnagh, who was taking a walk under the trees by the lake nearby, was thinking of me, watching the movement of wind on the water, noticing how the ripples moved across the lake like waves, and sending them on towards me: waves of strength and love.

Anna said, 'You came, dearest Lerryn.'

'I did. You called me and I came.'

'I did wonder if you would bring Taarnagh. I hoped you would.'

'Thank you. We'd been separated by circumstances earlier this year and I didn't want another separation. It was wonderful that we could travel here together.'

'Good. You have your boundaries now, Lerryn. That's good.'

'Boundaries, Anna?'

'Yes. You answered my call and you came on your *own* terms.'

'You understand that now?'

'I do, now. It took me a long time. These things take their own time, you know.'

'They do.'

'And you are happy now?'

'I am. Very.'

'Good. *Das ist sehr gutt.* She is very lovely, your Celtic lady. Warm and kind. I feel it. It gives me peace.'

'Have you found peace now, Anna?'

'*Endlich.* At last, dearest Lerryn. It has been a long and most passionate journey. Your rejection . . .' (I winced but she gripped my hand tight and smiled.) 'Your rejection set me on my journey to the centre of myself. And what I found was that I had never come to terms with a great loss. A loss that happened when I was a young woman, during the war years. I never talked to you of the war. Of my life story, my life as a young woman. But it explains a great deal; and I want to tell you now. Are you ready? To hear my story?'

Her eyes met mine with the question in them. I held her gaze steadily and nodded, perhaps also with a faint smile, though I had a sense that this was not going to be an easy tale.

So she began, and for the rest of the hour as she talked, her hand held mine.

'I was nineteen years old when the war began. Wealthy, with all my life ahead of me. We lived in Berlin, but we had houses in the country, in the north and in the south. I also had relatives in Switzerland, German-speaking Swiss, and in Austria. Sometimes at Christmas we would join my Austrian relations for the skiing. There were four of us, three sisters and one brother. We lacked for nothing.

'My father never joined the party, although I think he believed that some aspects of the ideology would save Germany. But we also had Jewish friends in our circle. Our closest Jewish friends left for London in 1938. Others went to America. But my special friend was a girl I had grown up with during my teens; the daughter of one of those families. Her name was Sarah. Her father was a lawyer. One summer in 1936 I took Sarah with me to our country house in the south. There was a beautiful lake. *Sehr schön.* We had a small rowing boat and we spent long lazy hours on that lake. No one disturbed us. In the shade of the old trees around the lake we found secluded places, sheltered and private, and there we were free to fall in love, to learn what we could be to one another. I was sixteen years old.

'As I speak, at this very moment, your lover is walking by a different lake, the beautiful lake here in Hamburg. It is no coincidence that I live *here* now, my dear Lerryn. I chose to live here by *this* lake.

'Sarah was only a month younger than me. It was a beautiful love. That autumn her parents began to plan their exile to London, and at first she fought them openly about it, refusing to co-operate with them, because she didn't want to leave me, or to end our relationship. We had told one another that we would be married, with a commitment to one another that would last a lifetime and would not be any less strong than if we were were a boy and a girl. We trusted each other completely; and neither of us ever betrayed that trust. Her parents could not understand that she would not go with them to England. There were many bitter arguments about it. She said that she would not leave Germany.'

Anna paused. She had pronounced the G in Germany the soft way, as if it were spelt Shj. Her voice was still mellow. I recalled then I'd always loved Anna's beautiful voice.

She lay back for a while, as if she needed a little time to absorb what she had told me so far and before continuing with her story. I held her hand and felt the power of those gentle words she had just spoken: neither of us ever betrayed that trust.

Then time shifted for me in Anna's peaceful room: I had fallen in love with Anna when I was twenty . . . many, many years ago . . . after what had seemed to me at the time a terrible betrayal of love by Lindsey, my childhood sweetheart.

I had fallen for Anna – and especially for her beautiful voice – after a period of deep sadness because my childhood sweetheart had not waited for me.

Now I sat beside Anna, who had her eyes closed for a few moments, lost in her remembered love for Sarah, meditating a while upon it. And I found myself drawn back to that time I had searched for Lindsey, my own first love.

I had sat with Moss and Biff in the kitchen behind the grocer's shop, and had been asked, 'Are you on holiday here, Lerryn?'

'Not really, Moss. I, er, I had a chance to join one of the short courses, at the Art Foundation here, and I, er, I thought it'd be good to meet Lindsey again after all this time. I'll never forget her or anything about those summers in Herton. They were important to me. Herton's a special place.'

I had noticed a look and smile that passed between Moss and Biff. They had seemed suddenly much younger, like teenagers in love. A fleeting moment then gone. Hidden under grey hair and tired bones. I had noticed Biff had a habit of tugging at his tie. Stress, maybe? I had babbled on about having had to learn hairdressing, but now I was going to stay at Aunt Harry's place in London, find hairdressing work, do some foundation courses, and try hard for a place at the Slade. I had been embarrassed at how much I had revealed of my hopes and dreams.

I had been about to ask if Lindsey would be home soon when they had said, 'Well, if you're going to be in London you can get in touch with Lindsey there. She's working in a factory near Old Street, sewing gloves, bless her. She'd only been in London two days when she started there. Peter's only on a grant so they're very short of money.'

I had flinched. They had seen, but hadn't been able to tell me who they were, or how it was that they understood. They couldn't take me in their arms and comfort me. Couldn't tell me that they knew of my love for Lindsey and that they were two women who loved one another.

'Who is Peter?' I had asked, as despair had overwhelmed me.

'He is a young man from Herton who asked her to go and live with him while he studies geology and geography there. His parents disapprove. But we felt she should make her own decision. She was very determined. You know her. She can be thunder and lightning if she's made up her mind.'

I had fled back to London and immersed myself in my attempts to get accepted at the Slade. Almost a year later, on my twentieth birthday, I had allowed myself to fall for the beautiful voice and wonderful loving on offer from my Aunt Harry's closest 'friend'.

Lindsey had married quickly and quietly when she had found she was pregnant. They had been driving north to tell Moss and Biff about the baby when there was a terrible car accident. Peter was killed. I didn't meet Lindsey again until the baby, Rosie, was four-and-a-half. I'd refused to accompany Anna to Europe and was on my own again.

In my reverie, I smiled, thinking about the sixteen years of living and loving Lindsey and helping to raise Rosie that had followed.

So many changes. So many worlds. Past and present and future. Now I was in love again, with a beautiful Celtic woman, warm and passionate and good.

Distant worlds moved and swirled in a kaleidoscope of bright images in Anna von Schiller's apartment.

Anna was ageing fast. I was approaching fifty, listening to Anna's story of her own childhood sweetheart, whom she had loved at the outset of the Second World War.

Such worlds apart we had been.

When Anna had loved Sarah, I had not even been born.

Anna opened her eyes, squeezed my hand, and continued, 'Outwardly, Sarah agreed to depart with her family for London. I wanted her to go. I knew she was not safe to stay in Berlin at the height of Nazi power there. But I knew that at the last moment she would not leave.

'Jewish people were disappearing, Lerryn. There are those who declare that they didn't know that this was happening. But they did know. They saw the empty houses in the villages and towns. They divided the contents up amongst themselves. They'd take home a fine table from an empty house, they'd sit round it and eat their food. They'd find themselves a new chest of drawers in an empty house and they'd take it home and would store their best clothes in it. Where did they think the family had gone whose table it was, whose chest of drawers they now used?

'Ordinary people did witness – though, perhaps, many did not fully understand the atrocities that awaited the disappeared.' Anna sighed. 'Perhaps.' Her grip tightened on my hand.

I saw that hers was an old hand with fine skin and veins on the back, leading towards a thin wrist. It was the kind of hand you would associate with an ancient mother. It was a hand that had once caressed every young and wanting inch of my very needy skin.

She began to speak again. 'We shall none of us ever know who betrayed Sarah's family. It was about a week before they were due to leave and the final papers were in order. Sarah and her mother were at home. I don't know where her father was nor her two brothers.

'The entire street was raided after dark. There must've been much shooting because the next day the apartments were open to the street and there was blood in the apartment above theirs. But theirs was uncannily tidy.

'It was the absence of mess that was the most ominous thing about it. Everything seemed to be in its place. Except for the people. They were gone. There was no sign of them. Mother and daughter. I imagine them even now, being held tightly, shoved harshly, marched out of there. Herded like animals. It seems they didn't have time to fight back, though Sarah was brave. She would have fought back if she possibly could.

'To this day I don't know where they were taken. Where they were sent. Neither of them survived though; after the war, the whole family searched every available list. There were many stories like that.'

Again Anna paused.

I had never seen the look that was in her eyes that day. As if the images of every piece of war-time archive were parading themselves on a film screen in her mind as she searched the lines of people for Sarah and her mother.

I didn't speak.

I waited.

I pictured Tarn by the lake, under one of old Hamburg's great and spreading trees. I thought of the still woods all over Germany. The Schwarzwald, with its immense hills and valleys of trunks and branches and spreading canopies; the woods that lined the railtracks, mile after mile stretching between the cities; the trees in the wide flat areas of the northwest, marking out the straight boundaries of the vast flat fields; the small areas of weekender woodlands near the cities where people escaped to breathe and to wander. Springtime in the forest of Waldfriedan, where we would walk tomorrow. To me it seemed – as it had always seemed – that Germany was a land of trees.

Old, rooted, down, down into the earth.

I sensed that Tarn was standing completely still, her eyes on the wide waters of the lake, her back leaning against the bark of a warm tree trunk. I could feel the connection with her, my new lover, as I waited to hear again the voice of the old woman, my first lover.

But, in Anna's room, a silence hovered.

Then into that silence came another voice connecting past times to present times, stories from a hidden history. And because I had spent many years searching through history, recent history, for the female identity of another ex-lover's grandmother, it didn't seem unusual or a coincidence to me, there in Anna's room, that from another lake, in another time, I sensed another voice with something specific to say.

Into my mind came the second verse of 'The Ballad of Ellan Vannin', and an image of Tarn, years ago, singing as a soloist with the collected strength of us girls in the school choir behind her, as if we were, in that instant, her tree trunk against which she could lean for strength. The second stanza of the ballad had an image of a lake across which the wind blew, disturbing the waters and revealing hidden truths: 'Hear the scream that surges, across the gentle lake. When women speak the earth must shake, still waters break, the truth to make.'

I took a deep breath, and shook myself back into the silent room. There was a very slight movement of the off-white curtains by the open window. Anna noticed, as I did.

She began to speak. She must say all that she needed to say. 'You may wonder what became of Sarah's father and brothers?' I nodded.

'They arrived in London about three months later. They had hidden in different houses trying desperately to get information about Sarah and her mother. They finally escaped by car to the Netherlands and then by boat to London, arriving in the spring of 1938. They were sheltered there by Jewish friends. Sarah's father and one brother were killed in the blitz on London. One brother survived. He died of natural causes in London fifteen years ago and never, during the whole of that time, did he give

117

up trying to piece together the story of the night that Sarah and her mother were taken. The family was very strongly bonded. If by the remotest chance Sarah or her mother had survived, be it in the camps or prisons, or even in the mental hospitals in which some survivors ended their days after the war, he would have known. No stone, as they say, was left unturned. My childhood special friend became one of the lost lesbians of the third reich. She and her mother were two of the lost Jewish women of that time.'

After telling me this part of her story, Anna was very tired. I sat with her, holding her hand, until presently she fell asleep. When I was sure that she was sleeping soundly, I eased my hand out of hers and, as quietly as I could, I left the room.

That night the phone rang. Margret answered it and held the receiver towards Tarn, saying, 'I think it's for you. Somebody wants to talk to Grandma.'

Tarn took the call. 'Hello? This is Grandma. Is that Yuki?'

'Hello, Grandma. I wanted to come and see you. But I'm in bed with Big Ted because I've got the flu.'

'Oh, sweetheart, I'm sorry to hear that. When did that happen?'

'Yesterday. I got it from school. Everybody's got it. My heads goes boom, boom. I'm like a jelly all over.'

'Oh, sweetie, what a pity. Everybody was looking forward so much to meeting you. Is school a bit easier now?'

'Yes, I've got a friend, Jutta, she's a new girl. They just came from Düsseldorf. Her dad's got a new job so she moved house. She's very nice. She's got the flu as well.'

'Oh dear, oh dear. Well I hope you'll both be better soon.'

'Then we can play together, can't we?'

'I expect so. But we're sad not to be seeing you. I shall try hard to come over here in the summer.'

'Mummy says she can bring me to Cornwall sometime.'

'That would be lovely.'

'She says I could have a surf board, Grandma.'

'That'd be fun. I don't have to have one, do I?'

Giggles. 'No, you're too old.'

'That's a good thing then. I don't mind swimming but I don't fancy surfing at all, Yuki.'

'I do. On a body board. But I've got to go now. Here's Mummy.'

'Helen?'

'Hello, Mum. What a pig of a thing. I'm really sorry about it, but she's just so wobbly. It's a nasty virus. All of us are having to take real care. Otherwise it lingers on.'

'You haven't got it?'

'No, thank God. I'm fine, Mum. You having a good time?'

'Wonderful, darling, thank you. We'll see what we can all do about the summer . . .'

'Don't worry, Mum. Wait and see about Joss's baby and then we'll sort out the timing. We can't do a lot until that's all happened, really. Anyway, enjoy your visit to Anna's. Give Lerryn my best and say I'm very sorry not to get to meet her this time, okay?'

'I will. Talk to you soon, darling.'

'Bye, Mum. Lots of love.'

'You too. Bye, love.'

During the following week, while I sat with Anna, Tarn walked by the lake, enjoyed long talks with Margret, and read the German magazines, newspapers and many books on Anna's well-stocked shelves. She was in her element.

'It was amazing,' she said one evening in our room, 'Margret was asking me what kind of day I'd had while you were talking to Anna. I said that I'd had a wonderful walk by the lake and that hearing the German language spoken all around me made me want to know more about German history and culture.

'She knows the women who run the women's bookshop here, so we began to talk about women's history here and lesbian history in general. Then I told her about Liesl, in Cologne, and her research on the Beguines. She'd seen the news about the stone box and the finding of the tiles . . . then Margret talked about healing. Did you know she's a trained nurse?'

I nodded. 'Yes, and it doesn't surprise me because Anna may need nursing before long.'

'Exactly. It's part of Margret's brief here. It put me in mind of that book you've got by the woman who nursed Georgia O'Keeffe when she was ninety-six. A gentle book about the friendship they developed.'

119

'Yes, it was a lovely book.'

'Well, the upshot of this conversation was that when Margret was doing her nursing training, years ago, she was *taught* that nursing originated with the rise of the first women's movement in Europe in the twelve hundreds . . . the Beguines.'

'They actually taught her that?'

'They did. Presumably the tutor was herself a feminist – or they'd have got a watered-down version.'

'I never heard of that before – I mean anyone actually *teaching* about the Beguines.'

'It came as a surprise to me too. Anyway, then Margret found me Fiona Bowie's book on the Beguines and this book here on Hildegard of Bingen, who was so famous as a scientist and healer in the twelfth century.'

Tarn handed me the book excitedly and I flicked through looking at the pictures. I said, 'I know of Hildegard of Bingen through Judy Chicago's massive art exhibition, *The Dinner Party*. Hildegard of Bingen was represented as one of the thirteen guests from the Middle Ages. Did you see the exhibition? It was fabulous!'

'No, I missed it. I wish I'd got there. But the thing is that Hildegard of Bingen's life must've run in parallel to the first Beguines . . . when the Beguinages were first being set up.'

'She composed music and was a writer too?'

'Yes. Her writing was linked with the land a lot; it's all about mother earth, mother nature. She's like the *intellectual* version of the everyday hedgewitch of the past, like Ellan Vannin. What's so exciting for me is that so much here is feeding into my own research. I came here to support you, but it's also becoming a rich and creative time for me. It's wonderful, Lerrie. I'm really learning such a lot. I still don't know when I'm going to the Isle of Man, and exactly how the Ellan Vannin material fits into the picture, but I know it does. Everything is beginning to fit into a whole. I'm so happy.'

'Come here.'

I drew her to me and we kissed for a long, sweet time. We touched each other's faces with soft fingertips, and held one another closely. It was as if Anna's blessing extended to us from the secret lake where she and Sarah had once fallen in love. We

120

were, in our middle years, alive, in love and delighted with one another. Ours was a rare and precious gift.

I said, 'For Anna, when they took Sarah away, there wasn't any certainty, no finality. She never knew when or how she died. She had terrifying images, horrifying things which might be being done to Sarah. Somehow Anna stayed sane. How? Later she was able to give and receive love with Harry and then with me. She was a very warm and loving woman. I loved her very dearly. Without her love in those two years I wonder if I'd really have been strong enough to search for Lindsey again and challenge Lindsey about her sexuality in the way that I did. I wonder if I'd have been open enough to be patient when Lindsey wasn't sure. I had opened up to Anna and it was a beautiful experience for me.'

'It still is. There's a lovely energy between you both. And it's in its rightful place now. You bring one another a lot of gifts. You're also a very warm and loving woman and your visit here will bring her peace and gladness. She'll be able to let go more easily.'

'Thank you. I love you Tarn. I really do.'

'I love you too, Lerrie.'

We began to kiss again and slowly we undressed and went to bed.

There are times when passion takes over and has its own urgent rhythms. There are other times, and this sweet night was one of them for us, when the intensity of the day lingers on, not unkindly, but with a gentle insistence on maintaining its presence and subduing libido. It doesn't subdue love itself. Love is like the canvas – large, patient, glad, and waiting. So, that night, as if in honour of Anna and Sarah, our caresses were those of knowledge and wisdom, with the enduring slow understanding that the artist has when she is preparing for a new work. She moves around her studio with experienced hands and a meditative contemplative soul. She shifts this set of brushes to the shelf by the canvas, she cleans the palette, she ensures she has the drawings set out from which she will create on to canvas the next day.

Similarly, the wise gardener, taking note of the weather, which is a little too windy this evening or a little too wet, goes to her garden shed and makes ready for an early start next morning. She considers the conditions and rhythms of this evening, this season. She touches each plant, each part of the garden, comparing the textures, the rough bark, smooth bark, soft leaves, curving branches, fragrant rounded mounds of thyme, oregano, marjoram, sage, soft furred surfaces, and those flowers about to open, touching each without passion and with infinite care.

So it was for us that night, easing ourselves from the day into a shared sleep, dreaming of Anna and Sarah and how it had been for them in their youth, when they had shared time and love and hope with one another.

In the dim light of early morning I surfaced from my sleep still curled on my side with Tarn curled around me, behind me. Without opening my eyes I heard her steady breathing and let myself drift down again. I must have slept because the next time I woke I realised I had been dreaming of the woodlands by the lake where Anna and Sarah had made love, but I couldn't recall any details of the dream.

Then I realised what had woken me this second time and that Tarn must be awake because her breathing had changed and without saying a word to me she was stroking the length of my curled body, her warmth still curved around my back and thighs.

Lazily, slowly, I yawned and turned over into the welcome of her arms until our lips met and there again was my familiar womb lurch and my breasts responding to her hands as the sensuous beauty of our lovemaking began.

We were on holiday, in a lesbian household, with our own room, warmth and privacy. There was no hurry. No work day ahead of us. No one to disturb us, no one to be concerned if breakfast was a little late this morning.

Tarn's hands, meanwhile, were strong, warm, passionate hands, hands that knew every inch of my body, hands that were reflections of my own, for many's the early morning I had reached for her in this way, stirring her from sleep into sensual wakefulness by some simple action of cupping her breast in my hand, playing with her as she surfaced from sleep, until there was that change of mood – that moment when the brush touches the canvas, that moment when the woman in the garden buries her face in the opening petals of a fragrant flower.

Slowly, steadily she began licking my breasts and sucking at my nipples until I stretched with lazy joy and lay languidly with my arms flung back on the pillows.

Then she stroked my inner arms with her fingertips, until my skin tingled and didn't quite tickle but sent shivers down through my breasts to my waist and belly.

She kissed my mouth and my neck, then moved her mouth back to my breasts and played her tongue around my breasts and nipples until I heard myself making moaning sounds.

She stroked my inner arms again and the hairs in my armpits, which made me shiver and wriggle my shoulders across the sheet, which was cool and fresh underneath me, and as I rubbed my back across the sheets, I heard myself whispering, 'More, more.'

So, for what seemed like hours, she stroked my body and played with my breasts until I felt I might not be able to bear it any longer. My clit demanded to be touched by her, my thighs were so hot and my skin so wanting and my hands were tingling with that exquisite blend of gentleness and hard want.

The muscles in my ankles were tensing up and my knees' muscles were shaking with energy and I thought my clit might explode if she didn't touch me there soon.

Then she did and I did explode, but not in my clit.

Dozens of colours poured into me. Waves and waves of colour. My mind flew high like a wild skylark hovering above the valley with the tumbling stream in it that meets the north coast on a rounded boulder beach.

The boulders hard and round, soft and round. Like my own breasts now. My breasts hard and round, soft and round at one and the same time. And the hardness was splendid, the hardness of full breasts sexy and full of lust pushing up into her hands, and at the same time soft and luscious like full fruits on a mature tree.

I started to come and come and couldn't stop. High sweet sounds and low guttural belly sounds from my throat, and the feel of her hot skin under my hands and the feel of the cool sheets under my bare buttocks as I was moving my buttocks side to side on the bed and arching my back upwards and thrusting my whole pelvis up towards her hand, offering and wanting and coming and offering and wanting and coming over and over.

Wetness everywhere and heat. Her mouth on my nipple, her hand on my clit. Everything was round; my body, her breasts, her body, my breasts.

Breasts and buttocks and faces and shoulders. Firm movements and soft simultaneously. All the need and want of the last years without her was pouring out of me. All the need and want that was buried when Lindsey left. All the compassion and need that Anna had buried. I was coming for Anna as well. I was myself and every woman who wants sex all at the same time. It was love and sex and lust and round and soft and hard and wet and hot in every moment. Waves and waves of it.

And presently I was on top of her making love to her with the same thoroughness, the same intensity, the same passionate need. This woman I could talk to. This woman who understood. This woman who was a match for me. This woman who loved and wanted and needed me.

Time passed but we were oblivious to time, taking turns or making love simultaneously. My mouth on her nipples, my hands all over her.

My tongue licking her ears, her eyes, her face, her mouth. Licking her neck and down again to her breasts. My hands rolling her buttocks and stroking her inner thighs. We couldn't stop. We didn't want to stop.

Eventually we must've fallen asleep because we woke very late morning, still wrapped together. Then we opened the curtains and marvelled at each other's faces, looking into one another's eyes without speaking, kissing sweetly and humorously, but not intensely, like intimate friends who had found a new friendship.

We showered and dressed slowly, luxuriating in the unaccustomed idleness, together on our first holiday, delighted with one another.

But something happened to me then in Anna's apartment.

It occurred to me that, at last, the absence of Lindsey Shepherd from my life was not of concern to me any more. The last traces of her long grey ghost-dress had flicked themselves around the firmly closing door of my bedroom; had slid away, during the night, along the long corridor and down the grand brown staircase that led to the street and wound through the trees to the edge of the deep wide lake.

At the lake there was a boat. The ghost in the grey robe untied the rope that fixed the boat to the shore. She stepped into the boat.

It floated out into the middle of the lake. The waters were vast and deep. Then, drifting down to the surface of the lake from the overhanging clouds there seeped a deep grey mist, swirling down, down, blending and merging with the surface of the lake.

The mist deepened. It thickened. It whitened until it was solid, dense, a low white mist, a silent cloud, enveloping the lake in a slow, white shroud.

It had absorbing qualities that white mist, that damp cloud, that ethereal shroud. Slowly, steadily it dissolved all that existed there upon the surface of the waters. It enclosed every edge, it slid on every ledge. Nothing was left solid in its centre. Nothing remained undissolved. It swirled. It moved.

It began to roll away, without speed, without hurry, with immense gracefulness. It curved and billowed, shifted and layered itself. Fold upon fold, wave upon wave. Flowing away now, as the dawn broke from the east. Evaporating and lifting and changing and shifting. Taking away with it all that it had enveloped until finally there lay the lake, gleaming and empty in the early morning.

Lindsey Shepherd had gone. *Endlich*. At last.

CHAPTER FOURTEEN

Tarn and I were in Germany for the whole of the Easter vacation. Tarn wanted space and peace, to walk and to read; she struck up a humorous and easy-going friendship with Margret. They found out that they both enjoyed cooking. They shopped and prepared delicious meals together, talking partly in German and partly in English because they were keen to practise the other's language, amidst much laughter and discussion of translation. Margret had been involved with a group of German women working against violence against women, so Tarn confided in Margret about her daughter's decision to stay with a violent man. Tarn spoke of Jocelyn and her pregnancy, about her fears for Joss and the forthcoming baby, and her distrust of Joss's boyfriend. Tarn simply did not believe that things would work out all right but, as Joss's mother, she was in a difficult position, partly because it was Joss's life and she must lead it her own way, and partly because, as a lesbian, Tarn was considered a 'pervert' by the boyfriend and kept at arm's length. The baby was due in August, and as time went on, Joss's situation was likely to become more and more intrusive on Tarn's peace of mind. Margret responded with understanding and sympathy, which Tarn found very comforting.

So, I was free to talk to Anna at length, of art and ideas and about my life in London with Tessa and Jules, about them and their art and music, and about Anna's thoughts on life in general.

Sitting up in bed one lovely sunny morning, with the windows open to let in the sounds from the lakeside and the busy city beyond, Anna said, 'So, my dear Lerryn, it is special, you know, this time with you now.'

'Yes, I do know that. It is for me too. The years with you were very healing for me. You were and are very important to me.'

'My dear Lerryn, that is wonderful to hear. I have gifts to give

126

you, contacts here, stories to tell. I have books for you and one or two cherished paintings. I have kept up to date with women's art and culture in Europe, and America.'

'Do you recall *The Dinner Party* exhibition?' I asked.

'Judy Chicago? I do. I stood before each place setting for long moments, absorbing the images, the embroidery – exquisite embroidery was it not? – the colours, the luminosity of the plates.'

'Well, I mention it because Tarn's reading up about Hildegard of Bingen. Coincidence, maybe. Anyway, Hildegard, it seems, held strong views about the greening of the earth, called it Viriditas. It's being suggested that she was still internalising the pre-Christian religions, earth as nature, all those ideas. And that her writings fed into the works of the early Beguines, whom Tarn is reading about. You know that it's Tarn's friend Liesl in Cologne who is writing about the Beguine Helga of Cologne?'

'Of course. It's very exciting. She was on breakfast television. A very dykey looking woman, if I may say so.'

'Helga? Or Liesl?'

She laughed. 'Liesl. Who's to say what Helga looked like?'

'So you haven't lost your touch of lust, then?'

A hearty belly laugh from Anna. 'Lost, my dear? One *never* loses it. One just doesn't follow it through these days.'

We both laughed.

'I have in fact followed Judy Chicago's work continuously since that exhibition. We used to be surrounded by artists, of course, when Margret and I lived in Cologne. The city is full of them.'

'I was wondering why you didn't stay?'

'Oh, life moves on, Lerryn. You know how it is.' Anna shrugged and gestured with her arms. 'I knew I needed nursing, or would before too long. I have friends here in Hamburg, so it wasn't an unfamiliar place. I'm a city person. Through and through. Margret met Renate at a festival in Cologne and Renate lives and works here. I was with no one at the time. But I love Margret as housekeeper. Love her dearly.'

'Oh, I can see that. You are wonderful together. This place is so peaceful.'

'Good. I think so. Margret needed work, but she wanted to live near to Renate. Naturally. She's only your age, Lerryn.

They have many years ahead together. So we thought long and carefully and I put it to her that I would move if she would stay as my housekeeper, and my nurse later when it's necessary, which it will be very soon. Already, I've stopped walking far; I'm more comfortable in my bed. So, we moved. I have always loved this lake and these apartments, and I had an old friend in this area many years ago. So here we are.'

'It makes good sense, put like that.'

'But we were talking of art and setting the world to rights, huh?'

'This is true.' I laughed, very happy to be with Anna like this.

'I am interested in Judy Chicago in particular. Her work on the Holocaust is very fine. And so is her work on the Birth Project – blood and mothers. But this concept is a problem here, now in modern Germany – blood and mothers. I have much I need to say to you about this, Lerryn.'

'Blood and mothers, specifically?'

'Yes. Pass me that book there, will you? It has a card in it. It was sent to me by a friend in America. You know how I love to get these parcels from all over the world. I always did, didn't I?'

'I used to be amazed at the things that arrived, I remember. Little sculptures in the post, packed so carefully. Every week there was something handmade!'

'It was a good life, Lerryn. You see I needed to live, really live. I think I was living for Sarah as well. And for her mother. Do you understand?'

'I think so.'

'Here is the card. See, it reads: "When women love each other it is the blood of the mothers speaking." It is a Caribbean proverb. Oh, I lived life to the full in those early years. After the war I threw myself into politics here in Germany. Rebuilding – with hope for the future. Then I burned out. And I began to flit around Europe – Paris, Vienna, until I came to England and met your beloved aunt. You know the rest. Of course I had money. The freedom to move around like that. And, of course, in love with you as I was later, I still understood your need for freedom and your refusal to live in my shadow. So eventually I came home here.'

She looked into my eyes. It was a good moment. Then she said, 'There are women artists here who would like to explore images of blood and mothers like in the Birth Project. But it is difficult here. We must maintain the frame around ourselves – a boundary between women artists now and the abuse of the idea of mother-blood by the fascists in the third reich. The terrible theft of important concepts holds us in its unfreedom in our art even now. The idea of mother-blood has been polluted by the fascists – it is also being re-used by the neo-fascists. The idea is corrupt and women will not be understood if they try to reclaim this here, yet.'

'Why are you worried about this in particular, during my visit here with you? There are so many things we could discuss. Why this one? I know you well enough to trust that you have good reasons, but I don't really understand them yet.'

'There are younger women now in Germany who want art *and* spirit. Good women, very young. I met some in Cologne and there are others who visit me here from time to time.'

'You are and always have been a well-loved patron of the arts, Anna. Aren't you glad to have such visits from young women artists?'

'Delighted, my dear Lerryn. Delighted. But these younger women, they go to all the new-found sacred places, Malta, Crete, Çatal Hüyük in Turkey, and they come back shining and inspired and they want to represent this in their art.'

'Why not?'

'I don't think they comprehend, not really. But then I didn't tell them my true story. Only for you, Lerryn. I wanted to save that story for you – and of course you may now tell them in your own way about my young love for Sarah, and how she was taken away. These young women – the third reich is a long way away from them. Back somewhere in distant time. Perhaps to them it is as far away as ancient Crete. But not to me. Perhaps they do not realise its legacies here. So I'm talking to you about it because I want you to make them understand. I want you to talk to them. I'm close to you. I can break my silence with you.'

She paused. I waited because I felt that something was missing. Some pieces of a puzzle. I didn't want to hurt Anna by revealing that I myself wasn't clear what connections she was making. I hoped my silence was supportive to her. I kept my gaze steady, on her face, smiling gently, and I waited.

She continued, 'The Nazis used all these things – white light, the Tarot, the I Ching, the stones, the symbols. They went to the women's sacred places – the ancient powerful shrines to the earth mother here in Germany – and cast their poison and fascist ideas of pure races around those very sites. They did it in the name of the mothers. Blood and mothers. They took the images of the earth mother, and the concepts of matrifocal societies and twisted them to their own purposes. To them the idea of woman was that pure wives and mothers would give birth to pure babies who would perpetuate the Aryan race and override all other peoples of the world. It was a travesty of the images of nurturing, sensuality, eroticism and femaleness. Every aspect of the original iconography became tainted. The swastika itself was the ancient Indian sacred sign of the four winds, the four directions. The wholeness of nature and the earth we live in, whose daughters we are, was contained in that symbol. The Nazis left nothing untarnished, nothing sacred. Then they took the bodies of the disappeared and destroyed them, often very slowly after medical experiments, or worn out from starvation and rape.

'In the name of the nurturing of the pure race, in the name of blood and mothers they took my own lover and her mother.

'I do not know where they died. They were sacrificed – in the name of that new spirituality. It was not simply politics, Lerryn, nor economics. The Nazis had a terrifying abuse of the spiritual as well.'

'I understand, Anna. I understand, now.'

'Millions and millions of people died – twenty-seven million in Russia – millions in the camps. And all in the name of purity of race – blood and mothers.'

'Are you saying that women's art as well as women's spirit can never be re-established here by women . . . because it is tainted by association?'

'They *are* both tainted by association. What can be achieved here and what is desirable, I don't know. There's an old saying, not a German one, never mind, that we can be part of the problem or part of the solution. That is what I am talking about.'

I shuddered. 'I didn't know they did that. A terrible abuse of those ancient places. I knew about some of the art symbols. There's an old stone up on the moors above Ilkley in Yorkshire called the swastika stone. An ancient stone with the old, old symbol on it. I hated being near it. Oh, it was years ago. I was up there with Lindsey once. Just seeing the symbol on the stone made my flesh creep and I couldn't photograph it or draw it. I couldn't get away from it fast enough. It wasn't reclaimable. But it must be awesome to be faced with the theft of the old cultures here, the incorporation of those places into the Nazi philosophy.'

'Well, I have to be true to myself, Lerryn. To me, Anna von Schiller. I do not want to be an unquiet ghost woman hovering in the glades and groves, endlessly circling the old stones and calling and calling for ever simply because in this life I was unvoiced for ever. You are aware of the statement that Audre Lorde makes, I am sure. She says, "My silences have not protected me. Your silences will not protect you." I have to break my silence when I see the young women wanting to dance at the stones, here in Germany. Waving their arms to the moon in some far-off sacred grove. They dance on Sarah's grave.'

'What exactly would you like me to do? Do you have something particular in mind?'

'Simply to tell my story. To talk. To ensure that, in their search for women's history, art and spirit, young women never forget what fascism has done and what it can do. To speak out when you feel it is the right time and in whatever way you feel is the right way. You will know – it is your way that matters now.'

'To paint? To make art?'

'Whatever you like, Lerryn.'

'I understand. I will speak. I will tell your story.'

'You are a woman artist of international renown, Lerryn. You are reconnecting with your homeland, Cornwall. Who is to say what direction you would decide to take your work? I need to share these things, Lerryn. You will, I am sure, heed what I say.'

'I have listened to you very carefully. I have a copy of that card myself, with the Caribbean proverb on it, from my friends Tessa and Jules. I have always treasured it. It's such a wonderful proverb. It's true that when women love each other it is the blood of the mothers speaking. Tarn is studying the ancestral story of the Isle of Man. There are things we need to know wherever we have come from. I will take care of the meaning of that proverb. And of your story, Anna. You have my word.'

'You will talk to Taarnagh?'

'I promise. She has brought me peace again and passion. I am alive again. You understand me, don't you?'

'Yes. And I want her to know my story. I want women to know. I have told you my story and I am asking you to pass it on. Simply to make it known. That's what I ask. That's all I ask. I am tired now, Lerryn. I would like to sleep now.'

'Sleep well, Anna. Dream whatever dreams would please you.'

CHAPTER FIFTEEN

We returned to Cornwall in time for Tarn's work just before the summer term began. Meanwhile, Cherry and Beech had been househunting without success. They had returned dismayed from several viewings of places to rent with land attached. Everywhere was expensive and it was now the start of the summer season, so they resigned themselves to waiting until September before finding a long let. The priority now was to help them sort and pack their belongings and move away from women's land and their beloved home at Eastfield Farm.

I was content to share the house with them, and when Tarn and I wanted time together I stayed at her place.

One evening Cherry asked me what I thought about her returning to Eastfield Farm to pot up some of the herbs that she'd left behind by mistake. I couldn't see a reason why not. They weren't Madeleine's plants, even though they were now growing on her land. They had been Cherry's seeds, tended and nurtured, and she hadn't meant to leave them there. I asked if she would like some company. We set off in my car but we left it at the local garage where it was booked in the following day for the exhaust pipe to be mended. From there we walked to Eastfield Farm.

It was calm and quiet as we made our way up the track to Cherry's old home. The hedgerows were beautiful and time seemed to slow down.

Behind us the pretty blue hills of Sancreed Beacon, Bartinney and Chapel Carn Brea were soft and silhouetted by the evening sun. There wasn't going to be much of a sunset though, too much mist and cloud over the sea behind the hills.

The lane, which resembled a dried river bed hoping to become a river, was boundaried on either side by twelve-foot-high Cornish hedges, topped with gorse and hawthorn bushes. We could hear cows the other side, heads bent down, tails swishing, mouths busy munching, cropping and grazing, their hot wet breath loud in the stillness.

There was no sign of anyone at the farm, though we were ready to ask permission if we bumped into Madeleine's estate agent.

Nor was there anyone home in Hazel Banyer's house, across the erstwhile farmyard. Cherry said, 'Rita, Hazel's tenant, has gone up country to visit her folks. It's eerie, isn't it, with our old place all closed up and not a living soul in the entire precinct? Listen, Lerrie, it's not just quiet, it's dead. There's no life now, as if the spirit of the place has gone. Because there's no one here to give and receive love. Oh, I can't bear this sensation, let's not linger near the houses.'

Cherry led me sadly to the bottom field where she and Beech had been so busy breaking in new ground, clearing brambles and planting onions, peas and beans in the early spring. A solitary golden larch, now about twenty years old, was in new bright gold-green leaf; some escallonia windbreaks were in full flower; we saw new shoots on the honeysuckle which Cherry had planted in the Cornish hedge; and we noticed that the bluebells were tall and straight with abundant deep-coloured buds this year.

In the third week of May they would carpet the edges of the bottom field. But no one would be there to be delighted. Except maybe the occasional would-be purchaser. 'I'll miss the bluebells this year,' said Cherry, as if speaking into my mind. 'I used to come out here every day throughout May and suddenly, there they'd be, again. And I would know that everything would be all right. What was it all for, I wonder? All the work and love we put in here? I suppose I should've known that one day it would be sold from under us. But I didn't think it'd happen. And I certainly never dreamed we'd be evicted in this way. I wake every day and it's real, it's true. She threw us out. Just like that. And now she'll sell it to the highest bidder.'

Cherry looked at me, tears of cold misery rolling down her face. There was no sound. I opened my arms and she came there and I held her. I thought, we must have land. We must have safe land for women for ever.

I thought of the deep blue tiles of Helga of Cologne. There seemed to be no boundary between then and now. As if the two worlds met and blended perfectly in that instant.

Then we sat for a moment on a large stone, stunned by the

peace and beauty of the place, aware of the story we'd been told about Helga and how she had left her childhood home to journey to women's land in a Beguinage hundreds of years ago. We had read the full translations of the tiles, now published and easily available. Just as the Beguines had been forced off their land and away from their familiar houses and gardens, so had Cherry and Beech been forced off this land, cast on to the vagaries of the private housing market, despite all the work they had done during their life of happiness here.

It was simply unbelievable that this place was going to be sold on. Why, oh why hadn't Madeleine at least put the fields in trust? For women. What if it was sold to someone who allowed hunting here? And even if, and it was only an if, a good woman bought it, and even if she encouraged women to return here, none of us would ever trust again that one woman's property was a safe haven for other women. Our trust was gone, broken, destroyed.

Cherry unpacked her trowel from her rucksack. Then she sighed and, slowly, sick at heart, she began to dig up small roots of marjoram, oregano, basil, comfrey, fennel, salad burnet, artemesia, medicinal valerian, borage and thyme. She handed me the roots, which I wrapped very carefully in the damp pieces of cloth we'd brought, and packed them in a plastic wrapper, placing them gently in our rucksacks.

Cherry clipped some sage branches and rosemary from the abundant bushes ready for drying. Then, unable to resist the temptation, we walked up through the middle field past the sycamores that shouldn't have been planted there. They were thugs and would take over given half a chance. Cherry and Beech had spent the winters coppicing them, to make them earn their keep as sources of renewable kindling. We walked the perimeter of the field, checking the bark on the conifer trees that had been cleared of brambles. Wounded trees, that had been shackled to the ground and chafed when the wind pushed the brambles against them, were recovering. Their new growth was zingy and the tips were healthy.

We reached the gate to the woodland. Cherry paused, searching the ground for evidence that the wild seeds they had scattered had taken, but it was still too early in the summer for much to show. We moved forward slowly along a curving secret path into the new woodland. The pines had bright green shoots and the silver birches that had been choked by brambles were growing up strong and glad. We ducked under some low branches of a ring of alders and entered a central circular space where we stood silently, absorbing the stillness in the circle of oaks and alders planted there to make a meditation area for women. Planted by women, many years ago. Two robins who always came to Cherry here when she was in this circle, arrived and sat on a nearby branch watching her. I realised that she was crying again. The hopes and dreams of many women were hovering in the young trees, but there was no security any more. The eviction and its abruptness had taken away any sense of purpose.

There was an unfamiliar air of disjuncture in the circle, as if it was trying to hold itself together, keep itself intact, waiting to find out what its future could be.

The trees did not know if they had a chance to stay alive. Someone might buy Eastfield Farm and turn the whole area into paddock, or cabbages. Oaks at twenty years old in the circle were only about five feet high. Five hundred years from now would they still be there?

I stood quietly, aware of the silence of the circle: it felt to me as if the trees had stopped to hold their breath, waiting. I was conscious of the slightest movement of leaves, the merest rustle, the waft of air across coconut-scented gorse, the whirr of a dragonfly's wings, the shift of a blade of grass. Nearby was the faint trickle of water from the spring, creating the only continuous sound, the only hint of continuity.

I opened my arms to hold Cherry again while she cried, though she made barely any noise, as she clung to me, shaking and trembling. Eventually she calmed, blew her nose on a tissue, and smiled at me ruefully without speaking.

We walked in separate directions and circumnavigated the tree circle, touching the leaves and branches of the young trees, bending sometimes to drink in the perfume of the gorse.

A little while later we left the circle and woodland, retraced our steps through the middle field and left the farm precinct by the back entrance. Someone was coming up the lane. Cherry recognised the farmer's son from the adjacent farm. Cordially he stopped to pass the time of day. He asked if she'd found somewhere else to live. She said not yet, because they needed somewhere with a garden, but they were hopeful for the autumn. The conversation was easy and brief and took only a few moments. There was no sign of Madeleine Gerrard, though she had come from the States to sort out the sale of Eastfield Farm and someone had said she was staying at her mother's, nearby.

Cherry was disoriented by her walk around Eastfield, so we decided not to go home. We went in the direction of Lamorna, walking towards the sea as if compelled to look out to some distant horizon, in the hope that grief might flow away to be dissolved once and for all in the expanse of ocean. At Lamorna we turned left taking the coast path back towards Mousehole and Penzance. It was dangerous to do so, as sunset was approaching, but we had a torch with us, and we knew the path in every detail. It had been Cherry's favourite long walk from Eastfield when she had lived there.

The coast path from Lamorna to Mousehole was my childhood path of hopes and dreams. It led to my stone seat where as a young girl I had watched the waves rising and crashing on the boulders below, and I had come here whenever I needed to think. I had grieved here for the loss of Lindsey just before Anna von Schiller and I became lovers; I had watched the waters here when Biff died in Herton; and I had fled to Cornwall when Moss died, and again when my Aunt Harry died, to walk these paths and put my memories in order.

Now, as I followed Cherry along the coast path, twilight deepened around us and the sea darkened to indigo to our right. I began to wonder whether, now that we'd lost Eastfield Farm, it might be possible to combine the land at Hermit's Hut Trust Fund – where women artists and writers came to visit and work – with women's land. Should I suggest it to Tessa and Jules? But, intuitively, I knew that Hermit's Hut was a different sort of land use and couldn't sustain both groups. I imagined trying to write, sculpt or paint with camping going on outside and women gardeners muckspreading in muddy boots. They just weren't compatible sorts of activities!

Ahead of me Cherry appeared to be defeated and sad, trudging along quietly. I thought about the death of Eastfield Farm and it seemed that part of Cherry had died there too. I wondered if Helga of Cologne had grieved like this for the loss of the dream of women's land. Is that why she had made her set of ceramic tiles, written on them, glazed and fired them, wrapped them in oiled leather and packed them so carefully in a heavy stone box with a stone inset lid? Did she intend the dream to be passed down to women some time in the future? Women who would understand the need and the longing.

We walked steadily along the beautiful path which rose and fell, dipping down in parts right to the sea level and rising again through Kemyel Woods and on past the quillets where people still sometimes farmed early flowers, then past the stone seat where Cherry, Beech and Molly had rescued me. I was glad that they had. It had been a close-run thing. And now I was alive, had wonderful friends, a full and rich life, and a warm lover. I walked on firmly, following the silent Cherry until we came to the hamlet called Raginnis.

Meanwhile, the sun had set, undramatically, behind us as we walked eastwards. It was several miles but we didn't mind. We were used to walking and we, Cherry in particular, needed not to be trapped in an unfinished house in Lescudjack Road, where she wasn't unhappy but didn't belong.

Turning to me, as we made our way down past the bird hospital in Mousehole, she said, 'I belonged at Eastfield Farm, I thought. So I think somehow, somewhere there must be a cosmic plan, some message for me as to why on earth I was catapulted out of the place in such a way. I'd have been willing to live and work for ever for women in those gardens, in that woodland, on those few acres of earth. I loved the place and now it's gone. P'raps I should make some tiles, write the story on them, glaze them, pack them in oiled cloths and bury them in an old stone box, carved with birds and animals. Bury those dreams and call the spirits for help and guidance.'

'We'll find land. We will.'

'Yes, we will. I am a modern witch, Lerryn, and I need to work our land. And when I find new land, I'll have a small statue of Helga of Cologne watching me while I plant my new herb garden.'

It was dark by the time we arrived in Mousehole and the last bus to Penzance had gone. There was nothing for it but to walk to Penzance. We met no one we knew to pass the time of day, or night, and we munched on apples and walked steadily up the hill from Mousehole to the road to Newlyn. Cherry said that she felt calmer now and aware that the walk was clearing her head, doing her good.

We had no idea of the events that were taking place back at Eastfield Farm.

It had begun slowly just after sunset. A small flame in the middle barn had smouldered quietly near to a scattering of dry leaves. A slight breeze caught them, swirled them, brushed them against the flame. It took. It breathed oxygen. It grew bold. It jumped from one leaf to the next. It multiplied. Many flames. Many leaves. The flames increased. Began to travel, jumping the gaps. Reaching out. Moving fast across the leaves towards a stacked pile of dry gorse. It sparked, crackled and burst upwards in a sheet of heat spanning easily the gap between the stacked gorse and the dry wood pile. It was alive; moving, jumping, leaping, growing. It reached the beams in minutes and the area along the top of the old barn where someone had once stored the old tins of paint and varnish. Flames popped and tapped at the outside of the tins, heating up the contents. One tin burst its lid and the varnish blazed, upwards and outwards. The other tins popped. One of them exploded off the ledge on to another wood pile. Heat and smoke filled the vortex of the roof where old bags of clothing had been left by Greenham women camping on the land. One by one they caught, opened, took light, blazed forth.

Scurrying creatures ran in all directions for the nearest cool, smoke-free crevice. Field mice dashed out of the barn for the wide open fields. The fire reached the wooden door that led to the house. Fierce chemical heat flew at the door, carving it and turning it to ashes in minutes. Then the fire met the air of the empty house and knew no boundaries. Every part of the living-room was quickly engulfed and the flames met no resistance as they flowed to the wooden stairs and upwards into the high dome of the roof and caught the polystyrene insulation material there. Smoke and flame mingled and blended into one enormous conflagration as Eastfield Farm went up.

*

We trudged through Penzance rather wearily. It had been a long way, worthwhile but tiring nevertheless.

We arrived home quite late, walking slowly up the front path and as we put the key in the lock, the door opened and there were Beech and Tarn, both of whom had been in from work about an hour, and were getting worried.

They made us some hot tea, as we told them about the whole walk, and how we'd felt and why we'd done it.

Cherry talked of the Beguines and the end of women's land. I told how, in the back of my mind as we'd walked, I'd seen Biff in boy's clothes leaving Manchester, and a group of young women waving and waving until at last the bicycle and cyclist were out of sight. I could see one of the young women crying and realised that Biff must have had a sweetheart back in her birthplace. Those she loved whom she left behind to go and find somewhere safe to live . . . over the hills and far away.

I had also seen Moss, walking south along the fringes of the Yorkshire Dales, pregnant and also in need of a safe place.

And I had seen Rosie, happy now, living in Sydney, Australia, not far from Lindsey and her new lover.

Silently Tarn picked up a copy of the *Cornishman* and handed it to me. Cherry and I read it together. There it was, on the property pages. Eastfield Farm – for sale on the open market to anyone who had enough money.

We were tired out, all of us. Weary with disappointment. Tarn had been at work all day and had had an evening of teaching languages. Beech had been helping a friend paint the outside of a house. Cherry and I had walked for miles. We all fell into bed and were asleep by midnight. We were woken before seven by a loud knocking on the door.

A policeman and policewoman stood there, on the doorstep. They asked if Miss Cherry Alexander lived there.

'If she did, why would you want to know?'

'We have reason to believe she can help us with our enquiries.'

'This is my brothers' house. I am Lerryn Trevonnian. I live here. What exactly are you enquiring about?'

'Is Miss Alexander here or not?'

They obviously weren't going to talk to me, but meanwhile Cherry had heard the police and came downstairs fully dressed.

'You'd better come in,' she said. 'I'm Cherry Alexander.'

'Where were you, Miss Alexander, yesterday evening, at about nine o'clock?'

'I was walking from Lamorna to Mousehole. On the coast path.'

'And before that?'

'I went to Eastfield Farm to collect some herbs.'

'Last night someone set fire to the middle barn there. The fire spread to the house and all the buildings are gutted.'

We all looked at one another in absolute astonishment.

'Are you suggesting I had something to do with that?'

'You were seen leaving Eastfield Farm. You had a conversation with the farmer's son.'

'Yes, I did. I'd just finished collecting my herbs.'

'We have reason to believe you were angry at being evicted and were involved in the fire.'

'That's ridiculous. I loved the place. I wouldn't dream of harming it.'

'Excuse me,' I said. 'I was with her. Didn't he tell you?'

'He didn't know you. He said there was a woman friend.'

'Well, it was me. And, yes, we are all angry. The eviction was a bad business and, no, we didn't torch Eastfield Farm.'

'You were seen there yesterday evening.'

'Yes, by the farmer's son, as we were leaving. The place was all shut up and empty. Hazel Banyer's tenant was away. Is her place all right?'

'Yes it is. Eastfield Farm itself was gutted, and you were seen.'

I talked fast, 'We went nowhere near the house at all. We collected the herbs and we went up to the woodland to make sure the baby trees were all right. Then we left. How dare you? How dare you come here into my house and accuse my friends? I want you to leave now, please. You don't have any right to be here. Now would you please just leave?'

Cherry patted me on the arm. 'It's okay Lerryn. Let them ask away. I've done absolutely nothing I'm ashamed of.' She turned to the policeman and woman. 'I'm angry about the trees, and

I'm angry about the wild animals that live on the land – foxes and badgers and many, many birds. I'm a conservationist, not an arsonist. I loved the place. I'd no more dream of setting fire to it than setting fire to Lerryn's house. Is that clear?'

'Well someone has, Miss Alexander. We'd like you to accompany us to the police station.'

'I haven't even had my breakfast and I haven't done my t'ai chi yet. I'm not going anywhere with you.'

'You were trespassing on Madeleine Gerrard's property and seen leaving there minutes before the fire began.'

'Well whoever did it, it wasn't me. I didn't go near the house. I didn't go anywhere near. I just want to collect my herbs, the ones I planted last autumn. I'd forgotten to bring them.'

'Your tenancy is over. You were trespassing on private property.'

Cherry was just about to blurt that it wasn't private property, it was women's land, she'd been its guardian and she loved it, when warning signals from myself and from Beech, who had just come into the room, silenced her. During the questioning, Tarn had been frantically slicing bread and packing us some sandwiches. I had a horrible feeling that we were going to have a very long morning indeed.

'I'll come with you,' said Beech. She glanced a question at the policewoman, who nodded. Beech dashed upstairs to finish dressing, as she'd only thrown on jeans and a jumper when she heard the police in the kitchen.

I knew that Tarn was working again that morning. 'I'll be ready in a minute,' I said, realising that to co-operate might get it all over with more quickly. I now wanted action and to go on talking. I'd grown up near Penzance and I vaguely knew the families whose sons and daughters had ended up working in the police station there. Not closely, but recognisably. I also knew that this wasn't London. The methods and conditions were not so intimidating as if we'd been in London with police on one side of the kitchen and me, Tessa and Jules on the other. This, by contrast, was a terribly white affair.

Beech came downstairs dressed and ready. Cherry said, 'I'd like you to stay here by the phone, please.' Later we found out that this was their code, from when they'd been involved with direct action years ago. It meant, Get rid of all documents, pack up our lesbian books, straighten out the place. Keep us safe.

So Beech stayed home. Tarn and I hugged, circumspectly. We all hugged, though what they made of that we didn't know. We had every reason, all of us, to have no trust for the straight world of police, anywhere on earth.

No, this was not London, but being accompanied out of the house and into the police car in full view of all Lescudjack Road wasn't funny at all. I had a sick feeling in the base of my stomach that this was not going to be an easy matter, simply solved.

The police arrived later that morning with a search warrant and turned over the contents of mine and Cherry's rooms. No, it wasn't London, but it was still them against us. I had plenty of police images to give me the heebie jeebies, and I hated being in a small interrogation room, tape recorder or not. I can't bear incarceration even for a few minutes.

Images of picket lines in Moss's Yorkshire town of Herton in the '84–'85 Miners' Strike . . . Rosie's photos taken whilst up a tree, hidden . . . pictures of blood and beatings, people trying to protect their heads and faces.

Images of me and Lindsey just before we broke up, amongst a crowd of men and women, some children too, with Tessa and Jules, and Tessa's daughters, there to challenge Clause Twenty-eight on a cold January day in the park near Kennington. Someone with a loud speaker told us to link arms, and, if we left, to stay linked in fives and tens. Cold earth. And blocked exits. Shut gates. The entrances and side streets thick with men on horses. The riders had heavy helmets with face protectors and they held riot shields. I had been standing next to a man in a wheelchair. How do you challenge a police horse from a wheelchair?

No, this wasn't London, but nevertheless they questioned us round and round for hours. Yes, we were allowed to eat. No, we weren't stood against the wall like Biff's sisters, Lucy and Sarah, until we fainted and were revived and propped up again. None of it was like that. But we had been trespassing and Madeleine Gerrard, it seemed, was in no state of mind to forgive us for that.

To add insult to injury, we were found guilty of trespass

when the case came to court; we were fined heavily; but acquitted of arson or criminal damage, through lack of proof. Madeleine Gerrard was well-insured. She did very nicely from the fire at Eastfield Farm.

CHAPTER SIXTEEN

Spring Bank Holiday was glorious weather. Tessa and Jules arrived as planned for a week at Hermit's Hut. We all went out into the landscape under blue skies in warm sunshine, walking, talking, having fun and working. Everywhere we went we took paints and pencils, easels and sketch books.

The weather was wonderful for early summer. A whole bunch of us parked near Molly's and made our way with her across the fields to Nanjizal. Where previously the land had been bare, stretching in long brown furrows across the contours, waiting for spring planting, now the fields were a bright patchwork of greens, in leys ready for summer silage, or planted occasionally with tufted rows of potatoes, and fringed with blossom on the blackthorn hedges and hawthorn trees.

Across the Bosistow Valley a cuckoo spread its two notes, calling and calling, its throat wide and its location secret. I was looselimbed and joyful after a night of lovemaking with Tarn. She was walking ahead, striding forward laughing and chatting to Tessa and Jules. Behind her was Molly wearing a backpack and carrying a stout stick, followed by Cherry and Beech.

I dropped back a little to enjoy the flowers, taking my time to examine a patch of white stitchwort through which some blue-bells were thickly growing, resembling a Laura Ashley fabric, unrolled and curled there on the ground. The gorse was coconut scented, wafting in the valley, and there were knee-high shoots on the foxgloves, in bud and ready to ping in the warm air.

As always, the sound of running water filled the valley before streams poured, collecting and gathering strength moving to the sea. Moss and Biff seemed very near to me, their ghosts free to roam at will. Perhaps they still visited the hills and valleys of Yorkshire, above Herton, and maybe they went for evening walks up into the Pennines and took picnics by the packhorse bridge. I don't know. But they seemed to be visiting Cornwall on that warm early summer day, happy for me that I had good friends, a sense of home and belonging, and my own valleys with tumbling waters in which to connect with the beauty of the land. They were peaceful and so was I.

I dropped further back and studied a foxglove closely. I was free and it was easy for me to do this for the others were a collection of artists, writers and land women who understood my involvement with these flowers in this landscape, and any one of them might at any time stop, pull out a sketch book and sit a while, sensing form and image, taking notes and making sketches for drawings and paintings to be worked on later.

Foxglove leaves are purple on the inside where the leaf joins the stalk and they formed a perfect green vase to hold the flower stem. At the tip of the stem the tight buds began green then gradually filled until the lowest ones were uncurling their sepals to reveal pink petals folded around each other.

I bent forward to touch. Once many decades ago, a woman herbalist had done exactly that, and sensing that the plant held important secrets had chanced to used it on one of her women patients who had heart trouble and had stabilised her. Saved her life. This foxglove was a life-saving plant, waiting by the edge of a path for someone to come along and recognise its wild medicinal beauty. Molly had told me that no herbalist was allowed to use this plant now. Digitalis was only available from a real doctor. Times change.

The buds were very lovely. Pink and hidden. Suddenly I was back in Herton, sensing myself in landscape, and I understood that I had swung like a pendulum to and fro in time until, grounded now here in this dazzling natural world, I had stopped oscillating and had come to rest, having found, as an artist, that central place again inside me, the source from which I could love and work.

I reached out to touch the foxglove buds.

I closed my eyes. I was leaning back in the armchair in Tarn's living-room when she had come up behind me and leaned over the back of the chair, which was padded soft between us. She had kissed the top of my head, then had slid her hands down over my shoulders until they cupped my breasts. She had whispered, 'Don't move,' and slid her hands around my breasts down and up again so that the cloth of my soft shirt rubbed over my nipples very slowly. I felt them rise up under her hands. She moved her hands down and over and up again, down and over and up again, caressing me, the cloth tantalising my nipples. My breasts rising and falling under her hands until I thought my nipples might explode with wanting, wanting this to go on, to go on. My nipples hard and full now, hard and full, my breasts soft and full, hard and full, soft and full, her hands caressing me down and over and up again, down and over and up again.

I was making small sounds in my throat meaning yes, yes, and then standing I turned to her to hold her, our mouths open and kisses wet and warm and wonderful. We had made our way to bed.

In the sunshine of Nanjizal Valley I reached out to touch the roundest of the foxgloves buds, as gently as the first touch of my finger on Tarn's clit. I looked up and saw her several hundred yards ahead of me, with the others on a rocky outcrop waving and looking back to see if I was all right. I stood up and waved and ran along the track past the blackthorn blossom that lay like summer snow, joyful with memories of last night's loving. Tarn held out her arms. I ran laughing into them and we hugged and kissed amidst much laughter and jokes about us being in love and lust. We didn't care. It was true.

We made our way down the steep valley side to the old mine workings, where once there had been an overshot wheel for tin-streaming fed by a long leat that had wound around the contours of the valley side from a channel upstream. We chatted a while about the remains of the old buildings and then clambered down to a wooden footbridge and up the other side a few feeet to join the coast path again.

From there we had a wide-angled view into Nanjizal Cove itself.

But it was very different from my last visit in the winter. The spring gales had removed a ten-foot depth of sand all along the coast and round as far as Whitesand Bay. Nanjizal had barely any sand left. It had become a boulder beach, with layers of granite interspersed with amazing veins of white quartz and fairy-lace patterns of minerals streaked with orange and red and dark shades of grey and black.

The tide was very low, for we had timed this to go caving, and out to sea a strand of white sand had been deposited which lay under shallow water reflecting brilliant pale turquoise, like I'd seen on the Isles of Scilly, bewitching us with myths of coral islands and treasure troves. Beyond that shallow lagoon, where three young girls were splashing and jumping about, lay the blue ocean, and the dark blue horizon curving, holding the scene together as if through a curved camera lens. The cove was framed by great jagged outcrops and rocks, shaped and weathered. On our left was a famous arch of stone over blue water not shallow enough to wade through. Nearer to us were seaweed pools and rock pools with red anemones and green fronds, jewelled and magical, tiny worlds within worlds, like a children's story book. In a twinkle of an eye you could drink a potion and become small and enter a boat and travel in those worlds to distant shores to have amazing adventures.

All around me on the boulder beach were egg-shaped boulders like breasts and buttocks, sexy and female, warm to the hands and ready for touch.

We had lain there on Tarn's bed as I wrapped my legs around her and held her breasts, squeezing them gently together until they touched, rounded and rolling a little as I moved my hands over them.

We had been blissful and abandoned, wild and free. Our limbs were no longer young, we took care not to be uncomfortable, and were not agile and nubile as we might have been in our late teens and early twenties. But art forms have a long apprenticeship and we were wildly creative women with plenty of imagination. Sure and certain, mature and experienced, we made amazing lovers for one another and were unafraid of expressing our passion for each other's female beauty. We shone with it. Dazzling and aflame with it. Hard and soft and round and unashamed. Half a century each of fingertip gladness, woman loving, warm, wet, sleek and shiny gladness. We knew exactly what we were up to and what we were up to was woman loving, hot, wet lust. We were two hot, magnificent women. And who is to say that the young have a monopoly on wild sexiness with each other?

The iconography was female: our hands were gentle, firm and sensuous, her body beneath my fingers was scented and warm with the full flowering of mature womanhood. She was the height of summer, there in my arms and I in hers, round and sunlit and full and flowing. And our harvest was plenty, plenty, sumptuous, glorious, perfumed, full-fruited, lips and tongues and breasts. Bellies and hips and thighs. Wrists and ankles, earlobes and shoulder curves. Our harvest was plenty, plenty.

Down on the rocky beach, Tessa said, 'So why is this cave called the Celtic Cross?'

'It just always is,' I replied. 'The tall part you can see there, the side pieces coming out from there, as you see, the long vertical cleft down to the level of the beach – well, where the sand would have been.'

'I can't see it as a cross,' said Jules, agreeing with Tessa.

'Seems to me that's just a Christian gloss,' said Tarn. 'They want to mark their name on everything.'

'But this is a female icon,' said Tessa. 'Dark in the cliff.'

'You're right,' said Jules. 'I can see a face in that top part of the stone. This is no Celtic cross. It's much older. This is a dark image, shining dark. I'm going to drum her. I'm going in there. Who's coming with me?'

'Not me, sweetheart. There's three feet of cold water in there. One slip and you'd break an ankle.'

'I shan't slip then, shall I? Right off, with the shorts, where's my drum?' She began to wade into the cave with her drum slung across the back of her shoulders.

'Okay, I'm following,' called Tarn and stripped down to her pants, picking her way over the boulders that led to the cave.

Tessa and I exchanged glances and began to unpack our sketch pads, choosing graphite pencils with extremely thick leads. We settled contentedly on a huge flat boulder, as Tessa pointed out what she thought she could see in the face of the dark female icon in the cliff in front of us.

'The cross pieces are rounded, are they breasts or are they wings?' she asked.

'If they were wings she would look like Lilith, and the long vertical part would be her long thin legs hanging down with her claw feet on the earth.'

'If they were breasts,' said Tessa, 'she'd be a Gimbutas bird-woman icon, wouldn't she? Her beady bird eyes would be looking at us sideways.'

'Oh, yes. Dark bird. Very dark.'

'Raven woman in the cliffs at Nanjizal. A combined bird and breasts image. How wonderful!'

'Listen. They're there, right inside.'

The drum beat began. Jules. Slowly the rhythm built up and then there came the sound of women singing. Tarn was using her voice as an instrument. Into my mind, naturally, came the school choir all those years ago. She was becoming the love of my life. Someone to journey forward with.

Their singing and drumming resonated from the depth of the dark cave in the cliffs. Beside me Tessa had her eyes closed, swaying slightly to the rhythm and the sounds. Then she opened her eyes, beamed at me with love of life, love of landscape, love of Jules, love of friends.

From behind us, in the flat lagoon, between us and the sea, came the sounds of laughing and splashing. Cherry and Beech and Molly held hands, jumping up and down in the water, getting soaked, revelling, playing, partying.

'Who has the power to name this cave?' said Tessa, picking up her sketch pad and beginning to draw. We fell silent, working companionably. We covered several pages each with sketches of different emphases, all the while surrounded by water and sky and drum beat and the voices of women singing.

Presently Tessa and I had finished.

We compared our drawings and were astonished to find the same dark face looking out at us from our different interpretations. Yet, as the minutes changed and the relationship of the cliff face to the angle of the sun changed, so did the face on the upper part of the icon. Her shadows deepened, her shape transformed itself slowly. But we had seen her. Separately and together. To us, from then on, she would always appear to be RavenWoman. She who belongs in the cliffs of Nanjizal. She who is dark and wise and knowing. Empowering and voiced, holding the key of transition between this world and the next. For me, sharing this with my dearest friends, this would be one of the special windows into my world view. Where did I belong and with whom would I journey? Where had I come from, and where might I decide to go?

The music slowly ceased and the drummer and singer

returned to the entrance to the cave, waving to us and blinking in bright daylight.

'It's amazing in there,' called Jules.

'Sounded fantastic,' called Tessa. 'Are you coming to eat now? We waited for you.'

'You bet, we're hungry. And thirsty.' They scrambled forwards over uneven boulders.

We showed them the pictures and waved to the others who joined us from the lagoon. We juggled with bags and cups, flasks and sandwich boxes, trying to find places to sit without letting anything fall down the cracks in the rocks, amidst much laughter.

'Only one problem,' said Jules. 'I got my bum soaked. I did slip, but only an inch or two. I'm all soggy. Yuk.'

'I've got a spare pair,' said Tarn. 'In my side zipper here.'

'You must've been a girl guide.'

'Actually, I was in the brownies. No it's just that I never know when I'm going to come on. Roll on menopause. None of this spare knickers nonsense.'

'Well, I'm glad of them,' said Jules. 'Here pass them over.'

She changed, and pulled on her shorts. 'Oh, thank heaven for that. I thought I was going to have a soggy bum all day.'

'So who are the crones here then?' I asked.

Tessa and Molly put their hands up.

'Well, we should have a ceremony. A croning.'

'Not yet,' replied Molly. 'It's supposed to be a year and a day after your last period, so I heard.'

'Maybe when we're next down here,' said Tessa. 'Do you remember that fire we had on the beach for Freyja, when Denny was still living at Hermit's Hut? That fire was a wonderful experience. The water and the night and the flames leaping up. I'd love something like that.'

'Sounds wonderful,' said Molly. 'I'd like it.'

'It was sad though,' said Jules, 'but the circumstances were different. We could have some very happy chanting and a real feast. A very joyful occasion.'

'Maybe we'll be able to celebrate having found a house with a garden as well,' said Cherry.

'Lots of good red wine,' added Beech.

Molly turned to me, 'Aren't you fifty this autumn?'

'Yep. Half a century. 5 September.'

'We'll need a carnival to celebrate all these events,' said Tessa.

'We'll have several celebrations. The croning, the house-finding, the half-century. All of them.'

'Sounds good to me,' said Jules. 'That's a spectacular autumn, all singing and swinging. I could go for that. Talking of good red wine, pass the bottle somebody.'

It was a wonderful picnic there by our RavenWoman cave. We had fruit and cheese and saffron buns, sandwiches and cool drinks with ice cubes in flasks and wine and more fruit.

We had to move though, because the incoming tide was creeping slowly around the rocks on which we were sitting and rising inch by inch, lapping and sucking, retreating and surging forward again.

As we made our way home from the beach, a bright film of our day out ran through my mind: images and sounds; the laughter of my women friends; last night's loving; a sense of summer magic; and of the meeting of many worlds in our changing and evocative landscape.

Next day, I received a letter from Anna in Hamburg. She wrote:

I am overjoyed that you and Tarn were able to have time here with me in Germany and that, at last, I had a chance to tell you Sarah's story. Now I feel that I can let go, both of the past and of this life and I prepare for my next world now. It is a relief to me to believe that this is not the end.

I feel very emotionally tired now, but contented and ready to let go. It is a strong and comforting feeling.

Margret has been reading to me, in German, from the works of Audre Lorde. I am thankful that they are translated here now.

I am moved by a very beautiful quote from *The Cancer Journals*, because she expresses better than I how glad she is that she has told her story. Margret has hung a framed copy of it beside my bed and every day I think happily of your visit here, my dear Lerryn, and of my relationship with Sarah, whose story is now 'transformed from silence into language and action'. Audre Lorde wrote, 'But for every real word spoken, for every attempt I had ever made to speak those truths for which I am still seeking, I had made contact with other women while we examined the words to fit a world in which we all believed, bridging our differences.'

So, my dear Lerryn, I too prepare. I have had a long, splendid life. I have been a very lucky woman doing exactly what I wanted to do and especially I had the chance to love women and live openly with that love. I can want for nothing better than that. It was my wildness and my freedom. Perhaps we will share times together in my new world. It is sometimes said that we have a group of nearest and dearest whom we keep on meeting in different ways, in different lives. It's a good thought. I send you my love and blessings for you, for your relationship with Tarn, for your dearest friends and for your creative work.

My love to you, Anna.

We had a phone call from Margret on the Friday of that week to say that Anna had died peacefully in her sleep. She had left a letter asking us not to attend the funeral but instead to spend the day walking in the landscape and painting something to remember her by. We took ourselves to Mulfra Quoit, from where we could see both the north and the south coasts and we painted the area of high downs, the curving hills, the distant coastline, the sky meeting the sea and the great moving banks of white clouds that shifted across the skyscape, casting shadows of light and dark on the heather and gorse.

It was a happy day, which Anna would have wanted. I sensed that different worlds could meet, through our use of language as well as our representations in visual art. I made a vow that I would try to transform my silences into language and action. That night I began to write this account of the events since my reconnection with Cornwall.

CHAPTER SEVENTEEN

When Tessa and Jules had returned to London, we settled back into a pattern of work and creativity. It was a summer of drought throughout Britain and it gave us a very busy tourist season in the southwest. We had to pick our places carefully if we wanted to avoid crowds and it was almost impossible to walk on the coast path without noticing great strings of folks bobbing along in the distance. But we knew the land so well and we had our favourite places.

Sometimes, in the evenings, we'd be up in the wilder parts of the downs watching the changing skies and glorious sunsets. However, on the longest day, we decided to picnic to the east of Land's End on the cliffs not far from Porth Gwarra.

In bright evening sunshine, deep shadows played around huge blocks of granite, which were natural but looked as if they had been carved and shaped; carefully stacked up against the towering cliffs. The dark gaps in between and the straight, parallel sides appeared to form a stone ladder with a seat on top.

We were in love, Tarn and myself, enjoying our private time together and aware of the height of the sun's powers, the zenith of summertime, and the expanding of our own powers and creativity.

Flaming hair spread across the sky from the lion-headed sun star. No wonder the ancestors had viewed her as dragon woman and had, across the world, known the sun as lion woman. The Aboriginal of Australia would sing to her: 'Sun woman you make the day; sun woman you show the way; you are a dreamtime creature with a wand of flaming bark; sun woman you light the dark.'

It was easy to imagine the most famous Cornish witch of them all, Maggy Figgy, seated on her chair watching the changing rays of the sun and preparing to fly along the coast on a stem of ragwort, to the Logan Rock, to join her legendary friends for midsummer celebrations.

154

I lay back with my eyes closed, the sounds of the sea far below, recalling that there was a sketch of this chair ladder and Maggy Figgy's seat in *A Week At The Land's End*, the antiquarian book that I'd carried with me on one of my first walks, just after I had met Tarn in the spring.

My land had given me all that I needed that spring. I had become grounded and whole again, and I was now working enthusiastically on my paintings.

Since then I had begun to teach myself the legends which had been long forgotten, but were recorded by my forebears, there for anyone to read. Complex legends and myths, bringing me to a rich and beautiful cultural heritage and back to myself again.

Now I was approaching my fiftieth birthday with renewed hope and vigour, the years dropping away, my self young and free again.

'Tell me a story,' I said, dreamily, with my eyes closed.

Tarn settled back against the warm stones and her sing-song voice floated around me as she began:

'Time was and time was not, when the old witch sat on her stone seat atop her chair ladder at Tol-Pedn-Du. She looked around and listened to the sounds of the waves crashing and falling on the rocks at the foot of the cliff.

It was the shortest day of the year, the winter solstice. It was already approaching sunset, although it was only the late afternoon.

Maggy Figgy regarded the clouds to the southwest which looked angry and were piling up near the horizon.

A storm, she told herself. A great and vigorous storm will brew from the Scilly Isles this evening.

The sun set splaying red hair as sun woman dipped into the sea below the horizon for her annual midwinter swim.

Maggy Figgy shivered. It was unlikely she and any of her friends would be swimming in the sea at such a time of year. Too much sense and the water cold as ice. But others would swim tonight from a great ship that would be driven on to this coast by the impending storm, and as usual some would perish.

There would be treasures by the thousand, gold, jewels and rich clothes. Pickings for the whole coven, there was no doubt about it.

Having foreseen the storm and the consequences she must depart from her stone chair with haste and warn the other women, who would by now be meeting on the Logan Rock, waiting for her, their leader.

So Maggy Figgy gathered up her skirts, pulled her shawl about her shoulders, fixed her hat firmly and climbed on to her stem of ragwort.

She muttered the flying spell under her breath and then three times more aloud as the stem rose into the air and she, astride, flew smoothly, following the line of the coast, admiring the soaring cliffs and the white, swirling, boiling waters far, far below her.

The flight took her swiftly to the Logan Rock where with practised expertise she alighted safely.

She was greeted by her friends in her coven and they sang and danced and feasted merrily, chanting for the sun to return on the morrow, which would herald the rising of the sun towards the equinox in the spring. The sun would reach her full powers for the midsummer festival six months hence.

But meanwhile the storm signs on the distant horizon were obvious and presently the group made its way down into the cove at Porthcurno. They were now certain that there, on to the bright stretch of white sand in the moonlight, would be driven the wreck of a fine vessel. It would bring all their hearts' desires. It would feed and clothe them all for months to come.

They were not wrong, of course. They had watched so many storms throughout their lives, and they knew how the tides and winds fared off this treacherous coast, where they lived and loved and made their homes.

Their women friends and men folk were also gathered on the shore, anticipating a fine night's wrecking.

No, they were not wrong. It was midnight when the Spanish galleon finally foundered and the bodies of the drowned sailors and their wives and mistresses were being hurled on to the rocks around the cove.

Men and women alike made headway with ropes and bags, boxes and sacks, stripping the clothes off the dead and even pulling the rings off their fingers and the earrings from their earlobes, in their haste and need.

For life was very tough throughout this very poor part of the

156

west country and many's the thanksgiving that had been made for a propitious cargo washed up at a time of want.

Maggy Figgy was the leader. She organised and supervised, gave advice and issued orders with equanimity. All obeyed her. Such was her authority and knowledge. She was trusted to bring in the bounty and ensure its distribution on a night like this. No one mistook her voice. No one offended her nor ignored her, not even her own husband.

Of course there were those in the cove who had no man. Lived and loved with other women and that was known and seen and validated too. But the leader, though wise and strong, was not one of these. Maggy Figgy was a woman who had a man, her own man, and they lived together peacefully.

The night wore on and the sacks were full. The bags were heavy, the boxes stacked, the trunks loaded on to the donkeys ready to be borne away to safe places in the moors and on the downs. But before the dawn came there was found one Spanish woman, head down in the water, her body in a cleft in the rocks. She was dead and cold and very, very well-dressed.

Do not touch that woman, came the order from Maggy Figgy.

They queried her as to why.

She is different, this I know. Do not disturb her clothes, her jewels, nor her shoes. Do not steal her purse nor strip off her cloak. I myself will attend to her. You two over there, you are strong. Take this woman to my cottage by Porth Gwarra, down from Tol-Pedn-Du. Lay her on my own bed. I myself will attend to her. Death will come to any who treat this woman without respect.

In due course, just before dawn on the first day after the winter solstice, the woman from Spain was laid out gently and firmly with honour in Maggy Figgy's own home.

Maggy Figgy sent her man away. Visit your brother over by Buryan, she told him, and return here tomorrow evening, when all will have been attended to. She hugged him and he departed as she asked, for she was a warm friend to him, and he trusted her, as if she were his queen. He was proud of being allowed to live with her. She commanded his respect and he paid it to her, always.

When she was alone with the Spanish woman, Maggy Figgy

157

blessed the woman. She cast preservation and protection spells upon her. She did not herself speak Spanish but she reasoned with herself that spirits do not need a particular language for they understand the intentions of the wise and will act accordingly, whatever the tongue that is being spoken.

Then Maggy Figgy undressed the woman carefully herself and laid the wet garments to dry in her home. Then she packed the jewels and the woman's purse in a wooden box and in turn this was placed in the trunk by the fireplace in the corner of the room.

Then Maggy Figgy covered the body in a clean shroud and carried the woman, who was not heavy without her wet clothing, and laid her in a sacred plot down by the hedge at the bottom of her garden. She put clean earth upon her and stones over the earth until she was satisfied with the work that she had done.

All the time she was muttering secret words under her breath. Then she strewed herbs from her herb wheel all over the stones and at the foot of the resting place she planted a young rosemary bush, for it is well-known that rosemary is for clarity of memory and she wanted the woman's spirit to go from thence and fetch her own loved ones to this place. Then they could come to claim her belongings and take her body to her own homeland.

Time passed. The weeks became months and the equinox came and went. The rosemary bush grew fine new shoots and as summer came it blossomed into blue flowers signifying a clean corpse under the stones and in the cool brown earth.

Many's the villager who enquired what had become of the Spanish woman's beautiful clothes and fine jewels, not to mention her weighty purse. In each questioning, Maggy Figgy stood firm.

Death will come to any who misuse the belongings of this woman. This I know. She is at peace and her loved ones will come to claim her and her chattels at the right time of the year.

To any who doubted her she would lift the lid of the trunk in the corner by her fireplace and there they could see for themselves the folded clothes, the box with the jewels and the leather purse on its long sash that had been girdled around the

Spanish woman's waist. All were there, in the rightful place, waiting.

The days lengthened and the sun rose and rose in the sky.

One day, it was the nineteenth of June, a ship was sighted off the south Cornish coast. On the evening of the twentieth it put into safe haven, and on the following morning a tall Spanish man came to knock on the cottage door near Porth Gwarra.

I have come to claim my loved one, Maggy Figgy was told.

Describe to me her clothes and jewels, she replied to the man.

This he did and she invited him in and there in front of him she opened the trunk and he cried on seeing the clothes folded and the box kept safely and the purse on its long drawstring.

These are for you said Maggy Figgy. And now I will take you outside to my garden into the dip at the end near the wild heath where the Spanish lady lies resting. And this I know, that you have come to take her home, to rest again on the land where she was born. This I know. In that land she was a woman like me — the leader of a group of women, wise and strong and knowing what they needed to know.

Thanking her, the man unfolded a canvas in which to wrap the remains of the Spanish woman.

Maggy Figgy organised the transport of the trunk and the woman's belongings back to the cove. There they were placed in a small rowing boat and then they were ferried across the stretch of water to where the sailing ship lay at anchor. It was completed on the afternoon of the longest day.

They hauled up the anchor and the sails caught the wind and the ship was seen in full glory leaving the safe haven and making for the open sea. All the people had gathered to wave goodbye.

After the ship had gone it was still light. Maggy Figgy made her way up to her stone seat and rested a while, watching the sun begin to dip towards the horizon.

Presently she climbed on to her stem of ragwort and cast her spells for flying. Following the coastline, with the setting sun behind her, she flew to the Logan Rock to meet the others of her group.

She alighted safely as usual and was met by the women, some of whom loved one another and lived with one another.

Maggy, they said, the Spanish lady has been taken home to her own land, where her soul will be glad to be re-united with the ancestors. One day she will again take human form and begin another turn of the wheel of life. But why did you do that on the night of the storm? How did you make your decision that no one must show any disrespect for her?

Join your hands with one another, said Maggy Figgy. For you are my friends, whom I trust. We are women and we are wise. There are things that we know; and things that must be done. We have made a vow to trust one another.

It's quite simple really, said Maggy Figgy. Tonight is the night of midsummer. Tonight we celebrate that one of us has gone home. I took care of her as best I knew how. She needed me to do that for her. She wanted me to recognise her. Now we can dance the longest night. When I saw her lying there, I recognised her. She was one of us. It takes one to know one.'

Dreamily, I opened my eyes. Tarn and I reached for one another and lay there safely, embracing each other in the hollow on the grassy bank, between great granite boulders. Tiny red and yellow flowers of kidney vetch clung to the earth around us, and far, far below us, waves crashed against the mysterious rocks forms of Maggy Figgy's stone ladder.

It was an old legend passed down by the storytellers, from far back into Cornish history, in which women figured hugely, both as legendary figures and as real witches.

'What did happen to the witches in Spain?' I asked.

'Surprisingly little, according to Barstow's book, *Witchcraze*. I love that book – well I mean I think it's excellent. I first heard of it when I was at Liesl's place, you remember?'

'Oh, yes. You were raving about it when you came home.'

'The book took me by surprise, I must say I had pre-conceptions because I'd heard so much about the Inquisition. I'd assumed that lots of witches were put to death there. But the records show something different for both Spain and Italy. It's rather hard to believe, but Barstow's work is *so* thorough, and the stats are in the back of the book. She must've ploughed through the Inquisition records in depth. It's awful work. I'm dreading it for the Isle of Man. Anyway, there were some accusations in Spain and Italy and some trials. But it seems that the Holy Roman Church was very confident, not openly being confronted by Protestants. The priests and bishops were a secure and thriving élite. They appeared to trust their own women. They seemed not to have turned on them or made them into a criminal class, as women, in the ways that happened in Germany and Bavaria and Switzerland . . . or in the Essex trials . . . or Scotland.'

'Presumably that's because they criminalised other races instead – Jews and Moors and, of course, the native Indians of South America. That was horribly brutal.'

'Yes. That's what I think happened. But the Spanish lady found her way into Cornish legend and I think that's absolutely fascinating, don't you?'

'I certainly do. I love our legends here. And I could stay here and listen to you telling them to me for hours.'

We lay there for a while talking about Tarn's research into the folklore of Ellan Vannin and the pull of the island which was now becoming strong again, as the summer holidays approached. But we didn't know exactly how this summer was going to work out because we were waiting to hear about Joss's baby which was due right in the middle of the August vacation. If that happened, Tarn would want to go to London to see Joss and the new grandchild, rather than going to the island.

Talking of Ellan Vannin led us naturally back to the women herbalists and healers of the past in rural areas like the Isle of Man and Cornwall, who had eventually lost their land and become part of a vast European underclass of poor and often homeless women.

Presently Tarn said, 'Yes, I shall want to go to the island before too long. Sitting here on the cliffs and talking of the island and Maggy Figgy, and listening to the sea here, I realise that the call is still there. It's strong in fact. What interests me a lot is that the witchcraze hysteria didn't arise in the island as it did across Europe. There were some recorded cases and some accusations, but some acquittals too. That makes the Isle of Man and Cornwall very similar, doesn't it?'

'Very. Cornwall was so isolated from the rest of England at that time – I mean at the time of the peak in the witch crazes, let's say 1550 – and witchcraft was very common. Everybody went to the healers and pellars, as they were called, to get spells lifted and unwanted "demons" expelled. It was so commonplace that it didn't cause hysteria. Cornwall and the Isle of Man seem to have been so rampantly pagan at that time. Christianity was a thin veneer, you know. Folk beliefs were part of the daily life and the social fabric.'

'There are cases in the gaol records though. Poor wretches. Conditions were awful. You remember they showed the prisons in the *Poldark* series. Any poor woman accused of witchcraft wouldn't do very well in there.'

'Yes, of course. But they did survive, you know, some of them. I'm thinking of the case of Jane Nicholas. She was accused of causing a small boy to vomit up pins and brambles and bits of straw on more than one occasion. But she was acquitted, eventually.'

'I wonder what cases I would find if I looked at the Manx records. You know, it's weird but every time I think of Joss, whenever she phones, whenever I think of the baby due in August, I get a feeling about her living with that vile man and I can understand why people consulted the pellars and witches, I really can.'

'You mean turn him back into a frog and have him hop back into his bog!'

We both laughed.

'Oh, I wish! Give me three wishes, Lerrie, and that's most certainly one of them.'

'Yes, and when I look up there to Maggy Figgy's stone seat I wish I could climb on a stem of ragwort and fly like she did. It sounds so silly. But that wonderful sense of being up there in the sky, hovering above these lovely cliffs, with the sun setting, and the colours on the water. What I wouldn't give?'

'I think we'd better get home before we have any more bright ideas. Come on. The temperature will plummet when that sun hits the horizon, and it'll catch me out tonight because I haven't brought my big jumper.'

'Okay. Home we go. And . . . I loved your story, Tarn . . . a truly wonderful midsummer night's tale.'

CHAPTER EIGHTEEN

July arrived in a blaze of summer heat. We let the garden into the house of an evening at Tarn's place by opening the french doors at the back by the dining-table. The flowers outside made a riotous display of heady honeysuckle, climbing clematis, and rambling roses in full bloom. Strands of creepers nodded themselves in over the open doors towards us as we sat there eating. It was delightful.

I poured some red wine, placed the bottle by the salad bowl, gave the jug of garlic dressing a good stir, and stood back to admire the colours and smells of the beautifully laid table. Borage flowers formed a circle of blue stars around a green salad, a small bowl of grated carrot with apple slices and marigold petals gleamed as if it were harvest, and a basket of brown rolls gave a rustic hint. We were about to celebrate Tarn's end of term and a month ahead of us without pressure. I sipped my good wine and Tarn carried in a lasagne, holding the hot dish with thick oven gloves. When the phone rang, I leapt up to answer it because Tarn had her hands full.

It was a man's voice. 'Is that you, Tarn?'

'No, I'm sorry. Who's calling, please?'

'Is she there?'

'Yes. I'll get her for you. Who shall I say?'

'Just get her will you?'

It was an unusual voice, a businessman's tone, loud and carrying, quite cultured, with a general south of England accent. No place in particular. I thought, Who the hell is that? I held the receiver away from me and pulled a face at it, then handed it to Tarn.

'Hello? Tarn Callister speaking.'

'It's Jeff.'

'Jeff? Hello?' Tarn put her hand over the mouthpiece and mouthed 'Joss's boyfriend,' wrinkling her nose as if there were a bad smell.

I could hear him say, 'She's had the baby. Five weeks early. It's a girl. It's all right but Joss isn't. She's had a Caesarean and she's not so good. The anaesthetic upset her. She can't phone you yet.'

'I see. Oh, goodness. You're sure she'll be okay?'

'Yes. They say so. She had it yesterday. She'll phone in a day or two. She wants to see you but no rush, she says. She wants to be home first.'

'Right. When will that be, do you know?'

'They can't say, yet. She's still in the delivery suite. She can be there for up to three days. It's called Victoria Ward. Then if they need to keep an eye on her after that she'll be on postnatal.'

'Is there just one postnatal ward?'

'No, there are two – Blundel East and Blundel West. She would be on East, they say.'

'And have you chosen a name for the baby?'

'Joss wants to call her Vorrie. Vorrie Marianne. Marianne was my mother's name.'

'Vorrie Marianne. That's lovely.'

'All right, then?'

'I'll write to her straight away and when she's ready I'll come up and stay with friends and come and see her and the baby. Will you tell her please?'

'All right then.'

'Fine. Thank you. Thanks for phoning.'

They rang off. No love lost there, I could tell. Tarn's face was thunder.

'She had the baby yesterday by Caesarean. He didn't let me know.'

'At least he rang now.'

'She'd have nagged him. He wouldn't otherwise. We can't stand each other.'

'Come on, love. We can drink to Vorrie Marianne. Five weeks early. How much did she weigh, did he say?'

'No, and I forgot to ask. How silly. My mind went absolutely blank. I couldn't think what to say.'

'You did fine, love. You can phone Guy's later on and see how they both are. You're her mother, so they'll talk to you, love. Come on, drink your wine, it'll do you good.'

Tarn nodded with tears in her eyes. She said quietly, 'Vorrie's a Manx name. When Joss was eleven, my parents flew out to Japan for a holiday. Joss became inseparable from her grandmother, my mother, and went to visit her on the island the following summer. One of the friends she made there had a new baby sister called Vorrie. Joss said then that if she ever had a little girl of her own she would call her Vorrie as a reminder of that magical time she spent on the island. I hadn't remembered that until now. It's so wonderful for me that Joss's daughter is linked to my island.'

'That's amazing. You see? You just never know what life's going to turn up. It's a lovely name. I'm glad.'

'So am I. I can't get over it.'

After that, Joss and Tarn talked on the phone every day. Joss was ecstatic. She said that the baby was absolutely beautiful and no trouble and that Jeff was as good as gold. It was all going to be all right now, she said.

Three and a bit weeks later Joss rang to say she was ready for Tarn to go to London to see her and the baby. Jeff was going to be abroad on business for five days. Tarn called Tessa and arranged to stay at the studio, and began to look forward to getting to know her new granddaughter.

I went to the station to wave Tarn off. I remember that it was an unusually breezy day, which was a relief because the summer was very hot and dry; and Penzance could be quite stuffy, especially down by the station in times of high temperatures. So we held each other close and then she stepped on to the train and we closed the door. Tarn stood above me, leaning down out of the window, and I held up my hands so that she could touch them. There we stayed, talking and joking until the whistle blew. I waved and waved as the train curved away, taking her to a city that I knew so well, three hundred miles away, to another part of her life that I knew not at all. I had no way of guessing what her experiences were going to be when she arrived there, though I knew that she could rely on Tessa and Jules, not only because they were now her friends as well as mine, but also because they already lived with the familiarity of being grandparents. Jean's second baby was due in a little while, on my birthday, 5 September.

*

Jocelyn's flat, for which, it turned out, Jeff was playing the rent, was on the south bank between London Bridge and Tower Bridge. It was a hot August morning, just after the rush hour, as Tarn walked from the underground to meet Joss. The area was full of surprises, like so many parts of London. The railway arches were enclosures for workshops – printers, car mechanics, storage rooms. But, turn a corner and there were offices, bright and shiny, turn another and old council estates with outside balconies and pop art graffiti, turn another to find pockets of green with clumps of mature plane trees and flowering shrubs, overlooked by the new luxurious apartments of those who had bought decrepit warehouses and reconstructed them into city dream homes with historical exterior character and interior beauty and comfort.

Tarn walked on, noticing that street names thereabouts gave glimpses of the craft of tanning and curing of leather, indicating a bygone industrial centre for leather work, then suddenly she came upon a narrow cul-de-sac where Joss's old-new warehouse butted straight on to the street. Tarn ran her finger down the list of buzzers on an entry phone.

Presently Joss's voice answered and the door clicked for Tarn to enter. The lobby was freshly painted in bright white and was lovely, alive with green plants. There were two doors to the ground floor apartments, and a posh staircase of new wood and an exceptionally clean grey Berber carpet led upwards. There was also a small lift, but Tarn chose to walk, enjoying the stair lights and the plants at each turn, until she came to Joss's landing.

Her daughter was standing in the open doorway, looking fresh and stunning in new slim-line trousers and a long fashionable shirt with short sleeves and a perfectly fitting collar and V-neck. Her blonde hair was tied back and she was wearing make-up and very expensive silver earrings from the Far East.

'Hello, Mum.' She was smiling hugely.

'You look wonderful, darling. You look really well.'

'I am. I'm happy. Jeff's always wanted this baby. I'm in my element.'

'Good.' They held each other. 'It shows, Joss. You really do look good.'

'That's why I asked you to wait to come and see me. I'm

trying to prove something to you, Mum. I haven't got my figure back yet. This shirt hides a multitude of sins, but I'm on my way. Come on in. She's in the nursery, sound asleep. She goes nine at night, three a.m., nine in the morning. So it's really not too bad, and she's such a contented little thing. She really is.'

The nursery was done predictably in lemon and white, taking no chances and firmly on the fence as to gender. Vorrie was asleep on her back in a crib near the window, her feet at the bottom of the mattress, and her head and shoulders free of the carefully tucked in blanket at the top.

She looked just like Joss had looked at the same age. She had her fist in her mouth and was sleeping like the proverbial cherub.

Joss whispered, 'Isn't she sweet? This is Vorrie Marianne.'

Tarn put her arm around Joss's shoulders. 'She's beautiful, darling. And she looks just like you. You were such a delightful baby, Joss. I've never known such a calm child. All the other mothers were so jealous. You ate and slept and gurgled and that was it. You slept through at four-and-a-half weeks and after that the only time you ever woke me at night was when you had tonsilitis.'

'I remember. I thought my head was on fire, not to mention my throat. I hope Vorrie never gets it. Anyway, what d'you think? You like her nursery?'

'Of course I do. It's charming . . .'

'And traditional? Well, maybe. But the rest isn't. Come and see.'

'Wait a minute. I want to look at her a minute more. Look at her tiny, tiny hands. You forget how small they are, you really do.'

'She's grown. I think she's a monster compared to when she was born. She seems really big now. She *is* peaceful. I'm so lucky, Mum.'

'I wish you both – you and your child – happiness and peace, you know I do. From the bottom of my heart.'

'Thanks, Mum. Come on, I'll put the kettle on and show you my new home.'

The flat was done in Joss's inimitable style, black and white with fabulous wall hangings and a Far Eastern flair, but subtle and artistic, with space and light and an absence of clutter. Joss had always been this way. Excessively tidy, almost obsessively so, and her place was always spotless. Even as a teenager she never had to be asked to tidy her room. Tarn had kept quiet about it in front of the other mothers. She didn't want to get into trouble for having a paragon of a tidy daughter when everyone else was moaning about young people and the awful phases they went through.

Joss's kitchen-diner had the same taste and lack of clutter. It was done out in very posh new units in black and white with all the latest high tech equipment and a brand new Chinese wok on the hob, next to the microwave, the coffee filter machine and the food processor. There was money being freely spent here. Tarn tried not to let it show that she had registered the quality and cost.

But it had shown; Joss knew her too well. In answer to the unasked question, Joss waved her hand at the gleaming surfaces saying, 'Jeff bought it all. He wants us to have a fresh start. He got someone in to do it and I love it.'

Then Joss bit her lip and held back the obvious words, 'And I love him too,' so they hovered silently, unspoken but very loudly audible, nevertheless.

'Could I have some jasmine tea, please, darling? I haven't had any for ages.'

'Of course, Mum. I'll join you. There's biscuits as well in that tin, or would you rather have some fruit?'

'Biscuits are fine thanks. Maybe I'll have an apple later.'

Presently, they carried the tea in its very pretty Japanese tea set through into the living-room, where Jocelyn placed the tray on a nest of blackwood tables, between two armchairs.

Tarn sighed and sat down. 'Oh, this is lovely. What a tasteful room. Mmm. Jasmine tea. This is bliss, isn't it!'

Joss laughed and they began to get to know each other again.

After a wonderful morning with Joss, Tarn spent an entrancing few hours with her new granddaughter. All her old skills with children and babies came back to her. She began to be caught up in Joss's dream-like existence, the euphoria, the peace and happiness which her daughter so deserved. She left there late afternoon, promising, as Joss had hoped she would, to go back each day while Jeff was away.

They didn't speak of him.

Every evening Joss received a phone call from Hong Kong. Usually she didn't talk about this to Tarn because Joss now recognised the need for a clear boundary between that part of her life and her interaction with her mother.

However, on Tarn's fourth day of seeing Joss and Vorrie, she sensed that Joss had something she needed to say. Joss was still very well and shining with health, but she appeared agitated. The three of them set off for a walk to the local market with Tarn playing proud grandmother and pushing Vorrie's pram, but knowing that something was wrong. Eventually, Joss said that there was something worrying her, that it involved Jeff, but not in a heavy way, and would Tarn mind if she talked about it.

'All right, darling. Let's have it then.'

'He needs to stay out there another ten days. There's a big contract and there's been a delay. It's not that I mind being on my own with Vorrie. I'm thrilled with her and I'm enjoying my time with her so much. The trouble is that I was going to go away one night next week, and I can't take Vorrie with me. Jeff can't help having to stay out there. I don't mind that. I knew it would happen from time to time – I'm just glad she was born early and that he was here then.'

'What's the event? It must be quite important if you were thinking of staying overnight?'

'You know I've been doing some weaving lately? This is a weaving exhibition in Birmingham, organised by the Weavers' Guild, and a dinner in the evening at one of the hotels. It's a chance for me to meet the friends I've made since I've been back here and it would make a really nice change for me. I could have left Vorrie with Jeff in London. He's very good with her.'

Joss paused and bit her lip, realising perhaps that this was a more than sensitive topic – Jeff and Vorrie were not likely to be a combination that would make make her mother feel at ease. 'I was wondering if you would stay at my flat and look after her for me so I could still go?'

'I'd be happy to, Joss. I'm used to her routine now and I'm pleased you felt you could ask me.'

'Would you? Would you really? Oh thank you, Mum. I've

been really looking forward to it. I love being with Vorrie, of course I do. You can see that. But there's nothing like a night off now and again. I'd be so grateful, Mum. Thank you.'

'It's a pleasure. It'll be a real treat. You sure it's all right for me to stay at your flat, though? I don't want . . . I don't want you to be in any trouble, Joss.'

They both took a deep breath and stepped back a little from possible confrontation.

'Like I said, Mum, he's changed. I've been trying to prove that to you. But I know deep down you don't believe me, do you?'

'If the truth be known, Joss, I'd like to believe you because I would like it to be true. I'm glad things are calm at the moment for you. But I have images in my head from your past years with Jeff. Those images will never leave me.'

'That's so sad, Mum. That means you never really have peace of mind.'

'That's right, Joss. That's the heart of the matter.'

'Is it because of your lesbian politics, Mum, that you don't think men can change?'

'I'm a lesbian, Joss, because I love women. It has nothing to do with men.'

'But you loved my dad?'

'Yes, I did. And we grew apart because of his changes and my changes. I don't need to wipe out the past. It wasn't awful. I don't need to. I need to know who I am now and to live my life openly now. That includes being a lesbian and being a mother and grandmother. The parts fit together fairly well,' Tarn paused. 'Most of the time.'

'But not my past. That gives you pain.'

'Yes.'

Joss looked down at the sleeping baby. Then with tears in her eyes she said, 'I'd kill anybody who hurt her, Mum. I'd swing for anyone who ever hurt her.' Then she thought for a moment, watching the people bustling up and down between the market stalls. 'Having this baby has changed me for ever. I will never be the same woman I was before she came into my life. She is my child and I will stand between her and the whole world if necessary to protect her. Do you understand me, Mum?'

'I hear the passionate feelings you have for Vorrie. And I

want you both to live long, safe and happy lives. Do *you* understand me?'

'I think we both understand each other better now, don't we?'

The days passed happily for Tarn, though she was missing me and we spent a fortune on the phone.

On Thursday 11 August, Jocelyn went to her exhibition.

She left on the tube just after the morning rush hour. Tarn walked with Vorrie to the park and chatted with the mothers and grannies there. While Vorrie slept between meal times, Tarn wrote letters and caught up on some reading. Joss phoned to say that she had arrived in Birmingham. How was everything at home? Everything was fine, fine.

The days passed very contentedly. Tarn played with Vorrie until the early evening, then bathed her, moved once again by the feel of the baby's new skin and the trust which Vorrie had as she lay in the warm water with Tarn's arm behind her, supporting her and holding her. Vorrie gurgled and splashed merrily.

A happy baby was dried and changed, fed and winded, sung to, and settled in her cot after the nine p.m. feed.

Tarn was exhausted. She'd forgotten how much one does with a new baby. Always on the go, feeding, washing, wiping.

Now it was all done. The 3 a.m. feed was prepared in a sterilised bottle in the fridge. Baby clothes were washed, dried and put away. The place looked as it would if Joss were there, immaculate and neat.

In Joss's bed, which felt uncannily strange because it was a double and she shared it with 'him', Tarn read for a while, then tiptoed to check Vorrie and when she was sure all was in order, she clicked out the light and went to sleep.

She had set her inner alarm for 3 a.m. but she knew she would wake anyway the moment that Vorrie murmured, let alone screamed lustily with the monster bellow lungs of a hungry baby as meal time approached. Besides, Joss had said that Vorrie was like clockwork. Wound up and ready to go off at two fifty-nine a.m.

Tarn woke with a start. She looked at the clock. Three ten a.m.

She pulled her jumper on over her pyjamas and, moving fast but quietly, she clicked on the lights and went into Vorrie's room.

Vorrie seemed to be sound asleep. Strange that it should be this night of all nights that she chose to sleep through, but Joss had done this at four-and-a-half weeks.

Tarn couldn't hear Vorrie breathing. Something cold hit her in the stomach. She clicked on the baby lamp. She stood over Vorrie's crib listening intently. Joss had been a silent sleeper like this.

No. Not like this. This . . . was . . . not . . . sleep.

She reached out her fingers and gently, very, very gently, touched Vorrie on the face.

Like someone in a horror movie she pulled her fingers away and brought the pads of them near to her face, staring and staring at them. It could not be true. It couldn't be true that the pads of her fingers felt . . . cold.

But she knew. In every coil of DNA in her own warm body, she knew.

Vorrie was lying on her back as the hospital had taught Joss to place her, feet touching the bottom of the crib, blanket tucked in exactly so. To the letter they had obeyed.

There was absolutely no reason why Vorrie should not be sleeping safely, in her own crib, breathing in and out, in and out.

Tarn couldn't move. She stood and stared at the baby's excessively still face, her small fists half curled, her arms exactly where they should be over the blanket. Nothing was too tight. Nothing was too loose.

There was no sound from the crib.

Nothing. No breath, no movement, no flicker of an eyelid.

There was no breathing. This was not Joss sleeping through.

This was Vorrie who was . . . not . . . breathing.

And . . . in the horror movie . . . though it was all true . . . not a film . . . not a dream . . . real life . . . Tarn knew it . . . real death . . .

If there was . . . no breath . . . then . . . there was . . . no life. No spirit. No child. No grandchild. Nothing.

No more Vorrie.
She *was* here. Living, gurgling, being. My grandchild.
My Vorrie.
This . . . is . . . my grandchild's . . . dead . . . body.

No spirit. No child. No grandchild. Nothing.
How is it that the descent to hell begins with . . . Nothing.

CHAPTER NINETEEN

Dearest Lerryn,

It's four in the morning and I'm at your studio.

It's all over and I will fax this to you first thing. I have plenty of support and Tessa and Jules have been absolutely wonderful. I hang on to sanity in this insane business by the tips of my fingernails.

Now, writing to you at this hour is what keeps me from falling into oblivion.

I dreamed that I was my daughter's baby. Joss's child. I dreamed that I was in her womb and that her body was being beaten up again.

She blamed me. She did not want me. She stuck a knitting needle into the sack around me. A sensation of enclosure and squeezing began. I felt as if all the breath was being forced out of me. I could hear myself screaming. Joss was sitting astride a grassy green and rounded hill. Her belly heaved and jerked. I was her child in her womb. Her belly heaved and jerked.

I was spinning in water and blood in her womb. Then a constricting sensation began as my limited space closed around me, forcing me onwards, forwards. I was surrounded by water and blood and I could not breathe.

I was pushed out of her body, but could not stop myself falling. I rolled over and over, bruised and chafed by the ground of the hillside. My body spiralled downwards and forwards till I lay in a blood-soaked heap at the foot of the hill. I realised that it was the witches' hill. It was Slieuwhallion Hill in the Isle of Man.

I woke up and lay in the dark here in your studio. I lay very still, but the sensation of spiralling over and over forwards and out of control stayed with me for a long time. I was very, very frightened. Ellan Vannin seemed close to me. I didn't understand why.

But let me tell you about Jocelyn.

Yesterday after the funeral and cremation she flew to Germany, where she will live for a while with Helen and Yuki. Helen has booked her into a therapy centre where she can have some counselling sessions. There is someone there who is known to Liesl – a woman who has done fine work with other young mothers who have lost their babies through cot death.

Joss blames herself for leaving Vorrie. She blames me for the death itself and cannot bear to be near me, to see me, or to talk with me. But she tells Helen that she knows that with help and over a period of time this will change. However, she has no way of knowing how long that might be. Helen says that Joss clings to sanity by a slim thread, but there are glimpses of hope because she has turned to her sister and seems able to trust her. In all the pain, grief and turmoil that is truly a blessing.

Jocelyn is entirely blamed for 'his daughter's death' by Jeff, who says he will kill her if she ever comes near him again. A strange and horrible reversal of the words from Joss to me that fateful market day when she said she'd swing for anyone who hurt Vorrie, then asked me to stay the night and care for Vorrie.

Helen tells me that Joss has asked if I will take Vorrie's ashes to the family grave in the Isle of Man. My parents – Joss's grandparents – were buried there after their car accident a few years ago. Joss was very close to my mother. I'm astonished that Joss trusts me with this task; and that she doesn't want to take Vorrie's ashes to the island herself. But Helen says that we should probably just do as she asks and question later. I wonder if she is punishing me in some way? Making me bury little Vorrie's ashes all by myself? Or if, somehow, she thinks it will help me to come to terms with what happened. Whatever the reasoning, I accept the reality of it. I atone by carrying out the task. I oscillate between guilt that I was unable to keep Vorrie alive and breathing and a personal need to say goodbye to her in this symbolic way.

In my life, dearest Lerryn, there have now been three boy/girl romances that have not fulfilled the romantic fantasy that we're fed as young girls.

Helen fell in love with the son of a well-to-do Japanese family in our locality when we lived there. He loved her truly and she

175

got pregnant with Yuki when she was eighteen. He was a little older, a university student, and was put under enormous pressure by his family not to marry her. They sent him away to a different university and two young hearts were devastated. I liked him. We all did. He was a fine young man and Helen was so broken-hearted that she said she'd never marry anyone else.

My own story is very mundane. Two university students met and married before either of them had a chance to find out what else life had to offer. Both of us were from the Isle of Man, from different parts of the island, and we didn't meet until we both went to Liverpool. At least that gives my children a clear Manx ancestry. Something I value and think they will learn to cherish. I wonder – is that why Joss wants Vorrie taken 'home'?

The third romance – Joss and Jeff – was never romantic at all. Jeff pursued Joss like the Duke of Bavaria pursued Cinderella, though Joss was not poor. But the analogy still holds in one sense – he kept offering her fairy tales and every one of them turned into a violent nightmare. Of course, he's not to blame for Vorrie's cot death, but he *is* to blame for accusing Joss of murder by leaving 'his daughter' with a dyke whom he despised. Those words and his steadfast hatred ever since have hurt Joss as badly as his fists once did.

Now she has to heal, no easy task. She doesn't want to return to Japan, though she could stay with her father there. She can't bear the flat in London, for obvious reasons.

Oh my dearest love, without you this would be a terrible tunnel leading ever downwards. Because I know that I have your love and support, I can get through this.

I'm going to the Isle of Man with Vorrie's ashes right away. I'll spend some time there, trying to come to terms with everything. Answering the call of the island at last, and hoping for healing from my ancestral land. I know you'll give me this time and space willingly, dearest. And I know that you'll be thinking of me, sending me strength over the waters. I'll write to you every day – I'll fax you, because it's quicker – sod the cost – and I'll be back in time for the beginning of September and your fiftieth, I promise.

All my love, Tarn XXX

BOOK THREE

Book Three

Chapter Twenty

Dearest Lerryn,

I've been here only a day and already I'm missing you. But I know I was meant to do this journey, and it is so different being here with your support than taking this great leap on my own with no sense of connection with anyone special. Our closeness warms me, even though we're apart. Loving you wasn't anything I could've planned but there you are in my life, in my heart, allowing me to cherish all our time together in Penzance before I left for London; and now, here, on little island, this gift of space and time.

Lerryn – oh, dearest, I am glad you are there for me. This would be a terrible journey otherwise. Somewhere, in a part of my heart that I can't access, somewhere there is 'the tragedy'.

I wish I could cry, but I can't. I wish I could wail and moan and shout, but somehow I can't. Sometimes I wonder if the tragedy is the start of an infinite expansion outwards and that I'll never contact my inner self again. At other times I fear that I may be imploding, contracting inwards until I am compacted so tightly that I'll become a mere pinpoint, falling into my own cosmic hole, never to be seen again.

I tried writing about Vorrie, but I couldn't make any progress beyond some questions of time. Who was I in relation to the universe, the stars, the great night sky? Why did Vorrie arrive and depart in that way? Where is she now?

Without your understanding and your love I wouldn't be here now, dearest Lerryn – I am on a long journey to the centre of the self. When I at last arrive, I will be able to return to you with love and beauty to offer once again.

Meanwhile, dearest, sleep well and work well, secure in the safety of my loving you.

Much love, always, Tarn XXX

> Dearest Lerryn,
> As soon as the wheels touched down, I felt safe. I was

on my island. The land of my foremothers. The stewardess had a soft voice and welcomed us in Manx. *Cur failt erriu gys Ellan Vannin.*

I stood, reached to the overhead locker for my hand luggage and moved slowly with the other passengers along the gangway to the exit. I had no expectations, no real idea what my next movements would be.

The cabin door opened, the steps were in position. I was on the metal platform, about to place my left foot down on to the first step, when without a shadow of a doubt, I was greeted in the old traditional manner, by my grandmother's mother.

It happens each time. And each time I don't expect it to happen again, though maybe I should, by now. There are warm hands, very lightweight, placing an invisible hand-knitted shawl, with a thick, hand-knotted fringe, around my shoulders. There are no words. There is no voice. No one else has seen or heard or felt a thing. But I am being smiled upon, and this I know, she is my great-grandmother on my mother's side, and she wants me here, on my island, again. The shawl will remain with me while I am here.

She will not come to me visibly or with words, but I will be comforted by the shawl; it holds her kind messages of love and continuity.

I am known. I am loved. I am wanted here.

I collect my heavy luggage, aware that my letters, telling of my arrival, will arrive after me. Contented, today, to travel by myself, I have deliberately set it up like this.

I simply want to be. So I catch the bus into town and watch the rolling fields and the wooded lanes, and hear once again the rise and fall of the voices. A sing-song version of the English language is spoken in these parts. Satisfied, I sit back and listen.

Our bus crosses the Fairy Bridge safely, so maybe other passengers are, like me, acknowledging the little people by paying silent respects.

My shawl is warm, silent, invisible. My grandmother's mother stayed behind near the airport. She never did catch a bus in any of her lives.

And, as for me, I have answered the call of the wise ones, voices across the ocean: I have returned once again to my beginning.

I am thinking of you, dearest.
All my love, Tarn XXX

Dearest Lerryn,
I have found a small wooden house with a veranda, down a remote and beautiful lane, where I can rest and grieve, absorbing the stillness of the hills and preparing myself to take Vorrie's ashes to the family grave.

I have a dim memory of being brought here by Aunt Ginny when I was in my early teens. It's not a holiday home – it belongs to a distant cousin on Aunt Ginny's side, who is away in Tuscany, so it is empty for the summer – I have been very lucky and allowed to stay here to work through my grief. My relatives here are very sympathetic. They don't intrude; they seem to understand that I need to be alone for a while. I saw my grandparents, both in their nineties, in the residential home, just briefly, which was a kind and gentle reunion.

Must dash to catch the fax place in town before it closes.
Will write again tomorrow.
All my love, Tarn XXX

Dearest Lerryn,
How are you, my love? Your new painting sounds wonderful. I can imagine you there at Botallack, sketching the old engine houses and thinking about the historical times when the men in your family were tin miners there. Your letter and description of the new painting seem full of strength and hope. I read your letters over and over. Your handwriting brings you near.

Today, after another sleepless night, I am frazzled and tired.

Night after sleepless night I ask myself, what more could I have done? I watch myself, over and over, back in London with Vorrie in my arms. My baby granddaughter, small, smiling, with huge, wide, vulnerable eyes and curly arms and legs. Mind and heart. Vorrie in my arms, looking up at me, unfocused but knowing. Bonding.

In my mind a pattern of words repeats itself: Vorrie. Child of the line of Callister. Grandchild. She was a grand little, wee little one. Was. Was. She was. Yes, she was.

Oh, Lerryn, the turmoil of it. My arrival here, feeling safe, is interwoven with such turbulent changes of emotion and mood.

Gwen Corkhill is coming to see me some time. She knows this situation from the inside because it happened to her daughter too. Gwen's one of the girls I grew up with, and I wrote to her when her grandchild died two years ago, never imagining that the same would happen to me.

Gwen and I started school together somewhere back in time. Little girls who loved to dance. She would take me into the glen behind her aunty's house near a farm by Groudle and there we'd listen for fairy music. Then, aware, we'd dance so quietly, all along the banks of the river, then, running with her dog, we'd emerge down the glen, where the water rattles hard over the pebbles to the sea.

Holding hands, skimming stones, not a care in the world, we romanced about growing up and having babies. We wanted girls, two each. We made up rhyming songs and we'd dance about: 'Two babies each – for them we'll care and tie bright ribbons in their hair.' I can recall our songs like yesterday! Motherhood was a central theme for each of us. Now, as a lesbian, that part of me is still there. I can't remember if I ever thought ahead to being a grandmother. Yuki took us all by surprise and is a source of joy. I became a grandmother early without having given it much thought.

This morning I think back to Groudle Glen and two little girls dancing and spinning fairy tales. And all those dreams came true for Gwen and me. But this is now and that was then.

Vorrie. Granddaughter. She was. She was. She was.

Oh, Lerryn, I knew this low time would come. I wish, I wish I could cry. Is this letter my way of crying? If so, it helps, it really does. I know I'll get through it. I can feel your love all around me.

And I love you so much, dearest woman.

Thinking of you.

Much love, Tarn XXX

Dearest Lerryn,

Sometimes at night, when I am grieving, I walk down the valley to a gap where I can hear the beat of the sea. I seem to feel its rhythm. But it has a weird and ominous quality, dip splash, dip splash, like a drum beat. It sounds like a Viking ships with oars. Dip splash. Dip splash. I feel the violence of the Vikings' arrival in this community. Slicing open our ocean: ripping open our island. I sense the plunder and pillage when pagan patriarchs were cutting open our matriarchy. Cutting open our Celtic homelands.

In the silence of the valley at night time, the rhythmic beat also sounds like a heart beat. As if my heart is a drum. I recall those times when Joss was in danger, being beaten. I would be unable to sleep when I was anxious about her, and would be aware of my heart beating faster and faster until I knew she was safe again. Sometimes I would get a midnight call from the hospital, where she had been taken again. It was a living nightmare for all those who loved her. On such a night her child may have been conceived.

Vorrie grew there inside Joss's womb until her own heart began beating too. Like a drum beat. Like a drum beat.

In the valley here, when I stand in the dark and listen to the beat of the sea, I hear a rhythm: M. Mother. Other. M. Mother. Other. M. Mother. M. Mother. M. Mother. Other.

The Other is the one I might have been if I hadn't become a mother. But I did, and then became Vorrie's mother's mother.

In the oars there is no gentleness. Time lines. Linear time. Beating. Beating. My daughter used to love a man who beat her. Beating. Beating. Invading. Pushing. Hell is this and hell is temporary. So I stand sometimes in that gap in the valley, aware of that distant beat, feeling angry, so angry about all the violence against women.

It is then that I make the connection – the oppression of the Beguines who lost their land; the degredation of the witches like those in the folklore here; the violation of the Jewish women throughout history and the story which we heard from Anna in Hamburg; the scorn and pain heaped on the suffragettes – your beloved Biff as a girl having to escape and disguise her femaleness and becoming trapped therein; the struggles of lesbians these days – yes, even these days – because the world doesn't want us to be honoured or real.

Oh, I hear the dip splash, dip splash of the Viking oars and I feel that I am here, reliving the Viking invasions and my heart beats faster and faster and I am afraid of this anger and this pain.

Then, full circle, I touch the snake tail to its mouth and cannot escape the reason for coming here. My baby grandchild is dead; her mother's ex-boyfriend holds me responsible; and my own daughter can't talk to me directly yet. My heart beats so fast then, with anger and despair; and, oh, how I miss Joss and our early years. Mother and daughter. So that is partly why I'm here in a wooden house, on the edge of desolation, to get over that, beyond that, through to the other side.

Then, at other times here the quietness of the valley comforts me. When the wind is gentle at night or in the early hours of morning, I lie awake with a completely different set of feelings. At those times I feel I am being rocked, and rocking myself, in the arms of the moorland. To the heart beat heart beat drum. Other. Mother. Other. Mother. Then I can imagine many women in the distant past on the island and that the first drums were the women's drums; and the Other is the person, the woman, I have become, the parts of myself healing here.

Then I seem to be a skin pulled tight at the centre of a drum beat, and it is all right to lie and listen to my own heart beat, because the fear is fading, slowly. I know that Joss is safe now, and I have hope that, because I was asked to bring her baby's ashes here, Joss and I will become friends again.

Then my heart beat steadies itself again and I am the Gaelic woman, conscious of the rhythms of the ocean, returning here to the long slow moon-sea harmonies. I am the strong woman who understands resistance. My connections are deeper, wider, fuller. The oars that splash beat splash beat are throbbing and they hold no gentleness, but I am the Celtic woman who has been here before and has survived.

I write to you, dearest Lerryn, and I send you my love from this complex place, my island.

Thinking of you,

All my love, Tarn XXX

Dearest Lerryn,

I dreamed of us in the night and woke with my skin aching for you. This is the end of my first week here and I'm missing you like crazy. But all my senses are acutely awakened by loving you and this opens me to intuitive reactions to everything around me here.

In this small wooden house with a veranda, down this lovely, lonely lane, I can rest and read, appreciating the solitude as I prepare to take Vorrie's ashes soon.

The distant view is across a gentle valley and is a real comfort to me because it isn't too intense or infinite. A charcoal line drawn across the sky provides a much-needed boundary for me. It holds the hills down in place so that they can't be blown away. They're held solid, pegged against the ground, like huge green tents, summits at the ridge poles, sagging. The view encloses the valley and gives me both distance, so that I don't feel too crowded, and containment, so that in my desolation at the loss of my grandchild, I don't simply dissolve away into nothing.

This morning it's like West Penwith here. Washed. Everything blowing dry in the wind. During the day it becomes very hot, like in Penzance, and sometimes there are storms at night. There are blue-grey clouds today and turquoise streaks on a sharply defined horizon. Near to the little wooden house dark ivy stars gleam and there are wet bars on the veranda black in silhouette against the morning light.

Once, several years ago, on one of my visits here, I stood and listened to the sounds in our Manx museum. Above me, glass roof lights, and on them, the softest splashes of rain, like fingertips. I heard the same sound from early rain this morning, and it took me back to my former research there in the museum, many years ago. In glass cases there were Celtic crosses, with runes and dragons, swirls and curls of intricate designs on them. They looked like Aran sweaters with dragons carved up the sides. They are so unusual because they also have Scandinavian markings on the thin edges.

I can recall the research I did, in the silent noises of that beautiful gallery, where I heard the sound of rain and of old books with creaking pages. The archaeologists found the Manx round houses and carbon-dated the organic remains. But they remained bewildered, for they could find no chieftains' dwellings. It seems that they could simply not imagine that the pieces are parts of a round puzzle. They could not comprehend such circularity. How could there possibly be a society without hierarchy? they asked.

I rest here and read and write ... but I must finish this now or I'll be late into town.

Thinking of you, dearest.

All my love, Tarn XXX

Dearest Lerryn,

Your wonderful letters arrived, two of them, by the same post this morning, full of life and love and vigour.

Supporting me, helping me, healing me. Bless you, dearest, for loving me. I am surrounded by your love of me and this sustains me, as we hoped it would, through these shifts of reality.

I have now taken Vorrie's ashes to the family grave where I buried them under the rose bushes. I knelt for a long time asking for blessing on Vorrie and all the family and my nearest and dearest. No particular words. Just a stream of thoughts and feelings. It was a cloudless afternoon, very sunny. I was alone there, though my feeling that the ancestors were near was very strong and comforting. I felt as if they were promising to take care of Vorrie.

Then I drove to the Dhoon Glen and climbed half-way down the valley and lay on a ledge thirty feet above the waters of the bay. There wasn't much wind, just a slight sea breeze playing around the waterfalls. Water poured past me, past the ledge where I lay, flowing water, down into the earth, to carry my loss away. After a week and a half here I feel I have accepted that Vorrie isn't coming back and that Joss will take a long time to change towards me.

Now I am back indoors, in the small wooden house, writing to you, dearest woman.

I am thinking of you.

My love, as always, Tarn XXX

Dearest Lerryn,

I had a comforting day yesterday with Gwen. As you know, we were at school together here, and our friendship goes back so far that I have, over the years, been unafraid of sharing my innermost feelings and changes with her. She wasn't at all surprised about you and me, just glad for both of us, and wants us to be happy. She said she'd been expecting that I'd sooner or later find another good woman, as she put it. I was able to talk openly and it brought me very close to you. I'm missing you incredibly – in every way.

Gwen and I drove north to the Point of Ayre and then walked on the low dunes and the long sweeping beaches there, until sunset. We watched the sun dip into the Irish Sea until streaks of crimson and orange spread upwards, pulsing up through some patchy clouds and reflecting in the ocean. These are the images I had held dear in my heart from life on the island before I was wrenched away from there and brought to Penzance in my teens.

Gwen has had grief of different kinds in her life and our conversation was special to me. Her caring and understanding of my shock and grief over baby Vorrie, and her outrage at the fact that Jocelyn blames me, did strengthen me through the day, calming me and helping me to adjust to the tragedy – a validation process. Our day together was a gentle and peaceful time.

Time moves differently here than in the city. I often think of you and me in West Penwith, how time seems to reach to us from behind the granite outcrops, pouring in through the gaps, taking us into other worlds and eras. It's like that here on little island. The meaning of time itself is continually being re-interpreted here, like films slowed down or warped into different realities.

The island, which has been calling me for a long time, is now holding me safely and I feel, strange as this may seem, that these hills and valleys make a cradle for Vorrie, where she can rest without any harm coming to her.

I talked with Gwen about all of this. Then she explained to me her feelings for this land, which she experiences as a very female place. I, in turn, told her how I felt that the island – Ellan Vannin – was both an island and a woman.

I held close to Gwen and we both cried, able to grieve together because we have been good friends for so long. Friends in childhood, until we were thrown apart, lonely and sad, when my parents moved away from the island. That was when I had first imagined someone I called Ellan Vannin, as if she had really existed and that image has sustained me ever since.

It was an important talk with Gwen, because we are

daughters of this island, both of us, and so was little Vorrie, in her own right.

Now, Vorrie rests, her journey completed. She has come home; and I sit here crying gently, comforted and wrapped around in my grandmother's mother's warm Celtic shawl, and writing to you about the ways in which I am beginning to heal.

Before falling asleep I went out on to my veranda, and watched the night sky, which was cloudless and full of stars. The entire Milky Way could be seen. I thought of you, my love for you and your steady love and support for me, our walks at night on the moors, and all the loving we will share on my return.

I love you so much, dearest.

All my love, Tarn XXX

Chapter Twenty-one

It was one of those heat-hazy days where light plays havoc along a smudged horizon on the north coast. I parked the car by the ruins at Bosigran, and walked out on to the cliffs until, turning, I could regard the length of coastline from where I stood.

It was beautiful. Far below me the waves crashed, sending up fine white spray. Out to sea the blue ocean blurred into indigo and then lost itself with no horizon. Beside me were tiny wild flowers and crisp lichens and dark red sedum with minute flowers clinging to sparkling granite.

Behind me, ironically, were Manx Loghtan sheep which had been imported from the Isle of Man to Cornwall. They grazed the cliffs to restore them to their original balance of low-cropped turf, gorse and heather. The sheep were bleating, nudging one another, dark grey and shaggy, bred to withstand a rough life, an island life of wind and salty air.

Above me sea birds were wheeling and calling over the cliffs, loudly, above the noise of the sea. I listened to flights of gulls flying inland, their plumage gleaming white and silver grey in a blurred blue daylight. I thought of Tarn; my thoughts flew out across the ocean to her.

Out to sea, the Scilly Isles were lost in the distance as if the water level which had once risen to separate the islands from each other, had risen further and further until they were all submerged, blended again into one complete land-mass.

I'd been taught our Cornish legends by Aunt Harry; stories of underwater Lyonesse – lost lands beneath the sea; and of mermaids who would call across the ocean on summer nights. Mermaids' voices from the curl of the waves. Mermaids who would sing and ride on seahorses, whose white manes would be flying in the wind.

It was such a lovely summery day. I felt light and happy because Tarn seemed to be healing steadily now in the Isle of

Man. She had phoned from the town the previous evening and sounded so much better.

It was now early morning and the summer tourists were finishing their slow breakfasts, so there was hardly anyone about. I was on my way to Zennor because Tessa, who was working on a series of legendary images of Black women, had asked me to get a good photo of the Black mermaid which was carved into the dark glossy wood of the mermaid's seat in Zennor Church. But there wasn't any hurry. I had the whole day to myself.

Listening to the birds which flew so wild and free above me, I lazed on the cliffs and had fun imaginging myself flying with the Celtic wild hunt. Flying with the night riders, though it was daytime. Great feathered wings moving me across skies of unboundaried fantasy, through openings in the summer air.

Down on the ledges at Bosigran spray was flying high. I laughed aloud and wanted to be a sea bird artist, a wild creature, flying out from the cliffs to distant lands, to far-off sandy bays. New wings for me, wings on my imagination. I'd fly and fly.

I lay there until mid-morning, letting my imagination go wild. Then, after all that effort, I fancied a cup of coffee, so I drove to the Wayside Museum at Zennor. I sat in the sun with my elevenses, and enjoyed the sounds of the mill wheels turning.

Later, I bought some postcards to send to Tarn, then I wandered round the museum, thinking that we must visit it together when she was home, because she loved the granite-built workshops and the displays of old tools. I lingered happily, thinking of her garden shed, and her old Aunt Ginny who had given her her first trowel.

Crossing the pretty, enclosed garden, then ducking through a very low, original doorway, I stooped and entered the main room, which was set out as a living room in traditional Cornish style, with a parlour off to one side. There was a huge inglenook fireplace with a cloam oven – for baking bread – built up inside the chimney place on the left. At floor level there were iron ladles and pokers; and in the granite lintel above the grate were swinging levers and hooks for kettles or iron cooking cauldrons. Some of them stood around on the slate floor.

A wooden settle stood nearby with a patchwork cover thrown over the back; and on the end of a tall, old dresser there was a card printed with the traditional tale of the Zennor mermaid.

I stood quietly reading it, though I knew it by heart from my childhood, because I had listened so often to stories from my parents and Aunt Harry. I imagined the people there around the hearth, storytelling in centuries gone by.

However, the card reminded me of the purpose of my visit to Zennor, so I left soon and made my way through the village uphill to the church by the pub. It was sunny and warm so I stayed out of doors for a while, wandering in the quiet churchyard. It was a peaceful place, with very old gravestones.

It was the kind of day when, in my early teens during the summer holidays, I would have been in Herton in Yorkshire. If it had been half-day closing there might have been a picnic out in the countryside with Moss and Biff. Looking around me outside the church now, I could see the backdrop of rocky outcrops, rugged hills and wild moorland that would at times resemble the Pennines near Herton.

Then I saw the dates on the gravestones and my mind flew back to the early twentieth century and to Moss and Biff's lives in the north. I wasn't at all unhappy, just very calm and still, recollecting and reconnecting. It was a good experience in the August sunshine.

In her life, Moss had been a staunch Methodist, and in a graveyard in Herton, a coded message still lingered: Here lies Biff, lifelong companion of Moss and friend of Frank. Rest in peace. 16 February 1981.

A young suffragette, Barbara Imogen Farley, had become an old dyke in disguise, Bernard Ian Ferguson. A woman disguised so that her reality was hidden.

From the bright sunlight outside I entered the dim interior of Zennor Church, and sat meditating on the exquisite wooden carving of the mermaid who held a mirror in one hand and a comb in the other. In a shaft of light through a high church window, the lovely fish woman's image now shone, carved with care into the dark wood, polished and treasured. She was not white, nor carved in marble, but was very dark, like one of the

191

Black Madonnas of European Christianity, which Tessa said had been borrowed from Egyptian Isis, and were still turned to as female help in time of trouble. Even the present Pope lit candles to Black Madonnas in Poland, said Tessa, who was searching and asking, Had anyone ever written about the mermaid of Zennor as a female Black image?

I concentrated on the mermaid with Tessa's voice in my head. 'It's a worldwide image, Lerrie. It occurs inland in Africa, too. Rivers and lakes all over the world have mermaids, and they don't have blonde hair. We have these glimpses of the old ways, despite the destruction of so many old images of women and power. Power of life, blood, song and bone. Hearth and home. We are left with these fragments, which give a hint of earlier worlds.'

I took up photographs of the mermaid carefully, paying attention to the light and dark in the church. What was she and who had she been before? She had become a mermaid of a local legend. A lovely, alluring creature.

The legend was that long ago a beautiful young woman had enchanted the congregations of Zennor by her sweet singing and perfect pitch at the back of the church on Sundays. She seemed to vanish after each service.

Mathey Trewhella was the churchwarden's son. One evening after church he followed the sound of singing to the stream which tumbled through the valley, over the mill wheels and onwards down to the sea. The sweet singing led Mathey down into Pendour Cove and he was never seen again.

Many years later, a passing ship dropped anchor in the cove and the captain heard someone calling to him. He peered down over the side of his ship, and saw a mermaid who asked him to remove the anchor as it was blocking the entrance to her cave and she couldn't get home to Mathey and their children.

Anyone who wants to hear the singing should go down to the cove on a summer's night and sit quietly, be patient and listen.

I smiled to myself in Zennor Church. Such a pretty, straight story. I finished taking my photos. What is it about women and the sea that makes these legends last so long? Are there really stories of inland mermaids in lakes and rivers? And in Africa and South America? I couldn't wait to see Tessa's new art works, because I loved her images of strong women, but the exhibition was still a long way off.

A straight mermaid in search of a boyfriend. Poor Mathey Trewhella, he didn't stand a chance. Are there any dyke mermaids frolicking through the sea and surf with womanly companions? What about a transformation into fish form? To be able to swim under water and live in caves with sandy floors and comb my seaweed hair and sing with a high and entrancing voice of pure pitch and perfect tone? I laughed aloud. If I were a merdyke, I would still be an artist and there I would paint under the sea. I'd decorate the walls of my cave with chevrons and meanders to show the tides and movements of the waves.

Merrily, I ran out of the church into the bright blue daylight, glad to be alive this summer's day. I had never been remotely interested in religion, but I had always loved the old Cornish stories. I was jumpy with life force, which was wonderful and was linked with my love for Tarn and my nearest and dearest friends.

Once I was back in the car it seemed to take itself back along the coast road, up over the moors behind Zennor until I found myself on a stretch of wild heather and rough grass in the area around Lanyon Farm. I took out my sketch pad and coloured pencils and small stool and, finding a sheltered spot by a granite hedge, I worked contentedly for a while. Warm hazy daylight surrounded the old farm and the adjoining fields, some of which were once called Parc an chapel. Barely any sign of the ruined chapel was now apparent. Just a few shapeless scattered granite stones which might or might not have been part of a building. It was impossible to say.

But now I realised that the old chapel was probably placed on an even older site, nestling in a part of the moors where, before the roads had been built, local people would have had an uninterrupted pattern of settlements and round houses. Who were they, my forebears, and how did they feel living in a wild part of an old landscape? A landscape that had inspired one of my heroines, Barbara Hepworth.

She had lived and worked just along the coast from here in her workshop at St Ives. My mentor, but not my ancestor, she had loved these wayward untameable places – had she flown over here in her mind, often, imbibing inspiration, whilst working on wood or stone in her Trewyn studio?

I completed my drawings, then, retracing my steps I followed my map carefully, taking inland paths until I came to the remote solitary standing stone known as the Men Scryfa.

There, I set up my stool, intending to sketch for a while. It was then in that remote area, littered with boulders that were very beautiful and encrusted with lichens I felt again the desire to fly, direct to little island to Tarn's side.

Up there on the moors I was seated by a stone known as 'the stone with writing'. The stone of a hero called the Royal Raven. There on the wild moors of West Penwith, the writings on the stone were Latinised forms of Celtic names. RIALOBRAN CVNOVAL FIL. Royal Raven. Famous Leader. Son of.

I knew the legend of Ryalvran, who returned to Cornwall to fight for his father's stolen land, and who had been slain and buried where the Men Scryfa now stood. But for me the raven was a superb and powerful female image. It had first arisen at the cave at Nanjizal with Tessa and Jules. Now I was here, at a raven-stone-with-writing, with a desire to fly to be with Tarn; to fly in a perfect straight line with wings outstretched like a bird; to fly with the power of a raven across land and sea to my lover's side.

At Men Scryfa, seated, I unpacked my sketch book and drew a female raven from memory. Her bright eye entranced me. I had read that there was a place, Mavilly, in Burgundy where people considered the raven to be capable of healing people's eyes. So they went there for cures. I pencilled in her glossy plumage and, turning to a new page, I drew her with the three mothers with whom she was associated in Celtic myth.

Around me the moor was still, with a mere hint of summer breeze playing across the heather. The sky was sunny with misty clouds in the distance. I was contented and I continued sketching for a while.

Presently, along a well-marked bridle way, in the lee of mighty Carn Gulva, some riders came into view. I watched as they moved on and out of sight. My imagination thus stirred, I turned to a clean page and drew the legendary Epona, a Celtic horsewoman who is often depicted with a raven. I added the raven and, page by page, as if producing stills for a cartoon, I allowed the horse and raven to trot and leap and jump and gallop. Together they sped and, gathering intensity, they moved towards the sea and re-emerged as Rhiannon on horse back. This time the horse was white as in the Welsh *Mabinogion*.

I paused a moment, pencil in hand.

Rhiannon was a beautiful woman who was going to marry her fiancé, a man named Gwawl. She was out riding one day on a white horse when, from behind her, she found herself being chased by Pwyll, the King of Dyfed. She outran him for many miles. However fast he galloped he couldn't catch up with her.

Eventually Rhiannon stopped, when Pwyll called. She agreed to talk with him. Months later she became his wife, though he had tricked her into marrying him by deceiving her betrothed, Gwawl.

Rhiannon was a generous queen, beautiful and bountiful, giving gifts to all around her. But she longed and longed for a child and couldn't bear one for many years.

Time passed. Eventually, she became pregnant and gave birth to a cherished child, Pryderi. Then came the festival of the First of May, Beltane. On that day Pryderi disappeared and no one could find him, though they searched everywhere.

Rhiannon, his mother, who adored him, was accused of murder.

She was forced to do a seven-year penance, for which she was to sit by the horse block outside the palace gate and offer to carry visitors on her back.

Seven years passed. One day Pryderi was returned to Pwyll and Rhiannon, alive and well. He had been cared for by a foster father who hadn't known who the little boy was when he first found him wandering about.

Later when Pwyll, the King of Dyfed, died, Rhiannon remarried, but magic was afoot and the land fell barren because of Pwyll's original betrayal of Gwawl all those years ago.

After some time the magician called Llwyd was forced to undo the spell and once again the land became green and fertile.

But always, by her side and in her gardens, Rhiannon was cared for and attended by three magical birds, whose singing could be heard from across the sea.

*

Without thinking, I drew more ravens. They multiplied until three female ravens were in the air behind Rhiannon, supporting her during her grief at the loss of her baby son.

I hadn't realised that I was drawing images that would link me to Tarn. I'd done it quite spontaneously, using my intuition as an artist. But it was a shock and I dropped the pencil. My sketch book slipped to the ground.

Rhiannon had lost her baby; Tarn had lost Vorrie. I closed my eyes and let Rhiannon move again through a film in my mind, calming myself until I dozed off in the warm sunshine.

I don't know how long I slept for. However, when I woke, the day had become hotter and I was incredibly hungry.

Far from wanting to fly like a bird, I simply wanted to go home.

I gathered up my sketch book, pencils and small stool, and, aware that Tarn was all right, and was coping with the events in the island, I felt calm as I thoughtfully retraced my steps to the car, drove home across the moors and soaked myself in a pleasant deep bath.

I wrote down all my experiences of my unusual day to send to Tarn, and I went to bed early.

I passed easily through a sleepy gateway into a storytale world of fantasy and legend. It was the world of Lyonesse, from the tales of my Cornish childhood.

It was a colourful land of wondrous beings and creatures, mermaids, seagulls, horses, and ravens, meeting one another on several serpentine pathways.

The paths formed interwoven strands, resembling Celtic knot work, and were painted in bright colours, including turquoise, silver and gold. The pattern was shining, intricate and very pretty.

Tarn and I were happy there, together. We walked along holding hands, passing through rolling hills with mythical animals and birds and numerous other creatures.

We went through lovely glades and across valleys, into caves and under the sea. We went to far-off shores of white sand and shells with gleaming interiors. There were many islands and tall mountains, green hills and rushing rivers, which led back to the sea. There were some more winding paths, which led to return routes under the ocean and up again on to familiar shores. Like the most detailed of traditional Celtic art work, the paths had no end and no beginning, and the mythical place had no past nor present nor future.

All was part of all and the effect was beautiful and peaceful.

When I woke next morning I realised that I had dreamed a happy dream about the legendary other place which the Irish call Tir na n'Og, and the Cornish sometimes call the Isles of the Blessed. It's another world where there is no pain or blame, no punishment or judgement, no stress and no sadness. No separation from loved ones and no anxieties of any kind.

Lying awake, vaguely aware that Cherry and Beech were moving about downstairs, but sensing no urgency of any kind, I lay back on the pillows, anticipating some new paintings, and thinking about the fact that other women lived in the old rundown house and that Tarn and I were now part of a new network of friends, building a life together. There was an easy reassurance in the mundane sounds of Cherry shutting the bathroom door, and water being run in the shower. I heard the post arrive, and Beech's feet going along the hall to pick up the letters from the mat. Daily life was going on around me and it felt so ordinary that it was a delight – certainly not part of a mythical other world. They were down-to-earth sounds.

It occurred to me, as Beech knocked on my door with a welcome cup of tea, that I was optimistic about life in general, and that Tarn would be home soon and she, too, would be all right.

CHAPTER TWENTY-TWO

Dearest Lerryn,

The middle of my second week here and I'm beside myself missing you, yet clear as always that I have to see this through. Lerrie, oh Lerrie, I need to be with you. But these long letters do help me, and bring me close to you.

I've been thinking a lot about the island; the name Ellan Vannin, which is the island's alternative name, and all the unnamed women in the island's folklore who were accused of witchcraft.

The thing is, Lerryn, that if Vorrie had died in my care all those years ago I would have been accused. If I face up to that, then something very powerful begins to happen to me. Inside me there builds a picture in which one of the unnamed women becomes clear to me and the name Ellan Vannin comes to me for her. Her story is inside me. I need so badly to tell it. It's strange, but I feel as if my healing depends on telling it. Something I have to do while I am here. I can't avoid it or sidestep it. It's as if a deep wound is there and only by bringing the hurt and pain of this story out of me can I move through this grief and come home to you.

Naming makes her real to me. She becomes visible in my mind and embodied here in this valley where I rest and heal.

Then I begin to feel that Ellan Vannin's name is a key which can help me to heal by unlocking a door to the unnamed women who were accused of witchcraft, revealing the hidden women wrongly accused of crimes.

It's not enough to be absorbing the landscape around me, to be walking and connecting with the hills and the sea. I know that little Vorrie was a daughter of the island, who had herself been conceived during a violent relationship, and who is now at peace, resting safely, and if I honour her by honouring those women of the past who have been dishonoured, then, and only then, can I heal.

Ellan Vannin's suffering is only slowly revealing itself to me, but she is so near to me. That's what makes it so heartrending. She is family. So close.

During these past few days I felt more and more beckoned towards the archives. As time passed I felt drawn away from the wooden house and the green valley, as if compelled towards the town and the Manx Museum, where I felt that I must delve into the old manuscripts and must read for hours.

It was good for me, giving me purpose and direction again as I studied both folklore and fact. They are not pretty stories – but I found while reading them that at last I was strong enough and empowered enough to face our legacy of violence against women and to place myself, my daughters, my dead baby grandchild and my island within it.

You may recall that Petronilla de Meath was an Irish witch put to death in Ireland in 1324, and is the nearest recorded case to those unrecorded women who passed into folklore in the thirteenth and fourteenth centuries in the neighbouring Isle of Man.

From that era onwards isolated accusations of witchcraft happened at different times and in different places all over the Continent in the century and a half leading up to the publication of the infamous *Malleus Maleficarum* of 1487.

In the Manx Museum I found five recorded cases of accusation and trial for witchcraft, and they disturbed me terribly so that I had virtually no sleep for three nights running. I kept pacing about and crying dreadfully, as if to grieve for my lost ancestors for the first time. I wanted to find their bones and bless them, put flowers on their graves and call up everyone to witness and attend, but I simply stayed in the little moorland garden here, reading.

I found, as I said, five cases. You asked me in your last letter to write the details and I will, though it's hard for us to absorb them. Without you to support me this would be terrifying work to be engaging with. I know that this won't be easy reading for you, for many reasons. The women suffered horrible accusations and trials and, as the hysteria gathered force, they were hunted and tortured. These are awful stories. This is not easy work. The emotions that arise aren't simple. Confusion and anger. Sadness and loss. Grief for all those many, many women, some of whom were lesbians like us. They are especially hidden in the records. But wherever there have been women, there have been women who loved each other. This we know.

The woman I know as Ellan Vannin died in 1264 – one year before the death of Magnus, last Viking king of the island – and between then and the end of the fifteen hundreds there were other tales of women who met the same fate as Ellan Vannin, but there are no details or any records. Only in the folklore can I find references to what people knew Slieuwhallion Hill was used for and to the swamp at the foot of the hill, which was called Curragh Glass.

Then, in 1617, a Manx witch called Margaret Quane was sentenced to death for witchcraft with her son. Together they were burned at the stake in the market place at Castletown. Also, at about that time, the beginning of the seventeenth century, there was a very unusual case dealt with by the Vicar of Braddan. He was called the Vicar-General because he was in charge of the Ecclesiastical court.

He may have been a sceptic about witchcraft and his decision in this strange case shows pure leniency at a time when European clergy were saying 'thou shalt not suffer a witch to live.'

The old woman before him offered to take herself into exile. Now this way of dealing with those found guilty was common practice across Europe. It probably save some women from death. But in this case the old woman spoke as follows:

'If you find me two new pewter plates that have never been used, sir, I will turn them into wings and fly from here to Scotland.'

The Vicar-General replied: 'There is no law against a woman flying from the Isle of Man to Scotland.'

The old woman was set free. There is no record of her name.

Her trial reminds me of some European cases where the priests and even the pope were themselves using magic or complying with magic. It also calls into question how far the church authorities really believed in witchcraft at all. Did the Vicar-General think the plates could be turned into wings? Or did he simply believe her innocence because he thought there was no such thing as witchcraft? Some priests obviously thought that witchcraft did exist – and some were going regularly to witches for healing and to have curses removed. But others behaved as if there were no such thing at all.

What they meant by 'witchcraft' seems to have varied widely, been amended and added to at will. The crucial issue in all cases seems to have been whether the authorities, whatever they were, actually felt threatened or not. If they thought they were in control they did one thing; if they thought things were out of control they tried to bring them under control, and so forth.

How barbaric they were in torturing for confessions and in gratuitous torture after confession seems to have varied enormously. What is certain is that individual women, and groups of women, suffered incredibly.

In the Isle of Man, after the pewter plates case, the records go silent except for two women: Elizabeth and Alice.

Elizabeth Black was found guilty of witchcraft some time during the seventeenth century. She was fined and set free.

Alice Knakill was found guilty in 1712 of scraping dirt from under a neighbour's door and making it into a drink to give to her own cows to increase their milk yield. She also made a love potion out of shiny rocks from the Foxdale area. Her punishment involved public humiliation by being made to stand in the open wearing special robes and a sash. Across it was written in large letters that she had been accused and found guilty of sorcery.

So, in the island, there were no equivalent mass trials or hunts such as those Marianne Hester found in Essex. Do you remember, Lerrie, that we talked about her book, *Lewd Women and Wicked Witches*? It's one of the few books on the witch hunts that really deals with the fact that nearly all the accused were women. Instead, in the island, there was an occasional use of the charge of witchcraft against individuals. No mass hunting. But it's still true that four out of five of those found guilty were women.

We talked near Maggy Figgy's chair ladder of the scattered accusations made against witches in the Isle of Man and Cornwall. It does seem to me that the inherent paganism of the population and relative isolation of both places did prevent the hysterical hunts and mass murders there. There were brakes of a different kind on mass hysteria in some parts of Europe, I think.

In Germany, where some of the most intense hunts took place, there was a strong history of public executions of Jews and other heretic groups and no state law against torture. But in some areas where the state was very centralised the central authority did sometimes function as a brake, or controlling factor, on local barons, clergy and princes. In such places, if feuds broke out between warring factions, vulnerable wives could be accused of witchcraft in order to attack the husbands' power base. Several cases were dismissed by the central authorities, who thus exerted control over both sides and probably some women's lives were thus saved.

Some writers put this forward as a way of explaining why the hunts came to an end, eventually. Rich men were not going to tolerate attacks on them via attacks on their rich wives.

It didn't save poor village women. The estimates are that over the period in question there were about two hundred thousand people accused and as many interrogated, with about a hundred thousand deaths.

Of those, over eighty per cent were women, and sometimes the percentrage was as high as ninety-eight. There was wide geographical variation in whether a mass hunt took off or fizzled out. It's ironic, isn't it, that state clamp down on local bigwigs was sometimes a restraining factor, since it was the structural control of the women, mainly the independent women healers who used magic every day, that the church and state so needed in the first place.

What I did find was that across Europe from the thirteen hundreds onwards single women, like my Ellan Vannin, were becoming poorer and poorer. Widows were very vulnerable, as were all independent women.

Before then they would have had gardens and small plots of land, part of the communal land. They would have grown their herbs and vegetables for their dependent children and sick or elderly relatives. But as farms grew in size the small peasants lost their land. And women no longer had Beguinages to flee to.

At the same time the craft and trade guilds were changing and becoming very male dominated. They were almost entirely in the hands of relatively wealthy and secure men in the towns. These economic conditions made things worse for, on the one hand, a class of poor men who had to seek work for wages and, on the other hand, a vast underclass of starving or very poor single women or widows.

By the fifteen hundreds such women could not find work in the trades, could not be admitted to apprenticeships and could not rely on their own gardens for food. In some countries such women were not allowed to trade from home either. They could not make things at home to sell in the markets – nor could they sell their labour for wages beyond the home. All this at a time when they couldn't rely on growing their own food in their gardens. These women would have often been healers and herbalists; now they were reduced to starvation or begging door to door.

If they were old they were deemed useless. They were sometimes an embarrassment, going from door to door begging. If they were young they were called sluts. What more effective method to get them out of the way than to accuse them of witchcraft?

So the reversal began – the healers began to be called witches.

What may have begun as rare cases of revenge or vindictiveness involving a few women in one area, peaked into a hundred-and-fifty-year-long torment. It was an attack on the folk beliefs of rural peoples by the church and its new definitions of who was allowed to do what.

The main point is that all the cases included accusations of use of magic. It didn't matter whether a healer had cured people or not – it was the process of using magic or being seen to use magic that the rich men sought to control.

But underneath all the so-called 'facts' there is something deep that disturbs me. And that is the strong sense I have of how terrified ordinary women must have been.

Nothing that you and I have ever faced in this lifetime comes near to that fear. We live with everyday fear, especially in the cities: fear of men and what any male stranger in the street is capable of doing to us if we are the right woman in the right place at the right time. The time when any man chooses to vent his anger or abuse his power.

But I can hardly imagine what it must have been like to fear helping a friend or neighbour in case she was persuaded to turn it round and blame me for her cow going sick or her husband having an accident, or whatever else might befall her or her family, and set up a witchcraft accusation.

I thought about that fear – that terrible, terrible fear – and suddenly I found myself in floods of tears. I cried and cried. It wasn't until later that I realised I was crying about baby Vorrie.

My own situation is not a regular one. It's specific. It's not an everyday fear that every grandmother has to deal with. I realise that I have been called here; that help in understanding about baby Vorrie is at hand. But I also feel that this will take me from the particular to the general: that my being blamed for Vorrie's death, in this very personal way, will link me to the blaming of women that occurred over three hundred years all over Europe – the direct result of men's political power over women.

Imagine any herbalist or healer or midwife or apothecary's assistant helping someone. The help might be a small packet of medicine or a spell or a potion. Then something goes wrong.

Anything at all. Someone's horse goes lame. Someone's husband has an accident. Someone's child dies. The healer suddenly finds herself blamed. Her act of healing is reversed into a witchcraft accusation, maybe years later.

Barstow writes that the effect of the knowledge of the witch trials in Europe would have set all the women on edge. It would have broken the trust that they would once have had of each other. It would have given them the urgent message: go home, stay home, obey your husband and speak to no one. Don't trust any other woman.

I've been blamed for Vorrie's death, though Joss blames herself as well. Joss has been severely blamed by Vorrie's father. Here on little island I understand how the scapegoating of women in general became a huge phenomenon in the fifteen and sixteen hundreds. The effect was a mighty attack on women's self-confidence and self-image for the centuries that followed.

Women could and did use magic in matters of sex. They were

closer to other women's bodies. They helped other women to control their fertility, raise their young and heal their sick. Men deeply resented this – the men of the clergy, the medical profession, and the law. Later the use of magic became identified with evil – linked to Satan and the devil in the minds of those who perpetuated the hunts.

At the beginning, when women like Ellan Vannin were being accused, it was their closeness to the cycles of birth, life and death, the growth of plants and the turning of the seasons that was what individual men resented.

My Ellan Vannin had that power. She was close to matters of sex and sexuality. Her woman lover was the magistrate's wife. Greba Kelly. Slowly, inside me, there is forming the story of their love for one another. Ellan Vannin was hated because the men could not control her. She was one of the first, I think. An isolated case. So very, very sad.

Well, dearest Lerryn, it's almost lunch time and I'm going to go into town to take this to the fax place. There's such a lot to think about and talk about with you. I am missing you so much, dearest.

Take care and know that I love you.

All my love, as always, Tarn XXX

Chapter Twenty-three

Dearest Lerryn,

Your letters have all been wonderful. Every day something in the post. I hear the van at the end of the lane, then the bump, bump as the wheels ride over the ruts, then there's the familiar envelope and the much loved handwriting . . . a message from you – a drawing, a card, one of your views of Cornwall. It's been marvellous for me. The daily contact. Just marvellous.

And the news. Whew!! To hear that you, Cherry and Beech and Molly have been offered some acres of agricultural land to buy as women's land is absolutely amazing. I'll put in as much money as I possibly can. And this time, no one woman to own it, eh? Oh, it's so exciting. Of course it doesn't solve the ongoing problem of housing for Cherry and Beech, but I think it's right to purchase land with no buildings on it. We simply haven't got the resources to raise the kind of money for land with buildings, nor to renovate them, nor maintain them, have we?

I look forward to seeing Cherry and Beech. I'm glad they're happy at Lescudjack. As you rightly say they need somewhere with a garden, because they're land women – but meanwhile they are safely housed and that's what matters first.

The future is open and that is a wonderful thing to know. Give my love to Molly, won't you? As an older woman she's one of the most open and hopeful women I've known.

There are some women of our age for whom the future feels closed. There's much disillusionment everywhere – in politics, of course, but also in everyday life. Years and years of Thatcher, then Major, have done that. Nothing is safe or secure. No job is safe. No government benefit is safe. No retirement plan is safe. Nothing.

You remember I wrote about my friend Gwen here? Well, it has been good to see her and re-establish our friendship but the death of her grandchild hit her so hard that she has given up hope of happiness. To her the future seems dreary and closed, but for me it isn't. I think that's because I have found love, deep love, with you, and gladness in my life. It has sustained me through these intense and sometimes searingly painful days.

These recent experiences have flowed out of me in one way or another into words on paper. I know you'll understand. It's the need to make something. To learn something. My writing is developing all the time and my sense of past, present and future as an integrated entity is fathoms deep. Deep as the ocean in the deepest part of the sea.

It seems that this year we have all been facing betrayal of one kind or another. But in the midst of that I met you. I have an intuitive trust of you and how we were with one another before I had to leave for London and the birth – and death – of my grandchild.

Again I have been pulled back to the Manx Museum, where I wandered through the peaceful galleries feeling so close to Ellan Vannin. I am nearer and nearer to drawing her story out of me.

As my stay here comes to a close, I realised it would be important for me to check the archives to see whether there would have been women involved in the making and inter-preting of the law. Unfortunately not. Surprise, surprise! In the Manx parliament the seats were reserved for freemen. This dated from the very first parliament set up by the first Viking king in 979. At that time there were thirty-two seats, which included sixteen representatives from the Isle of Man and sixteen from all the Western Isles. Later, the Hebrides were partitioned and only the northern group of the outer Isles remained, for a while, with the Isle of Man. The number of reps dropped to twenty-four, and it has been twenty-four ever since: Yn Kiare-as-feed (called simply, The Keys), which literally is the four-and-twenty. So there you have it. Twenty-four male landowners. What chance of justice for a solitary hedgewitch like my Ellan Vannin?

After I'd finished with the archive, I took myself to the swamp areas at the foot of Slieuwhallion Hill. There I sat and thought about the trial of witches by judges and juries made up entirely of men from the church and parliament.

I sat for ages in hot sunshine watching insects on the busy grasses of the boggy area. Its surface had dried out somewhat, due to the weather, but the swamp is deep, sustained by springs.

I imagined it after a long wet winter, with bubbles breaking on the muddy wallows of the area; imagined witches' bodies – bound hand and foot – sinking, sinking and the bubbles rising, rising. If they survived, that proved they were witches and they were sent for trial.

I'm sure that if I had lived then, Jeff would have accused me too.

I was going to finish this letter tonight but I'm hot and hungry, so I think I'll stop and have a cool shower and something to eat. Then I want to tell you my story of Ellan Vannin. I need to bring this out of me. To tell what I feel from the inside.

Thinking of you, dearest.

All my love, Tarn XXX

Ellan Vannin

Ellan Vannin you were waiting under the tramman tree. You had placed tiny flowers on the stone over your baby's grave. Spring flowers, real flowers. You stood under the tramman tree in the manner of the wise ones, and let its branches fold around you. Night closed over the dark moor, until the moon rose over the hills, illuminating your turf house on the edge of a soft valley in a green sea moorland. You were silent, waiting to hear the brittle twigs snapping underfoot as Greba Kelly approached you along the lane.

'I have come to hold you,' said Greba. 'I have known you since we were children. You are no more a murderess than I am. I am a friend who believes in you.'

'You are my only friend. My baby lies here buried. She died and no one knows how or why. Now I am hated by all. By the men who spoke the lies, who want me punished.'

'Come, Ellan. Come inside. Come away from the baby's grave.'

'It is dangerous to be my friend. They have marked me out.'

'Nevertheless, I shall hold you tonight.'

You went inside together and lay together in your bed in the firelight. She comforted you. She had her own grief to contend with, for she had wanted children. She had loved your child, and was her other mother. She held you all night, and for many nights after. You were open, needy, vulnerable. She stayed with you. You wept on her breasts. You curled small, and naked, in her arms. You were her child for a night or two. She was your mother, she was your child. You held one another.

In the neighbourhood, later, Greba Kelly, the magistrate's wife, pleaded your case. She was a good woman, whose opinion counted for something. She flouted her husband to help you. She insisted that you did not kill your baby. 'No,' she said. 'Has she not been punished enough?'

Her sing-song voice was raised in your defence.

Then, temporarily, the threat against you was withdrawn. Greba Kelly, the magistrate's wife, held sway in the village and she had influence over her husband, who was devoted to her. She was strong, beautiful and outspoken. Her word prevailed. She was your friend.

You were happier then, for a while. You went walking on the moors together, in the early summer, the wind in your faces, your shawls tied at the waist, your kirtle hems catching on the heather. Your green eyes were laughing, noticing that the hawthorn was in blossom and that the grass had a sheen when the wind shimmered it around the curve of the hill. You and Greba spread a rug and shared lunch together. She fell in love with you. You were real. You were beautiful. The two of you. No one can take that away from you. Not even after everything that happened.

Then, for a time, you were never without each other's company. Walking with your steps light, your shawls pulled around you, with baskets over your arms for collecting the gorse and early heather for dyeing the wool. Loving one another, as if everyone around you might be glad.

But they were not glad. People began to talk. Then, one man in particular was inflamed with resentment. Had he not spared your life at his wife's request? Yet all the while he had suspected you. He was certain that you had caused your baby to stop breathing by witchcraft.

He had let you go, freed you from the accusation, against all his better judgement, because his lovely wife pleaded so eloquently, and he never could resist her. It seemed to him that there was no punishment bad enough for an evil woman such as you.

He picked up his pen and began to write his revenge, for he had spared your life and it seemed that this is how you had repaid him. To him it appeared that you beguiled his wife, allured her and bewitched her. His anger flew high, beyond the thunderstorms.

At first, you were unaware of this, you and Greba, as if the future held no threat, and you shared your loving and your words, making plans and dreams with happy endings.

And even the hills reflected your bodies, such roundness and equality. The roundness of your breasts, the roundness of your bellies, the roundness of those female hills around you.

She commented on it, saying, 'In the circles and the spiral of our lives, we women draw close together. In the circles and the homesteads in the lives of our mothers' mothers' mothers there must have been love between women like us. We were the country ones, the cunning ones, celebrating our woman-love, and loving our island. She was our mother. We danced for her and sang for her and told our stories and buried our dead; and said be glad each day we are alive and wise. I hold you now, my Ellan Vannin, and say, come, woman-time, to settle in my bones again. Come settle here in all of us, women and mothers.'

You believed her and loved her. You had green eyes and dark brown hair, and you were lovely together, you and she, passionate too. You danced together by the Maughold stones, and the moon so bright and the night enclosing you, like the shawl of the old one, hugging you.

Then you cried, sometimes, pleading, Why, why? Why you? Why you and your dead child? Why did it happen? You wanted to know. But you had wisdom. The wisdom to let yourself heal. So you danced and wept and loved.

But Greba was not free to love you as a lover. Her women friends warned her to stay away from you. You were already marked out by the men of the church; and it was dangerous for you to love a woman who was not free. But by then you knew what body-heat and body-need was like and your love could not be contained in a rule or boundary.

But Juan Kelly hated you. He spoke acidly to his wife, telling her that in order to save your life she must return to his house, to remake her place there, without you. She didn't know what to do. Should she believe him? Could she trust that your life would be spared? She did not want to leave you but she could not take the risk. She returned to his side to take up all her duties as his wife. Then your skin was raw with need and your heart was broken for the second time. You grieved. It washed through you.

You were tempted, then, to wish him harm. Juan Kelly, your lover's husband – to wish him harm, for the times he hurt her, for the times he beat her, for the times he told her he would never accept you because you, a murderess, had no right to love anyone, especially not his wife. And how he hated you for having born a child. He told Greba that it was all he'd ever wanted, a baby.

Then Greba was also tempted to wish him harm. But if she did, it would come back to her. Threefold. Or three times three.

You stood, a solitary figure, as a dark and starry night enfolded you, under the tramman tree, asking for guidance: 'Ancestors, ancestors bide with me, bide with me. Ancestors, ancestors, bide with me, bide with me. I want to live. I do not want to die.'

Greba had a sense of you. She wrote to you: '*You are strong. You are wise. There is knowledge in your eyes. I was wrong to return to this house, to take up my duties as the magistrate's wife. I love you, Ellan Vannin, and we will both die. I take my spinning wheel and the fleece of our island sheep, and I spin skeins for a shawl for you. Then I spin some more for a shawl for me. The same wool, for matching shawls.*

From the west a storm gathers. The night sky has fast-moving clouds, and the wind is keen. My husband gathers the men together. He speaks to the church and parliament. The Bishop of Norway sanctions them, these Norsemen who invaded our island, and speak now of Christian laws. How I hate them all, now. I have tried so hard to persuade him. How I loathe myself. Not for loving you, but for believing him. I shudder to know him now. How he holds his shame inside so that it festers into a sore that will not heal; how the poisons in his anger burn like fever in his blood. How he slowly, insidiously, plans this revenge. The men will arrest you, and I cannot prevent it. I shall die still loving you. Here in this house, while the storm from the west moves towards us, we witness you, me and the moon. We know. We acknowledge.

He used to sit at his desk, in the old stone house, wielding his quill against the independence of women like you, with the Scandinavian gods of thunder beckoning to him. Of course the Viking invasions have long ceased. There is peace, trade and prosperity here in our island. But I do believe, dearest Ellan Vannin, that thunder gods live in the magistrate's heart.

My Ellan Vannin, I love you. I swear this to you, under the waxing moon whose silver shape floats behind the branches of my rowan trees. I spin the wool for your shawl and as I spin I sing a ballad of love, grief and deep reproach. I am your lover and when you go, my sweet woman, I shall die on that day, by my own hand. I am yours, Greba.'

Then you knew that they would come for you. You took flowers and wove them into your hair as a gesture of defiance. It was a hot August day, and from the morning the heat began to shimmer, with a promise of storm. You were terrified but ready. Beside you was the tumblerful of narcotics. You had grown and dried the herbs yourself.

They took you to the hill in the evening. You walked there with woven flowers in your hair. Strong unto the last. It was the day that Greba disappeared from the magistrate's house. You knew why she had gone. You could imagine her at the Maughold stones. You could see her there, also with flowers in her hair. You had her letter to you sewn inside your bodice. I love you, she had said. You knew it was real. It strengthened you.

It was a beautiful evening as the crowd gathered around you when you approached Slieuwhallion. It was windy and the green grass was waving there.

You walked in dignity, though they were taunting you. You were proud. You appeared to be silent and strong. When you reached the hill you closed your eyes. But your mind had gone. You sent your mind away with herbs – so that when it was time to take you away, you only had to walk as if on air.

But Greba was clear in her mind, knowing every moment how you were. She blamed herself for betraying your love, and left her words for all to know. She took herself to the Maughold stones and screamed there till your torment was over and done.

Then from the earth she lifted rocks and in the pockets of her skirts, heavy now and laden, she placed them. She struggled through the heather down the valley to the sea. It was a slow journey. In her pockets the stones felt cold, like your cold body, cut and broken.

She reached the shore and she knew that your voice was gone, your song gone, and the flowers were matted in your hair. No one could survive the worst fate that could befall a witch. For loving her and the death of your child, you paid with your life.

Downhill in a barrel. Downhill in a barrel. You paid with your life. In a spiked barrel. Let us not romanticise this ending.

Greba Kelly stood on a stony shore – in her hands the rocks were cold, sharp edged. In her despair, she drew a ridge right across her skin, cutting herself open. She called to you, 'Meet me, my love, on a distant shore, in another world, Ellan Vannin. I will meet you there. We will return to our island again, my dear, when the slopes of Slieuwhallion are safe.'

Chapter Twenty-four

Dearest Lerryn,

As I said at the end of my last letter, I arrived home here at sunset. It was a very warm evening after a very hot day, and I wrote my journal outside, surrounded by moths spinning near the light bulb on the veranda. When I had finished I sat there in the dark, waiting. I suppose I realised that thunder was imminent and I mused on my name, Taarnagh, which means thunderstorm in Manx Gaelic.

We have had one or two summer storms here – I have watched them gathering from the west, whilst standing on my veranda – but last night was of a different order.

It was a hot, close night; the heat had been building all day. Layer on layer of heat. I was watching as the light changed. Then, from the distant west came yellow and purple light, flowing across the green sea moor, filling every hollow and mellowing every purple leaf.

I waited on the veranda. I couldn't move. I felt compelled to remain there, surrounded by purple light.

Then the first low growl rolled in across the valley as if it were sliding along the edge of the eerie light. The sky darkened ominously, yellow was greening into a slimy brown glow, then became luminous brownish purple as the heat began to explode in the coming of the storm.

It cracked overhead and the sky was filled with lions pounding about and roaring, bouncing their energy from one rolling cloud to the next.

I didn't want to miss a moment so I grabbed a blanket that was airing on the wooden rail and wrapped it around my shoulders. I stood like Ellan Vannin with a shawl around me and the lions ran with other animals of thunder, whose paws and hooves raised great clouds as they charged about, with a noise to reach to Iceland.

Thunder rolling all around me. It was my storm. Ellan

Vannin's storm. Thunder and reverberations throughout the valley.

Then, above me, the sky darkened to indigo blue, slashed by great forks of lavender light.

Then the whole sky sizzled, cracking open the pride of lions, scattering them temporarily, their cloud manes flying about as they leapt away from the lightning shafts. Dazzle played over the valley from sky to earth and cloud to cloud. Jumping arcs of electric power, silver and yellow with blue edges, whipped across the arch of the sky aiming for the ground.

I was awestruck, fascinated and rooted to the veranda. I had to be there. It was my storm. It was her storm, Ellan Vannin's thunderstorm on a summer night with the sky on fire and the roar and rumble of great heaps of wrath piled against each other.

Thunder was overhead by now with deafening new sound. I heard the barrel maker, hammering the curved wooden slats together with a wooden hammer, and the great pincers holding white-hot iron hoops, plunging them fast into water then on to the barrel as they shrank into place.

I could hear worse than that. The spikes that line the inside of the barrel went into the wood with crashing splintering sounds. Light striking the blacksmith's anvil and spittle sparks flying.

It was my storm. It was her storm. They were making the barrel that killed Ellan Vannin last night. All night long they worked as the skies rocked and the rain slammed at the windows.

When I knew they were making the barrel which killed her I couldn't bear to watch them any longer. I hid my eyes by wrapping the woollen blanket over my head and I was weeping uncontrollably. All around me the splintering of iron on wood. The heat of the forge and dazzling fire to heat the iron hoops. The crash of the hammer on the anvil, shaping the great iron spikes. The noise and light, the intensity of fire and iron, and the sickening knowledge of the images made me shake and cry until I needed to scream, over and over with each thunder crack. Then I leaned over the veranda rail and vomited on to the garden. I couldn't help it. Then I ran indoors and put myself to bed and lay there with the duvet over me, shaking and trembling with the horrors of barrel making and what had happened to Ellan Vannin there in my island. My birthplace, my violent country of origin.

So I was indoors for the rest of the night as the storm raged around the valley and great forks of lightning seared the air around the wooden house. I was terrified that the house might be struck, but an inner voice told me that it wouldn't happen. It wasn't the purpose of the storm.

I was lying in my bed, but my bed itself was transformed into that self-same barrel and the inside of the barrel was lined with metal spikes.

Outside, the thunder rolled and charged forwards and backwards out of control, contained between the valley sides, like a moaning body in a barrel. Rolling round and round and the night sky screaming and the spikes invading the body of earth with blood and thunder and water.

I lay in my bed, trembling, as the unabated storm shook the walls around me, the floor underneath me, and the roof shingles above me. My wooden house became a shaking, rolling wooden barrel. Intense fear broke me as I felt the spikes piercing through me. Into my shoulder and out the other side. Through one thigh. Deep in my back and out through the front on my left side. That one missed my heart by inches. At its base it was four inches wide; it was ten inches long. It missed my heart by inches.

I heard Ellan Vannin scream out. She cried: I am a witch who refuses to die. And then she said to me: Remove that spike, Taarnagh.

There is so much blood, I whispered to Ellan Vannin. And this time she replied firmly, quietly, her voice insistent in its understanding: There is always blood at someone's birth. And the death of women's dreams is often violent. Face it, face it now.

'I am trying to face it,' I replied.

Then I lay very still and with intense effort I slowed my breath, holding and waiting, counting and waiting for the next breath, in and out, in and out. Into my mind came the garden at the back of my home in Penzance. I focused on the herbs there, the sage and rosemary bushes, the comfrey and calendulas. I imagined my hands full of healing leaves with which I

216

surrounded my body, covering each wound, closing each one, mending the broken skin. I pushed myself to the limit of my concentration, until finally there was no more barrel, no more pain.

I was calm again. No one was hurting me, nor was going to. Joss was safe, staying with Helen in Germany. Vorrie was safe, at rest, at peace.

Eventually, I drifted into sleep, and when I woke in the morning the storm had blown itself out, just as it does in West Penwith, when it rages from the sea, meets the moors, rises over the hills, and loses itself up country.

There are times when we realise we're on the slippery slope to that place where our mind goes beyond our control and we don't know the difference between fantasy and reality.

I reached the edge of that abyss last night and now, in the cool light of early morning, my night of terror over and done with, I can tell you that I am all right, that I don't need to make that descent; that I am able to maintain my boundaries between sanity and the other worlds beyond. I use the words carefully.

I recall that in the book *Wild Swans*, Jung Chang's father drifted between the worlds of sanity and madness – it was difficult for him to hang on to equilibrium in a world where he was under constant attack (of every kind); and that finally (despite the love and devotion of his family) he could not win his personal battle to stay stable and alive in a world gone crazy around him.

His daughter watched him as he struggled between the worlds of shifting, changing and terrifying realities. Her spirit emboldens my own. I am so grateful to her for that book. I shall always be so.

My world is not so terrifying as his was; nor indeed so terrible as Ellan Vannin's was. I am stronger now and I can face the realities of who our ancestors were, those wise women of Europe. The one hundred thousand and the two hundred thousand. I have never suffered the way any of them suffered. I have not suffered the way that Jung Chang herself suffered when she knew that each of her parents was undergoing torture.

But I suffered from the daily possibility of what might

happen again to Joss; and from never knowing when I'd get a phone call from a hospital to tell me that she'd been admitted again.

This is a very terrible world that we live in. That my daughter once volunteered to be with a man who beat her was beyond my comprehension. If I'm to stay sane I shall somehow have to learn to close myself off to what she chose to endure.

Do you recall that the church with the mermaid legend at Zennor is dedicated to St Senara? She was otherwise known as Azinore, who was nailed into a barrel and cast adrift with her baby off the coast of Brittany. The barrel landed in Ireland and the mother and baby were, miraculously, alive. Later, they returned to Brittany via Cornwall, founding the church at Zennor on the way.

It is the barrel that is my central image. I ask: who makes the instruments of torture and what does it do to them to be involved in such actions? It is this part of the Ellan Vannin story that had evaded me, but now I have caught up with it and have lived with it.

And I'm all right . . . and I will be home soon.

So, dearest, I'll phone you from the box in town and then we can sort out times of planes and trains and all that.

Won't be long now till we're together again. Your letters have been wonderful and have sustained and empowered me. As does your love.

All my love. Always. Tarn XXX

Dearest Lerryn

With the waxing moon in Sagittarius, I ask for clarification. I ask how to do this. How can I be a good mother to my daughters; and how can I learn to accept that Vorrie, my grandchild, is gone?

Jocelyn writes: asks me to phone her. I do so from the box in the town. She reaches out to me. We are careful. She has a tight knot in her stomach. We say there is no hurry. We plan to talk again. A glimpse of hope.

Early this morning I walked through the lanes to the post office, with a letter for Helen. Love and blessings.

Fuchsia is blood-red thick in the hedgerows now. My heart says 'home, home'. Suddenly and insistently my heart says I must prepare to leave my island, to leave Ellan Vannin. I must go from this place of ashes and graves.

So I think of this island where wild flowers cluster on the headlands and sweet briar roses line the path to this house, and where I trusted myself. I travelled here, where the sky meets the sea; where the land is legendary; where Ellan Vannin is and will always be. I came with the ashes of my grandchild; and found this wooden house, this sanctuary where once she lived.

I came here because it was the only place on the planet where I could heal a little of this pain. I would do so again.

But this is not home, except in the ancestral sense: here where Ellan Vannin lived and died is not the place where I should live and die.

After the summer storm, the day is calm and the heat layers itself upwards climbing the valley sides. The branches of the tramman tree shed their wetness, stretch their leaves out to the morning sun. The rowans breathe freely, the storm is gone. The wet wooden veranda dries out: this was a turf house once.

Here on the veranda I sit with my writing and recognise that my journey does not end here, even though it began here. The gift is the comprehension. If I had not come here, I could not know this.

Ellan Vannin and I met face to face. She is my island where I was born. I came here after Vorrie died, wanting to know Ellan Vannin as island, as woman, as mother of child, my birthright.

Now I come alive again after intense grief. For the sake of Ellan Vannin's pain, I'll heal my own. I sit in the sun here, the morning after the storm and I am very much alive.

All my love, Tarn XXX

EPILOGUE

EPILOGUE

I watched the horizon for the first speck to appear, sunlight glittering on metal wings. My heart was loud.

It's just a local airport, so I was very conspicuous as I stood there, agitated and flushed with excitement and holding a sizeable bunch of flowers.

The wheels touched down and a small cluster of passengers alighted. She waved as soon as she saw me. Her whole body was smiling. Tarn was home.

Talking and laughing, delighted with life and each other, we stashed her luggage in the boot and drove away from Newquay, south through the countryside beyond, in brilliant hot sunshine. Two days to my fiftieth birthday and the summer heatwave showed little sign of ending. There were still caravans and cars with trailers everywhere, so the journey was slow, but we didn't mind because we were together.

'Strange, isn't it?' I said, as we passed a laden car with two or three children in the back and loads of beach paraphernalia. 'There was a time when I'd have been in my element with all that. Me and Rosie with her mum; Jean and Sharon with beach balls and buckets; Tessa wandering off to get ice creams; somebody yelling that they'd dropped theirs into the sand and Jules trekking off for replacements.'

Tarn laughed at the thought of us packed like sardines on a beach with all the nuclear families. 'It was never quite like that for me,' she said. 'I was in Japan for most of my life as a young wife and mother. We knew some people who had a house by a lovely lake, with a backdrop of mountains. It was just like a tourist brochure. I remember it as a happy time before my marriage fell apart. The kids were in and out of the water. I'd be relaxing with a drink.'

'There were some good times then?'

'Yes, there were at first. I'd wanted Helen and Joss so much. That part of me was fulfilled. But now I know I was never cut out for that kind of life.' She paused. 'You mentioned you'd heard from Rosie. What's she doing? How is she?'

'She's become a professional photographer. Very independent. She's got a relationship – with a man – and she's decided to travel with him. She seems very happy. She doesn't want children. She wants her work. They plan to travel up through India, then perhaps to Europe. He is part-Indian, so he has lots of family contacts there and they'll have places to stay. She's very excited. Her letter is full of fun and life. She's a happy soul.' I smiled, then added, 'She reminds me of Lindsey in our early days – she had a propensity for happiness. I'm glad that Rosie's got it too.'

'That's wonderful, Lerrie. It's good that you can sound so positive about Lindsey and Rosie now.'

'Yes, strange but true. Lindsey's ghost doesn't hover any more. Freedom!'

We laughed and we'd have kissed again if I hadn't been driving. I didn't want to stop touching her. Her nearness was thrilling me. I was just smiling non-stop!

'It's been an amazing time, hasn't it, since we met?' said Tarn.

'Oh, it has. So much has happened. So many changes.'

'I still think of Vorrie,' Tarn mused. 'But it doesn't hurt so much.'

'I'm glad.' I pulled into the next lay-by and we kissed very slowly. Then we sat holding each other and kissed again, taking our time. When we had resumed our journey I said, 'I have peace of mind about Anna, too, now. And I think about the new friends she brought to us: a new life opening up.'

'Talking of new life, has Jean had her baby yet?'

'No, Tessa phoned and they're still waiting. She's due any time. They say they don't mind if it's a boy, girl or baby elephant just so long as she has it soon. But Jean's fine. They all are and they send love.'

'Thanks. That's great. I feel as if they've been my friends too for years.'

'Well, they will be, won't they, then!'

There is a place, one of our best-kept Cornish secrets, just a few miles south of Penzance; a perfect place to mark an end and a beginning. A between-the-worlds place where past and present meet.

We parked on a made-up tarmac area under some trees and we walked with our mini-packs along a lane, over a field and across a couple of inland stiles, until we were sitting on a gentle slope looking down into a deeply folded valley. The old hawthorns which lined the valley bottom had fat green fruits which would turn red shortly; and their ageing bark was encrusted with silvery grey lichens.

No one could see us and we were surrounded by a ring of soft hills. It was now late afternoon and we spread our picnic around us.

'So this is our new women's land,' she said, laughing.

'It's wonderful! I want to hear *all* about it! How *exactly* did this miracle happen?'

'It belongs to a couple from up country, people that Molly has got to know through The Gallery. They are conservationists, and naturalists. They bought the old house.' I paused and pointed to my left indicating the next valley. 'And they have out buildings which are derelict. After they moved in, they were offered forty-something acres more land. They didn't need it all but they had to buy it as one lot, and they want all this land restored to natural moorland and also to create wet lands for migrating birds. So they were talking to Molly about it in the shop. She let slip that we'd lost our women's land and they said their daughter's an ecologist and is living with women on an island off the New Zealand coast and they seemed okay about it. She is very happy there.

'Later, they came back and said that we could, if we wanted to, buy a couple of acres from them for our purposes, provided the land was used for ecology and conservation and so forth. It's not on the open market and they wouldn't sell to farmers, because of all the crop spraying and so on. They'll sell to us, if we want.'

'Where are the boundaries?

'Down that far hedge and following the edge of the trees at the bottom, and up this far side. It's about two acres. It costs four thousand.'

'For ever?'

'Yes. To be held in a Land Trust. So Cherry, Beech and Molly came and paced it out and they're drawing up a possible land use plan. We've found a woman solicitor . . . and there's another piece of amazing good fortune . . .'

'Which is?'

'That the very spot where we are sitting is on a water main that runs down across this land to the old farm buildings.'

'That is absolutely magic, Lerrie. We couldn't do women's land without water. We have got our own water! I can't believe that!'

'It's true. It costs about three hundred to have the hydrant put in and a stand pipe . . .'

'Well, what are we sitting here for? We'd better get home and get fund raising.'

'Tomorrow?'

'Go for it.'

We laughed and laughed then, because dreams can be made to come true. But you have to dream them first. We finished our picnic and left our belongings where they were and walked slowly all over the new land, bending from time to time to examine tiny flowers and wild grasses. It was a beautiful, peaceful place, and we knew without any doubt that we would raise the funds and would love it for many years to come.

We talked for a long time, until a most unusual sunset began.

Everywhere was silver. The grey rocks of the Cornish hedges became even darker by contrast, and the gorse bushes which grew out of them became partly shadowed and partly silvered in the unusual light.

Ahead of us was a silver sun setting behind veils. Slowly, as the sun curved down behind the ring of hills, the silver deepened so that every blade of grass around us became luminous and shining. At the horizon the hills were in deep silhouette and, into this thick duvet, the sun settled down. There was no green flash. Simply a final glimpse of silver disc, and then it was gone.

The afterglow began, pale silver orange with some yellow but nothing spectacular or dazzling. Almost a non-event. You can't plan your sunsets, not in Celtic countries. You can only wait and accept that they happen on their own terms, always.

The twilight came. We walked along the edge of the field, making our way back to our picnic place to collect our belongings. Then we sat in the deepening twilight listening to the singing of birds gathering, as the land began to prepare for night.

The temperature dropped and we pulled on tracksuits over our shorts. I took a couple of night lights in jam jars and matches from my rucksack. I lit the candles and put them nearby us in the darkening field. Then we lay beside one another kissing and murmuring.

Tarn was beautiful in the candle-light. Light and shadows played around us. We were contented and relaxed, talking quietly now about loving one another, anticipating our warm comfortable bed and some good lovemaking at home.

The stars came up and the sky was clear, and it began to get cold. 'I want to go down there to the old hawthorns,' she said, 'and touch them before we leave.'

'I'll wait here and pack these things. Here take this torch. I'll leave these night lights burning, just walk towards them up the hill when you're ready.'

'Okay. I just need to touch the trees.'

'Take your time. It's fine.'

I sat so quietly on our newly promised women's land, and the night enclosed me. The sky was clear and became very dark. The stars were out and bright, although I couldn't see the moon because it hadn't risen yet. In the distance I could see the faint bobbing of Tarn's torch as she walked downhill to the trees. I sighed with complete happiness.

It was on just such a night that Moss had gone out into her garden after Biff had died. It was quite late. Moss had made her way slowly to the wooden bench where she had used to sit with Biff. She had watched the dark, dark sky, recalling perhaps the night she had left Darlington at the age of sixteen, a headstrong and pregnant young girl. There under the cold night sky, which shone black like her best black boots, the stars like silver boot buttons, she had thought about her past, made a decision in the present, and chosen to let the cold night take her to spend all her futures with Biff.

Presently I saw the torchlight wavering as Tarn returned. We held one another closely. Then, gathering up our belongings, we made our way back across the land, to the parked car and home to our own bed.

The Women's Press is Britain's leading women's publishing house. Established in 1978, we publish high-quality fiction and non-fiction from outstanding women writers worldwide. Our exciting and diverse list includes literary fiction, detective novels, biography and autobiography, health, women's studies, handbooks, literary criticism, psychology and self help, the arts, our popular Livewire Books series for young women and the bestselling annual *Women Artists Diary* featuring beautiful colour and black-and-white illustrations from the best in contemporary women's art.

If you would like more information about our books or about our mail order book club, please send an A5 sae for our latest catalogue and complete list to:

The Sales Department
The Women's Press Ltd
34 Great Sutton Street
London EC1V 0DX
Tel: 0171 251 3007
Fax: 0171 608 1938

Also of interest:

Caeia March
Reflections

From the much-loved author of *Three Ply Yarn, The Hide and Seek Files, Fire! Fire!* and *Between the Worlds* comes a superb exploration of the power of legend, women's spirituality and erotic love.

Returning home after many months, Vonn Smedley dreams of the legendary romance of Tristan and Iseult. Forced by her father, the King, to make a marriage of political expedience, Iseult falls irrevocably in love with her husband-to-be's envoy. But dreams are no respecter of gender, and Tristan appears to Vonn as Tristanne – a beautiful warrior woman.

Then Vonn meets Rachel and, as the two women are drawn instantly together, myth and reality collide and coalesce . . .

'March is doing what novels ought to do, using the particularity of fiction to examine, expose, unfurl.'
Sara Maitland, *New Statesman*

'Hers is a unique voice, simultaneously poetic and colloquial.' Joanna Briscoe

'Tantalising, sensual, slow-moving, tender and romantic.'
Gay Community News

'Highly erotic.' *The Cornishman*

Fiction £6.99
ISBN 0 7043 4419 X